ROUTLEDGE LIBRARY EDITIONS:
CHAUCER

Volume 6

CHAUCER'S POETIC ALCHEMY

I0593020

CHAUCER'S POETIC ALCHEMY

A Study of Value and its Transformation in
The Canterbury Tales

SHEILA FISHER

Routledge
Taylor & Francis Group

LONDON AND NEW YORK

First published in 1988 by Garland Publishing, Inc.

This edition first published in 2020
by Routledge
2 Park Square, Milton Park, Abingdon, Oxon OX14 4RN

and by Routledge
52 Vanderbilt Avenue, New York, NY 10017

Routledge is an imprint of the Taylor & Francis Group, an informa business

British Library Cataloguing in Publication Data
A catalogue record for this book is available from the British Library

ISBN: 978-0-367-33583-0 (Set)
ISBN: 978-0-429-32068-2 (Set) (ebk)
ISBN: 978-0-367-35730-6 (Volume 6) (hbk)
ISBN: 978-0-367-35747-4 (Volume 6) (pbk)
ISBN: 978-0-429-34169-4 (Volume 6) (ebk)

Publisher's Note
The publisher has gone to great lengths to ensure the quality of this reprint but
points out that some imperfections in the original copies may be apparent.

Disclaimer
The publisher has made every effort to trace copyright holders and would welcome
correspondence from those they have been unable to trace.

GARLAND

PUBLICATIONS IN

AMERICAN AND

ENGLISH

LITERATURE

Editor
Stephen Orgel
Stanford University

GARLAND PUBLISHING, INC.

Chaucer's Poetic Alchemy

A Study of Value and its Transformation
in *The Canterbury Tales*

Sheila Fisher

GARLAND PUBLISHING, INC.
NEW YORK & LONDON 1988

Library of Congress Cataloging-in-Publication Data

Fisher, Shelia.
Chaucer's poetic alchemy : a study of value and its
transformation in The Canterbury tales / Shelia Fisher.
p. cm. — (Garland publications in American and English literature)
Originally presented as the author's thesis (Ph. D.—
Yale University, 1982).
Bibliography: p.
ISBN 0-8240-6388-0
1. Chaucer, Geoffrey, d. 1400. Canterbury tales. 2.
Chaucer, Geoffrey, d. 1400—Knowledge—Economics.
3. Value in literature. 4. Alchemy in literature. 5. Economics in literature. I. Title. II. Series.
PR1875.V34F57 1988
821'.1—dc 19   88-16477

Printed on acid-free, 250-year-life paper
Manufactured in the United States of America

ACKNOWLEDGMENTS

I would like to thank Professor Marie Borroff and Professor R. A. Shoaf, the advisors of my dissertation, for their valuable conceptual and stylistic criticism, for their helpful practical suggestions, and for their encouragement. Mary Christoforo, who typed the dissertation, deserves special thanks for the technical expertise and efficiency that made the last lap much easier. I am grateful to my husband, Dana Brand, for the intellectual advice and emotional support that constituted their own redefinition of gentillesse.

TABLE OF CONTENTS

INTRODUCTION

The importance of value and its determination and transformation
to The Canterbury Tales is evident from the two enterprises that
Chaucer defines as the motivating principles for his poem. The pilgrimage to St. Thomas's shrine which gathers the company at the Tabard
Inn should effect a transformation of their spiritual value. The
story-telling competition that produces the tales themselves is established to judge the value of the pilgrims' literary productions. Many
of The Canterbury Tales go on to address the problem of value and its
transformation. The Pardoner's linguistic dexterity transforms pigs'
bones into relics that bring him monetary value. The Second Nun presents a maiden whose spiritual value transforms her into a saint. The
Summoner shows how material value can vanish into thin air, while the
Canon's Yeoman rues his inability to transform the world's elements
into unlimited gold. If the Manciple questions the value of language
and if the Merchant tries to devalue marriage by commercializing it,
the Wife of Bath uses language and marriage to increase her material
prosperity and her own social value.

As these examples show and as Chaucer himself knew, "value" is a
word that operates within many frames of reference. In The Parson's
Tale, the Parson uses the word "value" to denote moral worth and social
rank: "Insolent is he that despiseth in his juggement alle othere
folk, as to regard of his value, and of his konnyng, and of his
spekyng, and of his beryng" (X. I, 398). The Franklin uses the word

1

"value" within a different frame of reference. Obliged to pay the magician, Aurelius "broghte gold unto this philosophre,/ The value of fyve hundred pound, I gesse" (V. F, 1572-73). The word "value" can thus have reference to both material and moral worth.

Value is, however, in itself, an end, the result of an act of evaluation. We ascribe value after an appraisal that constitutes, in fact, an interpretation of the thing to be valued. Specifically, we assign value by interpreting the relationship between phenomena. The value of a commodity is estimated in relation to other commodities or to a monetary system or in relation to human need and desire. An individual's social status is defined in relation to other individuals within his society. The spiritual value of the Canterbury pilgrims is estimated in relation to other members of their company and ultimately in relation (and through their relationship) to God. Finally, when we speak of an individual's or a society's "values," those values are synonymous with ethics, that is, with the standard of conduct by which an individual's worth is measured through his relationship to society.

If ethics provides a system for measuring moral worth, economics provides a system for measuring material value. In the Middle Ages, economic value and ethical value were not perceived as unrelated phenomena. Economics was a sub-discipline of ethics, for the way in which an individual valued, bought, and sold material goods was determined (ideally) by society's standards of just conduct and of the just and reciprocal relationships that should exist between individuals. Chaucer's concern with the interrelationship of material and moral value is apparent in the number of pilgrims who are interested in material value at the obvious expense of moral value. For many of the Canterbury pilgrims, the desire to amass material wealth determines the ethical values through which they relate to the world around them and to themselves. Their economics determine their ethics, rather than the other way around.

The economic changes and the growth of commerce in fourteenth-century England precipitated both social changes and a preoccupation with material wealth. In the following chapters, I will examine Chaucer's treatment of economic and ethical value in The Canterbury Tales within the context of contemporary economic and social change and in relation to the scholastic economic theory that attempted to formulate ethical standards for commercial conduct. The first chapter will briefly outline these changes in economic and social values in order to provide a background for the subsequent discussions of The Wife of Bath's Prologue and Tale, The Shipman's Tale, and The Canon's Yeoman's Prologue and Tale. Included in this outline will be a discussion of money's growing importance in the late Middle Ages and of the changing attitudes toward money, its utility, and the determination of its value. As money became more useful both to small business transactions and to international finance, a stable currency became crucial to national economies. The need for stable currencies raised the question of money's intrinsic worth. Was money merely a convention devised in order to measure the value of commodities or did money, in and of itself, contain an intrinsic value to which the names on coins necessarily referred?

The Wife of Bath's Prologue and Tale, The Shipman's Tale, and The

Canon's Yeoman's Prologue and Tale engage the question of intrinsic
worth at the same time that they emphasize the relationship between
economic and ethical value. The Wife of Bath, clearly a product of
her bourgeois milieu, presents ethical values that are synonymous with
her commercial interests. Yet, throughout her Prologue and Tale, the
Wife of Bath argues for her own intrinsic worth, for a worth existing
independently of the masculine traditions that would measure and name
her value. If the Wife of Bath believes in intrinsic worth, the Shipman, in his detailed account of the formation and breach of credit
transactions, shows that he does not. His Tale underlines the consequences of his disbelief to commercial relationships, marriage, and
friendship, and to the value of the words that his characters exchange.
The Canon's Yeoman's Prologue and Tale present yet another attitude
toward intrinsic worth. The Yeoman, as alchemist, would seek to transform the intrinsic value of base metals by turning them into gold.
Yet, because of his own material loss and the disillusionment caused
by his alchemical failures, the Yeoman ends by denying intrinsic worth.
He sees the world around him as counterfeit because it does not offer
him the value which he believed it promised.

In their concern with intrinsic worth and with the transformation
of economic and ethical values, these three tales reflect Chaucer's
interest in the value of the language that constitutes his poetry.
For if value can be defined within material and moral frames of reference, it can also be defined linguistically. A word's value is its
meaning, the signification assigned to it by its relationship to other
words within a linguistic system. Throughout my discussion of these

tales, I will examine the analogy between money and language and the similar ways in which the value of money and of language is determined. As these tales show, economic value not only influences ethical value; it also determines the ways in which individuals use language and the value which they assign to their words. In the quest for material profit, language is often used dishonestly, to hide intention rather than to communicate meaning. When language is used in this way, it becomes as counterfeit as the coin that misrepresents its own value. The Canterbury Tales demonstrate Chaucer's awareness that, if ethical values are transformed by changes within a social and economic context, a word's meaning, its value, is transformed by the context in which it is used. Moreover, if the Canterbury pilgrims' values derive from their interpretations of their world and of their experience within it, Chaucer's poetic value, as he well knows, derives from his interpretation of his material, of his sources, of his auctores. Chaucer's interest in the transformation of economic and ethical value reflects, as I will attempt to show, his concern with his own poetic alchemy, with his transformations of the value of language and literature within The Canterbury Tales.

Chapter I

"AL HAVE I NAT SET FOLK IN HIR DEGREE": THE QUESTION

OF VALUE IN THE WORLD OF THE CANTERBURY TALES

If Chaucer's age was characterized by economic change, commercial
growth, and the increased use of and interest in money, this economic
change also had social repercussions: a social fluidity arose from the
fluidity of wealth. Alexander Murray lucidly describes this phenomenon:

> Men's mutual relations shift, as if liquefied by their
> medium of exchange; men [like money] travel; social blocks
> split, like sums of cash, into changeable groupings of in-
> dividuals;. people herd in towns like coins in a chest . . .
> liquidity in wealth makes for social liquidity . . . .[1]

As the third estate, the commons, grew too large, too wealthy, and too
differentiated to be considered a single estate, the traditional medieval division of society into three estates (if it had ever provided a
viable stratification of society), weakened, and with it the foundations of feudalism itself.[2] The world that Chaucer represents in The
Canterbury Tales is in a state of transition between the economic systems of feudalism and capitalism. It is, consequently, a world in
which economic change has brought instability to social and ethical

_____

1. Alexander Murray, Reason and Society in the Middle Ages (Oxford: The Clarendon Press, 1978), p. 60.

2. Sylvia Thrupp, The Merchant Class of Medieval London (Chicago:
Univ. of Chicago Press, 1948), pp. 289-90, 295.

values.

Chaucer's interest in the influence of economic change on social relationships is not only reflected in the predominance of middle class pilgrims in the General Prologue. It is also reflected in his ethical and artistic concern with the instability of value throughout The Canterbury Tales. For when value is undefined, unstable, and ambiguous, the conventions that we use to measure and determine value are no longer adequate to their purposes. When value cannot be assigned by conventions or read from surface signs alone, we must begin a process of interpretation in order to discover value. The need to found valuation on acts of interpretation is at the center of Chaucer's interests in The Canterbury Tales.

The society that Chaucer represents in The Canterbury Tales is the product of a century of economic change and upheaval.[3] Between 1315 and 1317, poor harvests brought a famine whose demographic consequences were compounded by recurrences of the Black Death in 1349, 1361, and 1369.[4] Throughout the century, England's involvement in the Hundred Years War added its own political and economic repercussions

----

3. See the following works for summaries of the social and economic context of Chaucer's period: Harry S. Miskimin, The Economy of Early Renaissance Europe, 1300-1460 (New York: Cambridge Univ. Press, 1975); A. R. Bridbury, Economic Growth: England in the Late Middle Ages (London: George Allen and Unwin, Ltd., 1962); and F. R. H. Du Boulay, The Age of Ambition: English Society in the Late Middle Ages (London: Nelson, 1970).

4. It is estimated that England lost about a third of its population to the Black Death (Bridbury, p. 33). For a discussion of the famine of 1315-1317, see Bridbury, p. 23 as well as Henri Pirenne, Economic and Social History of Medieval Europe (New York: Harcourt, Brace, and World, Inc., 1937), pp. 192-93.

to the aftermath of famine and epidemic.[5] The combination of these
forces produced, in the fourteenth and fifteenth centuries, a contraction of the commercial and agricultural growth that had reached its
peak in the thirteenth century.[6] The general contraction within the
national economy did not, however, necessarily indicate a decline in
individual prosperity, for the contraction was accompanied by and, in
part, the result of population losses throughout the fourteenth century.[7]

In most instances, individual prosperity actually increased because there was more to share among fewer people. The way in which
contraction increased prosperity is illustrated by the changes in the
amount of land cultivated in England during the thirteenth and fourteenth centuries. Despite its growing commercial activities and interests, England, in the late Middle Ages, remained a primarily agricultural nation.[8] The economic expansion and prosperity of the thirteenth century therefore produced an increase in the number of cultivated acres (although often the lands involved in the expansion were

---

5. M. M. Postan "Some Social Consequences of the Hundred Years
War," in his Essays on Medieval Agriculture and General Problems of
the Medieval Economy (Cambridge: Cambridge Univ. Press, 1973).

6. M. M. Postan, "The Economic Foundations of Medieval Economy,"
in Essays on Medieval Agriculture and General Problems of the Medieval
Economy, pp. 14-16.

7. Du Boulay, p. 40. See also M. M. Postan's chapter "The Trade
of Medieval Europe: The North," in The Cambridge Economic History of
Europe, Vol. II (Cambridge: Cambridge Univ. Press, 1952), p. 216; May
Mc Kisack, The Fourteenth Century, 1307-1399 (Oxford: The Clarendon
Press, 1959), p. 347.

8. Mc Kisack, p. 347.

not suited to produce high yields).[9] Consequently, if the number of cultivated acres declined during the fourteenth century, that decline must be measured within the context of a smaller population and of the abandonment of the poorer lands into which agriculture had expanded.[10] Throughout the fourteenth century, individual wealth also increased because the demographic consequences of the plague placed labor at a premium. While the falling prices of staple goods made the necessities of life more accessible to a greater number of people, the cost of labor rose.[11] In response to the rise in wages, statutes were instituted in 1349 and 1350 that attempted to arrest the acceleration of labor costs. These statutes were, however, resisted not only by the laborers themselves, but also by the landlords who needed to establish competitive wages in order to procure labor.[12] In the fourteenth century then, the laborer had surplus income to spend on a better diet, on luxury goods, on possessions that would increase both his comfort and his status.[13] But the plague increased individual prosperity in yet another way. Men and women found emotional loss accompanied by material profit, for the death of family members distributed inherited property among fewer survivors.[14]

---

9. Postan, "The Economic Foundations of Medieval Eeonomy," p. 14.

10. Mc Kisack, p. 347.

11. Postan, "The Trade of Medieval Europe: The North," p. 214; Mc Kisack, pp. 333 ff.

12. On the regulation of labor prices, see Mc Kisack, p. 335 and Du Boulay, p. 14.

13. Du Boulay, p. 14; Miskimin, pp. 135-36.

14. Du Boulay, p. 34.

In England, the war with France did precipitate the contraction of certain areas of commerce, most importantly in the export of wool, England's chief staple.[15] Yet, in response, a native cloth industry developed which, because it provided employment and produced a finished product more expensive than the raw material, ultimately proved more profitable than the export of wool.[16] Through the use of technological innovations like the fulling mill, people in the countryside could make the prices of their cloths competitive with those of urban manufacturers. They too enjoyed the increased prosperity brought by the growth of the cloth industry.[17] But the manufacture of cloth not only influenced a greater cross section of the population than the export of raw material. It was accompanied by what Bridbury calls an "astonishing growth of the home market for English cloth . . ."[18] which spelled the end of Flemish domination in cloth sales. The magnitude of the growth of the cloth industry and of the home market is illustrated by the fact that, at a time when England's population had been reduced by a third, "as much English cloth was being sold on the home market as Flemish cloth had been sold there in the early years of the century . . . ."[19]

---

15. Mc Kisack, p. 356. See also Kenneth Ponting's The Woollen Industry of South-West England (Bath: Adams and Darl, 1971) and E. M. Carus-Wilson's "Trends in the Exports of English Woollens in the Fourteenth Century," in Medieval Merchant Venturers, second edition (London: Methuen, 1967), especially pp. 250-62.

16. Carus-Wilson, pp. 261-62.

17. Ibid.; Bridbury, p. 46.

18. Bridbury, pp. 35-36.

19. Ibid.

Much of the economic and social change of the late fourteenth century derived from this growth in industry and commerce. Directly related to the establishment and growth of commerce was the increased use
of that instrument which made large-scale commerce possible: money.
As many economic historians have argued, a "money economy" did not
emerge simultaneously with the "commercial revolution."[20] Money had,
of course, existed for centuries and had been used, in various forms
and to varying degrees, in commercial exchange.[21] But money in the
form of minted coin was not the only currency popular in the early Middle Ages. Because pepper shared many of money's advantages (it is
portable, it lasts, and it is rare), it was often used as currency.[22]
Yet as commerce grew, money became more convenient as a means of exchange; the increased use of money in turn facilitated economic growth
and development. With the greater frequency of monetary transactions,
however, it became necessary to define, or rather, to redefine the
nature and purpose of money. The primary reason for this redefinition
was, of course, purely practical. As national economies began to be
founded upon money, the monarchs and the merchants using money, as well
as the citizens purchasing the necessities of life with it, had to be

---

20. A phrase which I take from the title of Robert Lopez's book,
The Commercial Revolution of the Middle Ages 950-1350 (Englewood
Cliffs: Prentice-Hall, Inc., 1976).

21. M. M. Postan, "The Rise of a Money Economy," Essays in
Economic History, ed. E. M. Carus-Wilson (London: Edward Arnold, 1954),
p. 3. See also Alexander Murray's discussion of the forces influencing
the adoption of a money economy in Reason and Society in the Middle
Ages (Oxford: The Clarendon Press, 1978), pp. 28-29.

22. Murray, p. 33.

able to rely upon its stable value. In the mid-fourteenth century,
the French schoolman Nicholas Oresme wrote his treatise De Moneta
specifically to advocate this stability. Oresme, who has been called
"the father of modern monetary analysis,"[23] was the first medieval
economic theorist to discuss money in practical, economic terms.[24] He
was also the first to argue that money was the possession of the people
and to argue against the prince's right to devalue currency at his own
convenience.[25] According to Oresme, "Primo namque nimis detestabile
et nimis turpe est principi fraudem committere, monetam falsificare,
aurum vocare aurum quod non est aurum et libram quod non est libra"
("First, it is exceedingly detestable and disgraceful in a prince to
commit fraud, to debase his money, to call what is not gold, gold, and
what is not a pound, a pound").[26] For often, the prince's alteration
of the currency is done "propter emolumentum vel lucrum ex tali
mutacione sumendum" ("for the sake of the profit and gain to be got
from the change"--p. 23).

The belief in the prince's power over the national currency was
founded upon a monetary theory that located money's value in its

---

23. Odd Langholm, Price and Value in the Aristotelian Tradition:
A Study in Scholastic Economic Sources (Bergen: Universitetsforlaget,
1979), p. 113.

24. Émile Bridrey, Nicole Oresme: Étude d'Histoire des Doctrines
et des Faits Économiques (Paris: V. Giard et E. Brière, 1906), pp. 429-
430.

25. Bridrey, pp. 194-95.

26. Nicholas Oresme, De Moneta, ed. and trans. Charles Johnson
(London: Thomas Nelson and Sons, Ltd., 1956), p. 30. All quotations
from Oresme's treatise will refer to Johnson's edition and translation
and will be cited by page number within the body of the text.

utility as an instrument of measure. In his comprehensive survey of the monetary theory of Oresme and his predecessors, Émile Bridrey defines the value and function of money within a feudal economy: "Le numéraire est la mesure des valeurs, l'instrument des échanges . . . la fonction de mesure est tout son rôle, et il paraît oiseux de rechercher s'il a ou non une valuer réelle, puisqu'il n'est jamais destiné à emmagasiner en lui-même de la valeur, mais seulement à comparer entre elles des valeurs."[27] Alexander Murray gives an example of the way in which money was used as an instrument of measure: "Of the traditional functions of money, its role as a measure of value became uppermost . . . 'A tapestry worth ten solidi,' 'a candlestick worth ten denarii,' are typical phrases in records of payments."[28] Money could operate solely as an instrument of measure so long as economies were based primarily on exchanges in kind. When money became the chief medium of exchange in large commercial transactions, it had to contain a stored value that was fixed and reliable. Consequently, with the growing demand for stable money that accompanied the growth of commerce and with the shortage of precious metals that precipitated the successive devaluations of coinage by the prince, there came the awareness that the prince could not devalue money at his will or convenience.[29] The repercussions of these devaluations, in the form of severe inflation, threatened the national economy whose vitality was increasingly depen-

---

27. Bridrey, p. 107.

28. Murray, p. 31.

29. Bridrey discusses the economic conditions that lead to the formulation of Oresme's monetary theory on pp. 150-57, 430-31.

dent on commerce.[30] Money had begun to assume a function and an importance that the feudal monetary theory could no longer accommodate.[31]
These practical exigencies, accompanied by the advent of Aristotle's
works into western Europe in the thirteenth century, precipitated a
change in the attitude toward money, its use, and its valuation.

If Aristotle became a dominant influence in late medieval thought,
the fifth section of the fifth book of his Nichomachean Ethics virtually became the center of scholastic economic theory.[32] Although, as
Odd Langholm notes, Aristotle was more concerned with value and price
than with money,[33] his definition of money and its use also became the
source of medieval monetary theory. Aristotle writes of money:

> It is therefore necessary that all commodities shall be
> measured by some one standard . . . And this standard is in
> reality demand, which is what holds everything together,
> since if men cease to have wants or if their wants alter,
> exchange will go on no longer, or will be on different lines.
> But demand has come to be conventionally represented by
> money; this is why money is called nomisma (customary cur-
> rency), because it does not exist by nature but by custom
> (nomos), and can be altered and rendered useless at will.[34]

---

30. W. J. Courtenay, "The King and the Leaden Coin: The Economic
Background of 'sine qua non' Causality," Traditio, 28 (1972), fn. 25,
193.

31. Bridrey, p. 158.

32. Langholm, p. 12. Langholm's book traces the influence of the
Nichomachean Ethics V. v. on scholastic economic theory and specifically on the scholastic development of criteria for determining value
in exchange.

33. Langholm writes: "Aristotle has been much praised for his
pioneering venture into monetary theory . . . but in point of fact his
interest in money was only an indirect one; he was concerned primarily
with price, not with credit" (p. 24). Nonetheless, given the importance of the Nichomachean Ethics V. v. to the whole of scholastic economic theory, it was inevitable that Aristotle should be used as a
source for scholastic analysis of money as well.

34. Aristotle, The Nichomachean Ethics, ed. and trans. H. Rack-

In the Summa Theologiae, Aristotle's definition of money's nature and
purpose is repeated, essentially unchanged, by Thomas Aquinas:
"Quantitas autem rerum, quae in usum hominis veniunt, mensuratur
secundum pretium datum; ad quod est inventum numisma, ut dicitur" ("But
the value of consumer products is measured by the price given, which as
Aristotle pointed out, is what coinage was invented for").[35]

Bridrey, who finds in the Aristotelian definition of money a summary of feudal monetary theory, glosses the implications of this theory:

> Si la monnaie n'est ni la richesse absolument, ni même une
> richesse quelconque, si elle n'est pas un bien in rerum
> natura, si elle n'est qu'une valeur conventionnelle, c'est
> en réalité qu'elle est tout simplement un signe, le signe
> de la richesse, ou comme Aristote le dit lui-même, une
> futilité, un vain hochet . . . ce rapport du signe à la
> chose signifiée n'est en raison qu'un lien artificiel.
> Pure création de notre volonté, une convention l'a formé,
> une convention inverse peut l'anéantir.[36]

Such a monetary theory would, of course, allow the prince to alter
coinage at will, according to the conventions that he himself establishes. It would produce a monetary system based upon nothing but an
arbitrarily, if royally, determined system of signs. These signs, in
naming value, would, in effect, create it. It would make no difference
if a coin imprinted with a certain designation were "worth its weight
in gold." If a prince assigned the value of a gold coin to one made

---

ham, Loeb Library (Cambridge: Harvard Univ. Press, 1939), V. v. 11.
All quotations from the Ethics refer to Rackham's edition and translation and will be cited by section number within the body of the text.

35. Thomas Aquinas, Summa Theologiae, prepared by Blackfriars
(London: Eyre and Spottiswoode; New York: McGraw Hill Book Co.), Q.
77, a. 1, pp. 214-15. See also Langholm, pp. 91-92.

36. Bridrey, pp. 361-62.

from copper, the copper coin could circulate as gold. The feudal

theory of money could, in fact, produce a currency composed entirely

of counterfeits, of coins that do not deliver the value promised by

their names.

Although Aristotle's definition of money emphasized its conven-

tionality, he also provides the foundation for the late medieval argu-

ment that money functions as money and can represent value because of

its intrinsic worth. Again in the fifth section of the fifth book of

the Nichomachean Ethics, Aristotle writes:

> Now money serves us as a guarantee of exchange in the future:
> supposing we need nothing at the moment, it ensures that ex-
> change shall be possible when a need arises, for it meets the
> requirements of something we can produce in payment so as to
> obtain the thing we need. . . . it [money] tends to be com-
> paratively constant.
> (Ethics, V. v. 14)

Although, in the Politics, Aristotle writes that often "it is thought

that money is nonsense, and entirely a convention but by nature noth-

ing,"[37] he also writes that

> . . . for the purpose of barter men made a mutual compact
> to give and accept some substance of such a sort as being
> itself a useful commodity was easy to handle in use for
> general life, iron for instance, silver and other metals, at
> the first stage defined merely by size and weight, but fi-
> nally also by impressing on it a stamp in order that this
> might relieve them of having to measure it; for the stamp was
> put on as a token of the amount.
> (Politics, I. iii. 14)

This acknowledgment that, despite its conventional nature, money can

store value and must itself be made of a "useful" (that is, in Aris-

---

37. Aristotle, Politics, ed. and trans. H. Rackham, Loeb Library
(Cambridge: Harvard Univ. Press, 1959), I. iii. 16. All quotations
from the Politics refer to Rackham's edition and translation and will
be cited by section number within the body of the text.

totelian terms, a valuable) material leads to Oresme's redefinition of
feudal monetary theory.

Before Oresme, medieval monetary theorists had commented on the
bonitas intrinseca and the bonitas extrinseca (or valor imposita) of
money.[38] Oresme, however, was the first to develop fully the concept
of money's intrinsic worth and to use that concept as the basis for a
pragmatic monetary theory. In De Moneta, Oresme, like Aristotle in the
Politics, recognizes that money must possess certain qualities in order
to fulfill the function for which it was intended. Among these is the
need for money to be minted from materials that are valued apart from
their use as money:

> Et quoniam moneta est instrumentum permutandi diuicias
> naturales . . . consequens fuit quod ad hoc tale instrumentum
> esset aptum; quod fit, si sit faciliter manibus attractabile
> seu palpabile, leuiter portabile, et quod pro modica ipsius
> porcione habeantur diuicie naturales in quantitate maiori
> . . . . Oportuit ergo quod nummisma fieret de materia
> preciosa et rara, cuiusmodi est aurum (p. 5).

> (Now, since money is an instrument for the exchange of natu-
> ral riches . . . it follows that it must be a fit tool for
> the work. This implies that it must be easy to handle and to

---

38. Because Oresme was the first economic theorist to pursue and
articulate fully the implications of money's intrinsic worth, I have
concentrated on Oresme for the purposes of this chapter. Cynus, as
Bridrey writes "pose une distinction qui sera capitale dans la théorie
nouvelle, la distinction d'une bonitas intrinseca et d'une bonitas
extrinseca des éspèces. Mais . . . sa conception reste dans l'appli-
cation assez hésitante. Il lui arrive de dire que la bonitas ne con-
siste pas dans la matière même, mais dans le cours légal . . ." (p.
342). Giles of Rome, in his De Regimine, also addressed the question
of intrinsic worth but without using this new theory of money to replace that of his predecessors. I refer again to Bridrey, who writes
of Giles: "la preuve, dit-il, qu'il y a une valeur préexistente et
survivante du métal, c'est qu'il arrive qu'on fonde justement les
éspèces, pour en tirer un bénéfice, c'est que tout un genre de spécula-
tions, toute une serie d'artes pecuniativae, s'est fondée sur cette
propriété . . . avant d'être monnaie, elle est une chose comme une

feel with the hands, light to carry and that a small portion
of it should purchase a larger quantity of natural riches
. . . . Coin must therefore be made of precious and rare
material, such as gold.)

It is on the basis of money's intrinsic worth that Oresme argues

against the change of ratio through which a prince can devalue money:

"Nam secundum hoc quod aurum est de natura sua preciosius et rarius

argento, et ad inueniendum uel habendum difficilis, ipsum aurum equalis

ponderis debet preualere in certa proporcione" ("For as gold is natu-

rally more precious and scarcer than silver, and more difficult to find

and to get, gold of the same weight ought to excel silver in value by

a definite proportion"--p. 15).

Oresme also uses the concept of money's intrinsic worth to argue

against changing the names of coins in order to inflate their value

artificially. He writes:

> . . . ideo per sapientes illius temporis prudenter prouisum
> est, quod porciones monete fierent de certa materia et
> determinati ponderis, quodque in eis imprimeretur figura que
> cunctis notoria significaret qualitatem materie nummismatis
> et ponderis ueritatem, ut amota suspicione posset ualor
> monete sine labore cognosci. Quod autem impressio talis
> instituta sit nummis in signum veritatis materie et ponderis,
> manifeste nobis ostendunt antiqua nomina monetarum
> cognoscibilium ex impressionibus et figuris . . . . (pp. 8-9)
>
> (. . . it was wisely ordained by the sages of that time that
> pieces of money should be made of a given metal and of a
> definite weight and that they should be stamped with a de-
> sign, known to everybody, to indicate the quality and the
> true weight of the coin so that suspicion should be averted
> and the value readily recognized. And that stamp on coins
> was instituted as a guarantee of fineness and weight, is
> clearly proved by the ancient names of coins . . . .)

For Oresme, then, the names of coins must bear a direct and just rela-

---

autre, que la convention n'a ajouté qu'une utilité nouvelle à sa valeur
préexistente" (p. 382).

tionship to the value inherent in the material from which the coin is made. The _figura_ on the coin is determined by the value of the material and not the other way around. On the basis of a theory of intrinsic worth, Oresme argues for the stability of the sign.

It is undeniable that, as Aristotle wrote, man has final power over his conventions. Human need creates value and money is a convention invented by man in order to measure that value.[39] Oresme would not deny the conventionality of money, as the passage quoted above makes clear. But, as the passage also implies, once man has made conventions, he should respect them; he should not devalue them arbitrarily, for his own profit. Money should be minted from a valuable material, says Oresme. Gold is valuable because it is rare, a conception of value reflecting the human subjectivity that ultimately establishes value. Once the value of gold has been established and accepted, however, the name on the coin must indicate the intrinsic value of the metal from which it is minted. For only when the _valor imposita_ correlates with the _bonitas intrinseca_ can the coin's value be identified: "in eis imprimeretur figura que cunctis notoria significaret qualitatem materie nummismatis et ponderis ueritatem, ut amota suspicione posset ualor monete sine labor cognosci." Because the _figura_, the sign, is known to all, then value can be recognized easily. But only if the

---

39. The way in which human need creates and determines value is a complex question. Aristotle presented this formula for determining value in the _Ethics_, V. v. and scholastic economic theory addressed itself to interpretations of need that lead ultimately to the demand theory of economic value at the end of the scholastic period. I will take up the question of need as a determinant of value in Chapter II in relation to the Wife of Bath's formulation of economic and ethical values.

figura actually names the value of the coin can man be sure that he reads value correctly. Without a just correlation between valor imposita and bonitas intrinseca, money's purpose, the facilitation of the exchange of value, is undermined. An unstable correlation between intrinsic and extrinsic value produces economic instability in a world increasingly dependent on money and commercial exchange.

Oresme's theory of intrinsic value is not only relevant to monetary value and economic exchange. It is also applicable to language, to that convention which man has invented to facilitate the exchange called communication. Interestingly, in the gloss to his translation of Aristotle's Ethics, Oresme specifically associates money and communication: "Et monnoie est telle mesure comme dit est, par quoy il appert que usage de monnoie est aussuy comme necessaire en communicacioun civile."[40] A word, like a coin, consists of a figura, its signifier, and an intrinsic value, its meaning, its signified. A coin, because of its intrinsic value, defines the value of a commodity in relation to other commodities. Similarly, a word, because of the meaning assigned to it, names a phenomenon according to its relationship to other phenomena existing outside language. The coin cannot serve its purpose when a disruption of the correlation between valor imposita and bonitas intrinseca has devalued it. Nor can a word serve its purpose when it is not used to designate its own meaning. The prince who devalues money does so with false intention, for his own profit. The person who uses language falsely, in order to misrepresent his own

---

40. Bridrey, Appendix, p. 706.

intention devalues language. He disrupts the stability of the linguistic exchanges that constitute communication. The value and
stability of language is as important to the poet as the stable value
of his medium of exchange is to the merchant.

Nicholas Oresme introduced a monetary theory advocating the stable
value of the coin into a world whose social values had been rendered
unstable by money itself. The laborer, who could command higher wages,
enjoyed a higher standard of living that allowed him more purchasing
power. The artisans and tradesmen associated with the burgeoning cloth
industry amassed greater personal wealth. And, as Lester Little
writes, "the merchants, the bankers, the industrial entrepreneurs, and
the professionals . . . [were] dominant in urban life, not because
[they] constituted a majority of the population . . . but because
[they] were in command of the new market economy and eventually derived
therefrom considerable wealth and commensurate political power."[41] The
late fourteenth century was a period in which most people had more
money than they had ever had before. It was an age of a growing middle
class (even though that class had no name with which to define itself)
and upward social mobility. Money and material goods were admired,
coveted, valued because they could confer social status and people increasingly defined themselves and others by what they owned.[42] The

---

41. Lester K. Little, Religious Poverty and The Profit Economy
in Medieval Europe (Ithaca: Cornell Univ. Press, 1978), p. 24.

42. Du Boulay, pp. 14-15; Thrupp, p. 143.

desire for wealth, material goods, and the value which they represented was often stronger than the ethical values prescribed by Christian doctrine. In this age of shifting values, not even the clergy
could be relied on as the repositories of stable Christian morality.
The materialism that had infected the commons also beseiged the ecclesiastical estate. Pope John XXII decreed, in 1323, that belief in
Christ's poverty constituted heresy.[43]

The social fluidity caused by the fluidity of wealth went far
toward obliterating those distinctions between classes that, in fact,
create social classes. With more income to spend on luxuries, members
of the middle class could purchase the clothing, the houses, and the
material possessions that would allow them to resemble those in the
upper ranks of society. In social terms, the necessary relationship
between valor imposita and bonitas intrinseca had been ruptured and it
was no longer easy to determine social status. Nonetheless, there were
attempts, most often futile, to maintain the distinctions between
social classes. One such attempt was the institution, beginning in
1363, of a series of sumptuary laws which historians give us every
reason to believe were generally ignored. The sumptuary laws "'for
the reformation of excessive array'"[44] were ostensibly formulated for
moral and economic reasons: to arrest the flow of imported luxuries
and to arrest unChristian preoccupation with dress. But, as Du Boulay
concludes, "the social fear felt by men of estate for their ebullient

---

43. Rodney Hilton, Bond Men Made Free (London: Temple Smith,
1973), p. 104.

44. Du Boulay, p. 67.

inferiors was none the less strongly expressed in them. The statute

of 1363 certainly referred directly to the 'outrageous apparel of

divers people against their estate and degree' . . . ."[45]

If money had obscured social value, it had gone even farther

toward obscuring moral value. Wit, cunning, intelligence, and an eye

for a real bargain or a quick profit make a good merchant. Yet the

traits that constitute his professional value can undermine his ethical

values within a Christian moral framework. A financially astute priest

assures the security and the efficiency of his parish. Yet his pre-

occupation with clerical economics can become an end rather than a

means. In a world in which it was increasingly important to be a good

professional, it became increasingly difficult to determine an individ-

ual's intrinsic moral worth.[46] In such a world, money might well be

the only phenomenon that possessed a stable value deriving from the

correlation between valor imposita and bonitas intrinseca.

It is this world, whose social and economic currents I have out-

lined, that Chaucer recreates through the characters in his General

Prologue. Most of his characters manifest the materialism and the con-

cern with identifying themselves through property and money that were

rampant in the late Middle Ages. In most of the pilgrims, professional

and economic values vie with, if they have not obliterated, ethical and

moral values. Moreover, the microcosm of the General Prologue intro-

45. Ibid., p. 67.

46. See Jill Mann, Chaucer and Medieval Estates Satire: The
Literature of Social Classes and the General Prologue to the Canter-
bury Tales (Cambridge: Cambridge Univ. Press, 1973), p. xi; Traugott
Lawler, The One and the Many in The Canterbury Tales (Hamden: Archon
Books, 1980, pp. 33ff.

duces various and conflicting standards (personal, social, economic, professional, Christian moral) by which to measure value.[47] The conflicts between these categories underline the ambiguity and ambivalence prevalent in a world whose traditional modes of determining value can no longer accommodate the complexities and changes within the world itself.[48] Jill Mann concludes that "all these ambiguities . . . and the confusion of moral and emotional reactions, add up to Chaucer's consistent removal of the possibility of moral judgement."[49] I would argue that Chaucer's use of ambiguity in the General Prologue, rather than removing the possibility of moral judgment, specifically calls attention to its difficulty. For ambiguity demands that evaluation be based on interpretation rather than on a cursory reading of superficial signs.[50]

Chaucer emphasizes the necessity of interpretation in order to evaluate an ambiguous world through the character of his pilgrim-narrator and, specifically, through the pilgrim-narrator's interpretative inadequacies.[51] The pilgrim-narrator begins his catalogue of portraits

47. For discussions of ambiguity in the General Prologue, see Mann's Book, especially pp. 187ff; E. Talbot Donaldson's "Chaucer the Pilgrim," Speaking of Chaucer (New York: W. W. Norton and Co., Inc., 1972), pp. 1-12; and H. Marshall Leicester, Jr.'s article, "The Art of Impersonation: A General Prologue to the Canterbury Tales," PMLA, 95 (1980), 213-14.

48. See Leicester, 221.

49. Mann, p. 197.

50. See Judson B. Allen and Theresa Anne Moritz, A Distinction of Stories: The Medieval Unity of Chaucer's Fair Chain of Narratives for Canterbury (Columbus: Ohio State Univ. Press, 1981), p. 11.

51. The idea of a "pilgrim-narrator" derives, of course, from Donaldson's essay, "Chaucer the Pilgrim" and, throughout my discussion

with the promise

> To telle yow al the condicioun
> Of ech of hem, <u>so</u> <u>as</u> <u>it</u> <u>semed</u> <u>me</u>,
> And whiche they weren, and of what degree,
> And eek in what array that they were inne . . . .
> (I. A, 38-41; emphasis mine)[52]

The narrator will focus in his catalogue on the pilgrims' externali-

ties, their rank, their professions, their dress, as he sees them, as

he reads them, "so as it semed me." But rank, profession, and even

dress are not exclusively superficial signs; they can be indices of an

individual's personality as well as of his relationship to himself and to

his society. As the pilgrim-narrator's portraits show, his conversa-

tions with the pilgrims have gone far towards revealing the ways in

which dress, profession, and social status reflect personal attributes

and moral values. But if his portraits show that a correlation between

exterior and interior does exist, the narrator does not interpret this

correlation accurately. He does not use it as the basis of an adequate

evaluation of (most of) the pilgrims. If it is difficult to assess the

intrinsic worth of the Canterbury pilgrims because of the conflicting

standards of value that the General Prologue itself presents, it is not

impossible. Or rather, it is only impossible for the pilgrim-narrator,

---

of the pilgrim-narrator, I rely and elaborate upon the suggestions
within Donaldson's essay. Recent critics have, however, questioned
the literary existence of such a pilgrim-narrator. See H. Marshall
Leicester, in the article cited above, 218ff, and Allen and Moritz in
A Distinction of Stories, pp. 11-12.

  52. All quotations from the General Prologue refer to the second
edition of F. N. Robinson's Works of Geoffrey Chaucer (Boston: Houghton
Mifflin, 1957), and will be cited by fragment and line number within
the body of the text.

whose own standards of measurement are subjective, reductive, and
morally confused.

As he concludes his presentation of the pilgrims, the narrator
offers an apology for failing to order his catalogue:

> . . . I prey yow to foryeve it me,
> Al have I nat set folk in hir degree
> Heere in this tale, as that they sholde stonde.
> My wit is short, ye may wel understonde.
> (I. A, 743-46)

Although critics have discovered a variety of orderings within the
General Prologue,[53] it is significant that the pilgrim-narrator himself
believes that he has allowed disorder, and specifically, disorder in
the matter of "degree," to invade his catalogue. He begins his catalogue on the right, that is, on the traditional, foot. After describing the knight and his retinue, he presents the ecclesiastical estate.
Although the narrator could have maintained an ordering by "degree" by
placing the Parson among the ecclesiastical pilgrims (rather than after
the Wife of Bath), he moves, instead, from the Friar to the Merchant as
he begins his presentation of his bourgeois companions. Nor are the
bourgeois portraits arranged in any discernible order, except insofar
as the catalogue concludes with those pilgrims who are neither so
wealthy nor so socially prominent nor so physically attractive as the
Franklin or the Seargeant of Law or the Physician.[54] The pilgrim-nar-

---

53. For two recent interpretations of the order within the General Prologue, see Allen and Moritz, pp. 89-91, and Donald Howard, The
Idea of The Canterbury Tales (Berkeley: Univ. of California Press,
1976), pp. 150ff.

54. Donaldson, pp. 5-6.

rator's catalogue fails to follow a traditional social or literary order in relation to degree because Chaucer has used disorder to reflect the instability of social value within his milieu.

In a world in which monetary fluidity has created social fluidity, the definition of "degree" itself becomes problematic. Just as a syntactical system is organized according to the different functions of words, the structure of medieval society had been founded upon distinct differences between classes, between "degrees." Uncertainty about the functions of words produces a syntactical disorder, the consequences of which are ambiguity at best, and at worst, meaninglessness. The social fluidity of the late fourteenth century, which obscured the traditional differences between classes, manifests itself in the fundamentally syntactical disorder of the General Prologue. The pilgrim-narrator, uncertain about what constitutes the differences between the elements of his catalogue, cannot order them according to a syntactically coherent system.

The pilgrim-narrator, who cannot order by "degree," resolves the ambiguities of his world and simplifies the problems of evaluation that it presents, by assigning value on the basis of a cursory reading of superficial signs. His reading not only denies the complexity of the pilgrims; it also produces inaccurate interpretations of value. His mode of measuring value is analogous to that of feudal monetary theory. If the figura signifies to the narrator a certain amount of worth, it does not matter if a corresponding bonitas intrinseca validates this designation. The General Prologue portraits may not reveal a traditional social or poetic order; they do, however, demonstrate the way in which the pilgrim-narrator's consciousness responds to and organizes the world around him. The growing materialism and professionalism that have created social and moral ambiguities have also influenced his consciousness. He responds to surfaces; he admires wealth and good clothes. For him, a sufficient amount of material value and personal attractiveness can compensate for moral failings.[55]

The pilgrim-narrator's penchant for assigning value on the basis of superficial readings may produce relatively venial errors in his assessment of the Prioress; it may lead him to oversight and omission rather than gross miscalculation.[56] But his bourgeois attraction to wealth and professional skills can produce more serious moral errors in the case of pilgrims who have little but their possessions and their competence to recommend them. It is doubtful whether the piratical Shipman, who devalues a "nyce conscience" (I. A, 398), is simultaneously a "good felawe" (I. A, 395).[57] It is doubtful whether the crooked Physician, who "lovede gold in special" (I. A, 444), is also "a verray, parfit praktisour" (I. A, 422). Throughout the General Prologue, the pilgrim-narrator demonstrates his inability to interpret and thus to evaluate through his misuse of epithets that conventionally name not only value, but, specifically, moral value. The knight is called "gentil" (I. A, 72), a designation appropriate to both his

---

55. Ibid., p. 4, 5.

56. Ibid., pp. 3-4.

57. Ibid., pp. 6-7. Contrary to Robinson's gloss of this phrase as "a rascal," Donaldson notes that a "good felawe" can just as easily be translated into its modern English equivalent.

social rank and his moral worth. But the Manciple (I. A, 567) and the Pardoner (1. A, 669) are also called "gentil" when the word correlates with neither intrinsic nor extrinsic worth. The pilgrim-narrator's most glaring misuse of the epithet occurs in his virtually oxymoronic description of the Summoner as "a gentil harlot and a kynde" (I. A, 647). At this point, the pilgrim-narrator himself seems to feel that he has gone too far. He proceeds to condemn the Summoner, not for his pimping but, ironically enough, for his cursing, for his misuse of language.

The narrator's misapplication of these epithets shows both his moral confusion and his interpretative reductiveness. The fluidity of language that these epithets imply reflects, of course, the social fluidity and the fluidity of value within the world of the General Prologue.[58] Through the repetition of words like "gentil" and "worthy" within different and often incongruous moral contexts, Chaucer demonstrates that words are subject to the same multivalency as everything else in this world. But Chaucer also shows that, when the word is not used to designate the meaning conventionally assigned to it, it can become a cipher; it can become meaningless. What, after all, is a "gentil harlot?" Ironically, the pilgrim-narrator, who puts into practice what we might call a "feudal theory" of language, apologizes for repeating bawdy tales verbatim with the excuse that "wordes moote be cosyn to the dede" (I. A, 742). The pilgrim-narrator's excuse suggests the need for referentiality that Nicholas Oresme had advocated

---

58. Mann, p. 196.

in his theory of money's intrinsic worth. Yet the narrator's own use
of language within the General Prologue, his own failure to associate
words with their designated meanings, undermines the validity of his
excuse.

In a world in which the signs that should designate value have
themselves become multivalent, it becomes increasingly necessary to
derive assessments of value from clear-sighted interpretation. In an
ambiguous world, cursory readings of surfaces are not sufficient to
produce adequate evaluations. If Chaucer used the pilgrim-narrator to
underline the necessity of interpretation, he also uses another unlikely character, the Host Harry Bailley, to emphasize this theme.
The shrewd bourgeois innkeeper, Harry Bailly is, in effect, the Muse
inspiring The Canterbury Tales; it is he who suggests that the pilgrims
tell stories to amuse themselves on the way to Canterbury. But his
suggestion does not stop there, although it might have. The Host goes
on to place the stories within the framework of a competition, in order
to determine which of the pilgrims "bereth hym best of alle" (I. A,
796). A competition is an enterprise established for the sole purpose
of determining value. By using the competition as the inspiration for
the pilgrims' stories, Chaucer underlines his own interests in the determination of value throughout The Canterbury Tales. But a competition also needs a judge, someone to interpret value, someone to determine merit on the basis of the relationship between the competitors'
performances. Significantly, Chaucer has established the bourgeois
gentilhomme Harry Bailley as the literary critic of The Canterbury
Tales. The predominantly middle class pilgrims will be judged in their

own terms by one of their own kind.

But amusement and concern for literary value are not Harry Bailley's primary motivation for establishing the story-telling competition. The winner's prize will be

> . . . a soper at oure aller cost
> Heere in this place, sittynge by this post,
> Whan that we come agayn fro Caunterbury.
> (I. A, 799-801)

Harry Bailley wants to make sure that thirty pilgrims find their way

back to his Tabard Inn at the end of their journey.[59] In a world whose

values have been influenced by the growth of commerce and the rise of

a money economy, even literature cannot escape the profit-motive. It

is more than fitting, as Chaucer well knew, that a poem concerned with

economic transformations of ethical and linguistic value should be

founded upon Harry Bailley's commercial contract. Nevertheless, the

story-telling competition is not the only inspiration for The Canter-

bury Tales. There is also the pilgrimage itself. Although, by the

time Chaucer's company turned towards Canterbury, the moral value of

pilgrimage had itself become ambiguous,[60] the tension between the

spiritual and the economic inspirations of The Canterbury Tales under-

lines the primary cause of the instability of value in Chaucer's world.

---

59. Robert W. Hanning, "The Theme of Art and Life in Chaucer's
Poetry," in Geoffrey Chaucer, ed. George D. Economou (New York: McGraw-
Hill Book Company, 1975), p. 27.

60. For a discussion of late fourteenth-century clerical ambivalence toward pilgrimage, see Muriel Bowden, A Commentary on the General
Prologue to The Canterbury Tales (New York: The Macmillan Company,
1954), pp. 23ff.

Chapter II

WHAT WOMEN MOST DESIRE: VALUE AND ITS DETERMINATION

IN THE WIFE OF BATH'S PROLOGUE AND TALE

In the General Prologue, the pilgrim-narrator's use and abuse of
the word gentil reflect both his interpretative limitations and the
difficulty of determining value in his multivalent world. At the end
of The Wife of Bath's Tale, gentillesse is again at the center of Chaucer's concerns as the Loathly Bride offers her disconsolate young groom
a sermon on that subject. The sermon's presence in the bourgeois
Wife's Tale has troubled some critics nearly as much as the hag's presence in his bed troubles the young knight. For many critics, an ir-
resolvable incongruity exists between the substance of the hag's sermon
and the acquisitiveness, materialism, and cruelty of which Alison has
boasted throughout her Prologue; for these critics, the morality of the
sermon serves only to condemn the Wife.[1] More recent critics, who are
more generous in their evaluation of the Wife's temperament, have not
been so puzzled by this alleged incongruity. While some have posited
a thematic relationship between the Prologue and the sermon on

---

1. For critics who note the incongruity between the Wife's behavior and the sermon on gentillesse, see R. M. Lumiansky, Of Sondry
Folk (Austin: University of Texas Press, 1955), p. 128; Kemp Malone,
Chapters on Chaucer (Baltimore: The Johns Hopkins University Press,
1951), p. 216; and B. F. Huppé, A Reading of The Canterbury Tales (Albany: State University of New York Press, 1964), p. 134.

gentillesse, others have seen, in the sermon, a revelation of previously hidden qualities in the Wife of Bath. Dorothy Colmer locates the
thematic connection between the Prologue and Tale in Alison's member-
ship in the growing middle class; the sermon is thus "a bourgeois ob-
jection to showing deference where no superiority is apparent . . . ."[2]
In a different vein, Robert Burlin believes that the fiction of her
tale frees the Wife of Bath and thereby allows "a surprising extension
of the Wife's fantasy to include refined sentiments and immaterial
values . . . ideals she could not easily appropriate to her public
self."[3]

The issues which the hag presents in her sermon do reflect Alison's concerns throughout her Prologue and Tale. Yet these concerns
derive not only from her position as a member of the new middle class,
but also from her status in a world whose values are determined by men.
Moreover, as I will discuss in this chapter, the concerns of the
Loathly Lady and of the Wife closely resemble the artistic questions of
the poet who created them. An interest in revaluation unites the
Loathly Lady, the Wife of Bath, and Chaucer: the revaluation and redefinition of convention that allows convention to represent new meaning.

The young knight candidly offers his bride an ungrateful, if not
unnatural, explanation for his reluctance in the marriage bed:

        "Thou art so loothly, and so oold also,

---

2. Dorothy Colmer, "Character and Class in The Wife of Bath's
Tale," JEGP, 72 (1973), 336.
3. Robert Burlin, Chaucerian Fiction (Princeton: Princeton University Press, 1977), p. 223.

> And therto comen of so lough a kynde,
> That litel wonder is thogh I walwe and wynde.
> So wolde God myn herte wolde breste."
>   (III. D, 1100-03)[4]

The hag replies by redefining gentillesse for the knight. She locates

the virtue in one's temperament and not, as her husband would, in

worldly attainments: in birth, wealth, or beauty. She argues that one

is gentil from the inside out and not the other way around. Society

cannot make one gentil, because the attainments valued by society are

transient. Only one's heavenly, not one's earthly father can grant

gentillesse.

The hag does not provide a radically new definition of gentillesse

(although her definition seems unfamiliar to the young knight).[5] More-

over, her sermon itself possesses a distinguished lineage.[6] It takes

its details in part from Lady Philosophy's advice to Boethius and in

part, as the hag tells us, from Dante.[7] Chaucer himself wrote a short

poem "Gentilesse" that essentially restates the Loathly Lady's argu-

ment. But if the substance of the hag's speech is not new, its context

---

4. All quotations from Chaucer's text are taken from F. N. Robinson's Works of Geoffrey Chaucer, second edition (Boston: Houghton Mifflin Co., 1957), and will be cited by fragment and line number within
the body of the chapter.

5. See Robinson's notes on gentillesse in his edition of Chaucer's
Works, p. 704. In Kingship and Common Profit in Gower's Confessio
Amantis (Carbondale: Southern Illinois University Press, 1978), Russell
A. Peck discusses the differences between The Wife of Bath's Tale and
Gower's Tale of Florent (pp. 46-49).

6. Robinson, p. 704.

7. See Boece, iii, pr. 4 and ii, pr. 7. I refer to and quote
from Robinson's edition of Chaucer's Boece throughout this chapter.
Dante's Convivio (fourth Tractate) and Purgatorio, vii, 121 ff. are, as
Robinson notes, Chaucer's primary literary influences in the sermon on

is. Without its context, the Loathly Lady's speech would have no further resonances than does Chaucer's short poem. Both would restate an analysis of gentillesse with which tradition (both literary and ecclesiastical) would have acquainted the medieval Christian. The way we read the Loathly Lady's speech is determined by its context within the narrative of the tale itself, by the personality of the tale's teller and, above all, by the social context to which the Wife of Bath belongs.

Economic growth, as we have seen in Chapter I, not only demanded a redefinition of the value of money in order to accommodate its increasing importance as a medium of exchange. It also produced a social fluidity that demanded a redefinition of social values in order to accommodate the growing prominence and power of certain classes. One such value was gentillesse.[8] The word gentillesse assigns and measures value; it attributes excellence to those who are designated gentil. Gentillesse had traditionally been an aristocratic attribute belonging to those who possessed property, rank, and power, who fulfilled the criteria outlined by the knight in the Wife's Tale. The middle class, with its growing wealth and political power, questioned their own right to this designation. There was, however, another denotation of the word gentillesse. In a Christian world, gentillesse entailed more than material or ancestral excellence; it also designated spiritual excellence, charity, magnanimity. Yet this Christian conception of

----

gentillesse.

8. See also Sylvia Thrupp, The Merchant Class of Medieval London (Chicago: University of Chicago Press, 1948), p. 245 ff., for a survey of the various prerequisites for gentility in the fourteenth and fifteenth centuries.

gentillesse was accompanied by the social assumption (made automati-
cally by the young knight) that a necessary correlation existed between
birth and wealth and spiritual integrity. We need only examine our own
usage of the word "noble" to see this linguistic correlation at work.
"Nobility" means more than bloodlines and bankbooks. It is a moral
state accompanying the security that bloodlines and bankbooks give. It
is a graciousness, a tolerance, an openhandedness characteristic of
those who possess economic and social distinction. For the medieval
bourgeoisie, a question arose concerning who had the right to be called
gentil. The middle class saw that power and prestige were defined, for
the aristocracy, through material possessions. If one were able to establish oneself through such possessions, would *gentillesse* become a
part of this newly established identity?[9]

The members of the aristocracy were not, however, willing to cede
their title to *gentillesse* to those who were rapidly approaching them,
if not surpassing them, in material wealth.[10] Consequently, they emphasized those aspects of *gentillesse*, ancestry and manners, that the
nouveaux riches could not buy. In her comprehensive study, The Merchant Class of Medieval London, Sylvia Thrupp writes that "[t]he author

---

9. As Thrupp points out, the wealthy burgesses who had recently
come to political power were not loathe to make moral distinctions on
an economic basis. The official terms for men of their own rank were
"pluis sufficeauntz" and "potentiores, pluis vaillantz" (The Merchant
Class, p. 14). Thrupp writes: "The better people are the more honest,
the wiser, the more prudent, and the more discreet. All these qualities are assumed to be present in maximum strength in the richest of
the citizens, the best, the most sufficient, and to be at low ebb among
the poorer citizens. On occasions of political disturbance the latter
were sometimes called the plebs or the lower people (de plebeis,
inferiores)," p. 15.

10. Thrupp, p. 301.

of a dictionary completed in about the year 1440 looked on manners as the very essence of nobility or gentility."[11] Such manners, as Thrupp notes, are, of course, dictated by social convention and bestowed by social rank;[12] they are possessions as surely as wealth and land. Yet it was a commonly held belief (perpetuated, undoubtedly, by the aristocracy) that such manners, the hallmark of gentillesse, could not be imitated by those who had recently acquired material wealth and power.[13] These manners were considered the outward manifestation of spiritual integrity.[14] Gentillesse, then, was a growing concern in an age which experienced a social fluidity dictated by the fluidity of wealth.

The Loathly Lady's discourse on gentillesse underlines and answers a question central to the Wife of Bath's Prologue and Tale and to the social and economic context of Chaucer's middle class woman-clothier from Bath. Through these characters, Chaucer asks his audience: Wherein does value reside? Is convention always an adequate means of measuring value? In the Loathly Lady's sermon, Chaucer studies the problem of determining value. It is a problem which haunts the Wife of Bath, who has struggled to define her own value and values in a world whose masculine traditions would determine those values for her. The Loathly Lady repeats her answer (and that of Alison) firmly throughout

---

11. Ibid., p. 303.

12. Ibid.

13. Ibid.

14. Ibid., pp. 303, 305. And evidently the members of the rising middle class concurred. As A. R. Bridbury points out, etiquette books for the bourgeoisie became increasingly popular as "they struggled with novel and perplexing social difficulties" (Economic Growth, p. 105).

her sermon. Value resides within the self, within one's own personality.

In relation to the hag's subject, gentillesse resides within the
self's capacity and willingness to cultivate a virtuous temperament.
She tells the young knight: "'he is gentil that dooth gentil dedis'"
(III. D, 1170) and "'Thanne am I gentil, whan that I bigynne/ To lyven
vertuously and weyve synne'" (III. D, 1175-76). The hag not only redefines gentillesse for the young knight. She offers him a means of
evaluating gentillesse that replaces the conventional indices of wealth
and birth with the correct signs for determining spiritual value:

> "Looke who that is moost vertuous alway,
> Pryvee and apert, and moost entendeth ay
> To do the gentil dedes that he kan;
> Taak hym for the grettest gentil man."
> (III. D, 1113-16)

In the General Prologue, the pilgrim Parson is described in the terms
that the hag has just presented:

> A good man was ther of religioun,
> And was a povre PERSOUN OF A TOUN,
> But riche he was of hooly thoght and werk.
> (I. A, 477-79)

Her definition of gentillesse would allow the knight to see the Parson
as "'the grettest gentil man.'" The hag, then, divorces gentillesse
from the evaluation (which is, she implies, a devaluation) established
by the conventions of the aristocracy. The aristocracy can, of course,
be gentil. But gentillesse cannot be measured by material and social
privileges, because the worth of gentillesse specifically transcends
those privileges.

The central issue in the hag's sermon, then, is bonitas intrinseca
and the correlation between convention and value. She will assign the

name gentil only to the man who has sufficient intrinsic moral worth

to merit the name. As we have seen in Chapter I, Nicholas Oresme re-

defined feudal monetary theory on the basis of money's bonitas

intrinseca. Oresme's redefinition is analogous to and illuminates the

Loathly Lady's redefinition of gentillesse in The Wife of Bath's Tale.

In his treatise, De Moneta, Oresme writes, in language that recalls

that of the hag in her sermon:

> Et iterum, dedecus est principi irreuereri predecessores
> suos; nam quilibet tenetur ex Dominico precepto honorare
> parentes. Ipse autem progenitorum detrahere uidetur honori,
> quando bonam monetam eorum abrogat, et facit eam cum eorum
> ymagine scindere, et loco monete auree, quam ipsi
> fabricauerant, facit monetam eream in parte.

> (And again, it is a disgrace to a prince to dishonour his
> predecessors, for we are all bound by the Lord's commandment
> to honour our parents. But he seems to detract from the
> honour of his ancestors when he cries down their good money,
> and has it, and with it their image, cut up and in the place
> of the gold money which they coined makes money which is
> partly brass.)[15]

Gentillesse, like money, is devalued by those who continue to use a

name (whether of a family, a virtue, or a coin) after they have debased

the value behind the name. Like the hag's sermon on gentillesse,

Oresme's De Moneta argues that there is an intrinsic value which a name

(whether of a coin or a virtue) should indicate. There should be a

stable value associated with each sign or name, a value determined by

the nature of the object to which the name is applied. In an insight-

ful interpretation of the implications of Oresme's theory, Bridrey

writes: "Oresme . . . tres nettement y reconnait une chose, un objet

---

15. Nicholas Oresme, De Moneta, trans. and ed. Charles Johnson
(London: Thomas Nelson and Sons, Ltd., 1956), p. 31.

naturel, doué par convention de certaines fonctions spéciales, mais un objet préexistent par lui-même à la convention, ayant par lui-même une certaine valeur intrinseque."[16] And in a statement which illuminates the shared concerns of the hag, the Wife, and Nicholas Oresme, Bridrey writes: "La verité, c'est donc que la monnaie n'a pas qu'une valeur purément fictive, c'est qu'elle a aussi une valeur intrinseque réele . . . Si elle est de par son origine une création conventionnelle de l'industrie humaine (instrumentum artificialiter adinventum), il y'a pourtant en elle quelque chose qui échappe à la convention."[17]

There is something in it which escapes convention. That "something," we hear from Oresme and the hag, from the Wife of Bath and from Chaucer, is intrinsic worth. The idea that intrinsic worth exists apart from convention is central both to Chaucer's creation of the Wife of Bath and to the way in which, I believe, he intended us to read her. Chaucer underlines the importance of intrinsic worth in a striking image that appears in the Loathly Lady's sermon in order to illustrate her own argument about gentillesse:

> "Taak fyr, and ber it in the derkeste hous
> Bitwix this and the mount of Kaukasous,
> And lat men shette the dores and go thenne;
> Yet wole the fyr as faire lye and brenne
> As twenty thousand men myghte it biholde;
> His office natureel ay wol it holde,
> Up peril of my lyf, til that it dye."
> (III. D, 1139-45)

The image of fire as something whose nature does not depend upon exter-

---

16. Émile Bridrey, Nicole Oresme: Étude d'Historie des Doctrines et des Faits Économiques (Paris: V. Giard et E. Brière, 1906), p. 201.

17. Bridrey, p. 206.

nal circumstances occurs in the Boece.[18] Lady Philosophy tells

Boethius (in relation to the failure of high offices to insure respect):

"'Certes yif that honour of peple were a natureel yifte to dignytes,

it ne myghte nevere cesen nowhere amonges no maner folk to don his

office; right as fyer in every contre ne stynteth nat to eschaufen and

to ben hoot.'"[19] On a different occasion, as Lady Philosophy discusses

the relativity of fame and of human conventions, she cites the Caucasus

mountains as an example of a distant region into which even the fame of

the Roman Empire has not penetrated.[20] In the hag's speech, Chaucer

conflates the two images--the image of fire retaining its own nature

and the image of a distant place not ruled by familiar conventions--

that appear separately in the Boece. The same conflation does, however,

occur in the fifth book of the Nichomachean Ethics, in the same book in

which Aristotle offers the definition of money and its function that

ultimately produced the scholastic theory of money's intrinsic worth.

Aristotle defines money in the fifth section of the fifth book. In the

seventh section, he uses these two images in his discussion of the de-

termination of justice by nature and convention:

> Some people think that all rules of justice are merely con-
> ventional, because whereas a law of nature is immutable and
> has the same validity everywhere, as fire burns both here
> and in Persia, rules of justice are seen to vary. That
> rules of just vary is not absolutely true . . . there is
> such a thing as Natural Justice . . . .[21]

---

18. See Robinson's note on Chaucer's use of fire on p. 704 of his
edition of the Works.

19. Boece, III, pr. 4.

20. Boece, II, pr. 7.

21. Aristotle, The Nichomachean Ethics, ed. and trans. H. Rackham,

In the fifth book of the Ethics, then, Aristotle associates money and justice through the problems of evaluation that both present. Given our discussion of gentillesse and its place within the hag's sermon, we need only substitute gentillesse for "justice" to see the appropriateness of using the same methods to analyze the nature and value of virtue and money. For justice, gentillesse, and money all make us question the relationship between convention and an independently existing intrinsic worth, just as Chaucer makes us question this same relationship throughout The Wife of Bath's Prologue and Tale. Fire is fire wherever it may burn. It retains and acts in accordance with its nature whether it burns in a palace on in "the derkeste hous" in the Caucasus. And whether gentillesse exists within a rich man or a poor man, within the body of a beautiful woman or of an old and ugly hag, the gentil nature retains its distinguishing characteristics.

In her sermon to the young knight, the hag has "coined" a meaning of gentillesse that revalues the word on the basis of intrinsic worth. She seeks to attribute to gentillesse a value as rich and rare as its name promises. The Loathly Lady wants the word to indicate intrinsic virtue just as Oresme wanted the name on the coin to indicate the intrinsic worth of the metal from which it was minted. Nonetheless, the external signs that we use to measure and to read value can never be wholly sufficient for their purpose. There is an internal nature, an intrinsic worth which exists independently of our conventions and which

Loeb Library (Cambridge: Harvard University Press, 1939), V. vii. 2-3. All quotations from the Ethics refer to Rackham's edition and will be cited by section number within the body of the text.

we must interpret in order to understand. We can only hope, with the hag, that the signs which allow us to read reality are just and stable indices of intrinsic worth (whether of virtue or of coins), of the intrinsic nature that will always defy our ability to fix it through signs.

The question of intrinsic worth and its relationship to convention explains the presence of the sermon on gentillesse in The Wife of Bath's Tale. The preoccupation with her own intrinsic worth is the Wife of Bath's primary motivation for telling her confessional prologue and the exemplum of her tale. And, in case her audience did not pick up this preoccupation in her long and rambling prologue and in the justification of women's rights that is the substance of her tale, Alison clinches the argument for intrinsic worth with the hag's sermon on gentillesse. It is much easier for the hag (and the Wife) to demonstrate the importance of intrinsic worth in a sermon on the virtue of gentillesse. It is not quite so easy to argue convincingly for the intrinsic worth of that which is less virtuous, like the Wife of Bath's own personality. The Wife of Bath knows perfectly well that she is not gentil and we suspect that she would not want to be gentil even if she could. She would no more want to fit the hag's description of the gentil person than she would want to fit Jerome's description of a virgin. But if gold is gold and has its use and therefore its value among men, then copper is copper and tin is tin, and these substances, despite the abundance that would decrease their value, also have their use and their worth. To put it in the Wife of Bath's own terms:

> "I graunte it wel, I have noon envie,
> Thogh maydenhede preferre bigamye.

```
It liketh hem to be clene, body and goost;
Of myn estaat I nyl nat make no boost.
For wel ye knowe, a lord in his houshold,
He nath nat every vessel al of gold;
Somme been of tree, and doon hir lord servyse.
God clepeth folk to hym in sondry wyse,
And everich hath of God a propre yifte,
Som this, som that, as hym liketh shifte."
                        (III. D, 95-104)
```

In order to justify herself, of course, the Wife presents her intrinsic worth as God-given and therefore unchangeable. She must act,
she believes, according to the dictates of her personality as surely as
fire must always burn in order to be fire. Later in the Prologue, Alison again acknowledges the differentiation of value within the created
universe:

```
"Lat hem [i. e., virgins] be breed of pured whete-seed,
And lat us wyves hoten barly-breed;
And yet with barly-breed, Mark telle kan,
Oure Lord Jhesu refresshed many a man."
                        (III. D, 143-46)
```

The Wife's self-justifying statements advocate a "live and let live"
philosophy whose tolerance may approach moral laxity. But they also
advocate something more. Each of these statements argues for the usefulness and therefore the value of a substance which men take for
granted because the substance is not rare. According to Aquinas, usefulness is the primary (although not the only) criterion for determining economic value and the Wife, in these passages, tries to gain acceptance of and value for herself according to that economic usefulness. Aquinas writes:

```
. . . sicut Augustinius dicit, pretium rerum venalium non
consideratur secundum gradum naturae, cum quandoque pluris
vendatur unus equus quam unus servus; sed consideratur
secundum quod res in usum hominis veniunt.  Et ideo non
oportet quod venditor vel emptor  cognoscat occultas rei
venditae qualitates, sed illas solum per quas redditur
```

humanis usus apta . . . .

(It is Augustine who points out that the price of commercial
commodities is not assessed in accordance with their relative
position on some absolute scale in the natural world, for a
horse is sometimes sold for more than a slave, but in accordance with their usefulness to men. A seller or buyer need
not, therefore, know the hidden properties of an object of
sale; he needs to know only those that pertain to its suit-
ability for human use . . . .)[22]

The Wife begins her argument for her intrinsic worth on the grounds of

her economic usefulness in order to justify to her audience her place

in the multiplicity of God's creation.

But the Wife's justification of herself on these grounds is merely

her foot in the door, as it were. If she can gain her audience's ac-

ceptance on these economic and practical grounds, perhaps she can gain

what she really wants: an acceptance of the value of her personality,

of the "occultas rei" that she proceeds to reveal throughout her

Prologue. Alison wants the wood to be valued apart from the vessel and

its utility. She seeks an acknowledgement of the value of the barley

from which the bread is made. For Aquinas has also pointed to a dis-

tinction between economic and natural value: ". . . aurum et argentum

non solum chara sunt propter utilitatem vasorum quae ex eis fabricantur

aut aliorum hujusmodi, sed etiam propter dignitatem et puritatem sub-

stantiae ipsorum" ("Gold and silver are prized not only because they

---

22. Thomas Aquinas, Summa Theologiae, Vol. 38, prepared by Blackfriars (London: Eyre and Spottiswoode; New York: McGraw-Hill Book Company), Q. 77, a. 2, pp. 220-21. All quotations from the Summa in this
chapter refer to the Blackfriars edition and translation, and will be
cited by question, article, and page number within the body of the
text. For a discussion of Aquinas's use of a natural and an economic
standard of value, see Odd Langholm, Price and Value in the Aristotelian Tradition: A Study in Scholastic Economic Sources (Bergen: Universitetsforlaget, 1979), pp. 86-88.

can be used for the production of vases and such like but on account
of their inherent purity and excellence"--<u>ST</u>, Q. 77, a. 2, pp. 220-
21).[23] Alison wants this recognition of value extended to her and to
her personality, to that intrinsic value which masculine traditions of
valuation would deny. For fire, the Wife of Bath believes, remains
fire, no matter where it burns. It has a nature of its own which will
prevail in any circumstances "'til that it dye'" (III. D, 1145). Similarly, Alison will be Alison despite the attempts of the antifeminist
tradition to define, and thus, confine her, or at least to control her
into usefulness. Having lived her eventful life according to her temperament, the Wife of Bath now wants that temperament to be known and
to be valued for what it is. Alison will stamp the coin of her own
personality. But, unlike the young knight who would name <u>gentillesse</u>
where none is to be found, she will stamp no false images upon the
coin.

   Alison's argument for her own intrinsic worth begins with the
memorable opening lines of her <u>Prologue</u>:

>   "Experience, though noon auctoritee
>   Were in this world, is right ynogh for me
>   To speke of wo that is in mariage . . ."
>   (III. D, 1-3)

She asserts the value of her own experience against the clerical devaluation of that experience and of the woman who lived it. Jerome has
decreed that Alison "'ne sholde wedded be but ones'" (III. D, 12),
thereby invalidating four of her marriages. Because the Wife of Bath
is essentially her marriages, his decree would effectively invalidate

-----

23. Langholm, pp. 86-88.

her, her temperament, her life. Alison confronts Jerome with a battery
of authoritative texts, glossed with her own pragmatic vision of the
world, in order to legitimize her many marriages. As the Prologue
progresses, the Wife of Bath turns her attention to subjects even
dearer to her own personality: sexual pleasure and woman's supremacy
in marriage. The clerics would condemn her on these counts, too; they
would judge as sinful the actions and appetites that she interprets as
the manifestations of her God-given personality. Using Saint Paul as
her auctoritee, Alison defends her sexuality and her desire for power
over her husbands. As many critics have noted, Alison adopts both the
texts and the methods of the antifeminists in her refutation of them.
She fights them on their own turf, with their own weapons. Many
critics have been doubtful of Alison's success in justifying the ways
of woman to God (or to the clerics).[24] If they have not joined the
clerics in a condemnation of her morality, the critics have found in
Alison's diatribe an example of Chaucer's double-edged irony as he
satirizes both the sinful woman and the narrow-minded clerics.[25] Without question, the Wife of Bath's assault is funny in its daringly irreverent manipulation of texts. But more is at stake than humor or ir-
reverence or even Chaucer's elusive irony. Alison's self-assertive
bout with the antifeminist tradition is closely associated, in its concerns, with the hag's sermon on gentillesse. Before Chaucer thrusts us

_____

24. See, for example, D. S. Brewer, Chaucer, third edition (London: Longman, 1973), p. 139.

25. E. T. Donaldson, Chaucer's Poetry: An Anthology for the
Modern Reader (New York: The Ronald Press Co., 1958), pp. 1075-76.

into a _Prologue_ and _Tale_ densely woven from literary, moral, and economic conventions, he presents Alison's challenge to authority in order to show us how to read his character and his poem.

The Wife of Bath attempts to revalue the antifeminists' texts according to her own intrinsic worth just as the Loathly Lady redefined _gentillesse_ on the basis of the virtue inherent within one's personality. The aristocracy had claimed _gentillesse_ as a designation which belonged, by birth, to the upper class. The hag reappropriates the word and revalues it on the basis of intrinsic worth. Similarly, Alison appropriates the texts that provide the antifeminists with an authoritative voice and she uses those texts to justify her own personality. The antifeminist tradition allows men a means of defining women, of categorizing them, of evaluating them. Just as money allows us to measure the value of goods, the antifeminist tradition allows men to measure a woman's value. In its definition of women, the antifeminist tradition would imprint a woman's character with its own image, whether or not her intrinsic worth correlated with that image. It would define a woman's worth according to its own standards. But there is an intrinsic worth that exists independently of convention, an intrinsic worth that, in the case of women, the antifeminist tradition does not accommodate. The antifeminist tradition, in fact, resembles the feudal theory of money. Both allow those who have power to name value, not on the basis of intrinsic worth, but on the basis of their own expediency. Both fail to found their conventions upon an evaluation of worth. The standards of the antifeminist tradition do not accurately measure and therefore do not accommodate a woman's personality, her energies, her emotions. They do not offer a just indication

of Alison's intrinsic worth. In her confrontation with the antifeminists, Alison appropriates their conventions in order to redefine them.
She reinterprets their auctoritees to accommodate her own personality
and to align those auctoritees with her own intrinsic worth.

As Alison challenges the clerks, Chaucer not only demonstrates
that the antifeminists have failed to define (let alone subdue) the
Wife of Bath. He also uses her bout with the antifeminists to show
the arbitrariness of conventions. A convention reflects the needs of
its creator, just as a coin bears the image of the monarch who minted
it. For every Biblical or patristic text which the antifeminists can
quote to condemn the Wife, she can find another from the same sources
to exonerate herself. She recoins the antifeminist tradition to suit
her own needs. Alison says of a wife's relationship to her husband:

> "I have the power durynge al my lyf
> Upon his propre body, and noght he.
> Right thus the Apostel tolde it unto me;
> And bad oure housbondes for to love us weel.
> Al this sentence me liketh every deel."
> (III. D, 158-62)

If the Wife seems to be making a convention to satisfy her own needs,
the same critique can be made of the antifeminists' conventions. The
Wife of Bath takes up this point later in her Prologue as she demands
a woman's right to use language:

> "By God! if wommen hadde writen stories,
> As clerkes han withinne hire oratories,
> They wolde han writen of men moore wikkednesse
> Than al the mark of Adam may redresse."
> (III. D, 693-96)

Through the Wife of Bath's encounter with the antifeminists, Chaucer
demonstrates his own awareness that conventions are arbitrary, that

they are subjectively determined.[26] But if conventions are the only
means we have for structuring our lives, our literature, our economies, we must be ready to re-evaluate and to revalue those conventions
when they fail to accommodate the very complexity of the world that
they should help us organize and understand. We must formulate our
conventions upon our just attempts to understand and interpret intrinsic worth.

If Alison's acts of revaluation are central to her desire for
self-definition and self-determination, they are also central to Chaucer and to his art.[27] It is no accident that Alison of Bath is such
a vital, engaging, and complex character. And it is no accident that
critics, regardless of their evaluations of her behavior and her morals
(or lack thereof), cannot get Alison out of their systems. Chaucer
wanted to engage us and our sympathies in the Wife of Bath's character
because, in her Prologue and Tale, he presents his own relationship to
the auctores and conventions of his artistic enterprise. Chaucer uses
Alison as the spokeswoman for his own interpretation of the need to revalue conventions in order to accommodate one's own artistic purposes.[28]

If the Wife of Bath possesses an abundance of self-determining
energy, she derives that energy from Chaucer's revaluation of conventions when he made her. The Wife of Bath belongs to a long line of

26. David Aers, Chaucer, Langland, and the Creative Imagination
(London: Routledge and Kegan Paul, 1980), p. 84.

27. Alfred David, The Strumpet Muse (Bloomington: Indiana University Press, 1976), p. 135.

28. See Robert Burlin, Chaucerian Fiction, p. 180.

crones who constitute the Old Whore tradition. Her grandmothers are
as old as Ovid's Dipsas and as familiar to Chaucer's audience as La
Vielle in Le Roman de la Rose. But Alison is memorable specifically
because she bears only a family resemblance to her literary grandmothers. She is neither old nor a whore. As Jill Mann writes: "The
uniqueness of the Wife of Bath is that, although she contains certain
traits in common with the vetulae, Chaucer presents her as attractive.
Our impression of her complex personality derives from our inability
to categorize her as a temptress or a bawd."[29] In her own confession
of her materialism, her sexual appetites, her lying, and her badgering,
the Wife of Bath proves that she conforms to the antifeminists' stereotypes.[30] But in his adoption of convention, Chaucer also transformed
it. As he redefined and remade the elements of the Old Whore tradition, he created a character whose intrinsic worth exists apart from
and cannot be evaluated solely in the context of this tradition.

The Wife of Bath's acts of revaluation are, then, Chaucer's own.
If she argues with the antifeminists in order to assert her own identity, Chaucer transforms literary conventions in order to define his
own poetic individuality. Without conventions, we would lack means to
measure and name value. Chaucer deliberately composed Alison from the
materials of the antifeminist tradition in order to emphasize the ways
in which she differs from and transcends that tradition. By measuring
Alison according to convention, we can discover the intrinsic person-

---

29. Jill Mann, Chaucer and Medieval Estates Satire (Cambridge:
Cambridge University Press, 1973), p. 126.

30. Burlin, p. 227.

ality of the character and, what is more, the intrinsic worth of the artistic vision which created the vital, nagging, oversexed, pathetic, and resilient Alison of Bath. If we must measure value by the conventions which we make for that purpose, in art, as in money, something exists which convention cannot name.

Alison is a coiner; she mints new definitions in order to accommodate her intrinsic worth. She, not the antifeminists, will name the conventions that define her and she will seek her auctoritee, not in the Church Fathers' teachings, but in the stars. She uses her birthmarks and the zodiacal influences that are their source as an explanation for her personality:

> "Gat-tothed I was, and that bicam me weel;
> I hadde the prente of seinte Venus seel.
> . . . .
> For certes, I am al Venerien
> In feelynge, and myn herte is Marcien.
> Venus me yaf my lust, my likerousnesse,
> And Mars yaf me my sturdy hardynesse;
> Myn ascendant was Taur, and Mars therinne.
> Allas! Allas! that evere love was synne!
> I folwed ay myn inclinacioun
> By vertu of my constellacioun;
> That made me I koude noght withdrawe
> My chambre of Venus from a good felawe.
> Yet have I Martes mark upon my face,
> And also in another privee place."
> (III. D, 603-20)

The Wife of Bath reads the marks on her body in order to apprise her audience of her temperament. Moreover, the language in her description of her birthmarks clearly raises the question of bonitas intrinseca. For, if Alison is a coiner, within her social context, she is also a coin.

Alison believes that the astrological influences signified by the marks on her body have determined her character from birth. She is a coin whose faces are imprinted by Venus and Mars respectively. Just as the name on the coin should indicate its weight and worth, her birthmarks, Alison believes, signify the two major components of her character. But, as Walter Clyde Curry noted, even the signs that the Wife of Bath uses to justify her temperament would condemn her.[31] According to astrological lore, the person blessedly born under Venus is pleasant and gracious, loving and lovely, and, above all, sexy.[32] These attributes would have been Alison's had Mars's ominous influence not exaggerated her Venerian assets and turned her into a large-hipped, broad-faced, insatiable woman.[33]

The Wife of Bath, however, is not trying to seem better than she actually is; nor does she lament her personality. Rather, she rues the antifeminists' values and conventions that would condemn her temperament and her behavior: "'Allas! Allas! that evere love was synne!'" (III. D, 614). Yet, if the Martian-Venerean temperament were as unappealing as the medieval astrologers postulated, the Wife of Bath would be less attractive to her audience than she, in fact, is.[34] Al-

---

31. Walter Clyde Curry, "The Wife of Bath," Chaucer: Modern Essays in Criticism, ed. Edward Wagenknecht (New York: Oxford University Press, 1959), pp. 169-70. All information about the influence of astrology on Alison's temperament is founded on Curry's research.

32. Curry, pp. 170-72.

33. Ibid., pp. 174-75, 178-80.

34. Ibid., p. 182. Curry also uses astrology to explain the nature of the Wife's Tale: "the fineness and delicacy which achieves expression in the story is but the resurging as it were, of the artistic Venerean impulse . . ." (p. 183).

though Alison might find, in astrology, a satisfactory resolution for the two conflicting impulses in her temperament, it is obvious that Mars and Venus are not the only influences inscribing her character. The Wife's zodiacal signs, like any signs belonging to and constituting a convention, only begin to measure the complexity of her temperament. Once again, Chaucer's character has escaped measurement by conventional standards, even when she herself names the convention by which she wishes to be measured.

Despite the failure of a zodiacal explanation to accommodate Alison's personality, an important point emerges from her discussion of her birthmarks. The Wife of Bath believes, correctly, that she has been influenced by an external force, larger and more powerful than she. Of course, Alison's chronicle of her life shows that she has exerted considerable influence over herself and her world. For example, her "'sturdy hardinesse,'" given to her by Mars, describes not only her cruelty toward her first four husbands, but also the will to self-determination that she demonstrates throughout her Prologue. Yet Alison does not attribute her personality to those conventions, medieval marriage and economics, that go far toward explaining her motivations as well as the presence of the Martian qualifications of her Venerean temperament. The strength of her will to self-determination exists, in part, as a reaction against the weight of the masculine traditions that would dominate her.

As Jill Mann has demonstrated, the Wife's sex defines her estate, her career, and her function within fourteenth-century society.[35] Al-

_____

35. Jill Mann, Chaucer and Medieval Estates Satire (Cambridge:

though Alison's General Prologue portrait begins with a mention of her

cloth-making activities, "Of clooth-makyng she hadde swich an haunt,/

She passed hem of Ypres and of Gaunt" (I. A, 447-48), the importance of

her cloth-making to an interpretation of her character is problematic.

Chaucer does not allude to this aspect of her active life in The Wife

of Bath's Prologue. Noting "the assumption that cloth-making is the

duty of the feminine estate," Mann writes: "The fact that we never

hear again of the Wife's 'clooth-makyng' strongly suggests that the

only reason for introducing it here is to emphasize her estate func-

tion."[36] Indeed, in the prologue to her Tale, Alison appears as a

tradeswoman only in the sphere of marital economics. Yet, in a recent

article, Mary Carruthers fully documents the considerable power and

profit that a clothier in England's burgeoning cloth industry would

have enjoyed.[37] Unlike the woman involved in spinning as a "house in-

dustry,"[38] Alison, as a clothier, would have managed a group of workers

and would have been in charge of her own share of this vital English

---

Cambridge University Press, 1973), pp. 121-22.

36. Ibid., p. 122.

37. Throughout my discussion of the Wife of Bath's socioeconomic
status, I am indebted to Mary Carruther's well-documented article, "The
Wife of Bath and the Painting of Lions," PMLA, 94 (March 1979),
209-22. Although my conclusions about the Wife's motivations, her
"lion painting," and her relationship with Jankyn are often different
from Carruther's, I agree fundamentally with her interpretation of the
effect that Alison's milieu has had upon her personality. See also,
A. Abram's early article, "Women Traders in Medieval London," Economic
Journal, 26 (1916), pp. 276-85.

38. Eileen Power, Medieval Women, ed. M. M. Postan (Cambridge:
Cambridge University Press, 1975), pp. 62ff. Carruthers, p. 210.

industry.[39] Even if Alison had inherited this business or the money
to establish it from her husband(s), her profits would have accrued to
her through her own industry and effort.[40] Chaucer's reference to the
Wife of Bath's cloth-making, even if it does not play a central role
in her Prologue, increases our awareness of her capacity for self-determination.

Alison does mention cloth-making once in the prologue to her Tale.
After she has delivered the monologue with which she badgered her old
husbands, the Wife says:

> "For al swich wit is yeven us in oure byrthe;
> Deceite, wepyng, spynnyng God hath yive
> To wommen kyndely, whil that they may lyve."
>   (III. D, 400-02)

Her statement, as much an articulation of proverbial wisdom as a comment on women's economic condition, supports Mann's conclusions about
the relationship of cloth-making to woman's estate function. Through
her emphasis on "kyndely," the Wife presents deceit, weeping, and spinning as components of woman's intrinsic nature. She attributes woman's
possession of these skills, outrageously and irreverently enough, to
the same God who bade us not to bear false witness. Moreover, Alison
believes that God gave her these gifts as means of self-preservation
and self-determination. The ability to manipulate language (whether to
quite clerks or husbands) gives women bargaining (and therefore, economic) power in their world. The presence of spinning in this list

---

39. Carruthers, p. 210. Carruthers writes: "The term 'cloth
maker' refers to that person, the clothier, who manufactures cloth"
(p. 210).

40. Ibid., p. 210.

associates economics with language, and women's economic activities

with their linguistic abilities. It is, however, interesting that

spinning occupies third place in the Wife's list. If the manipulation

of language and the spinning of stories fail to provide one with power

and profit, then the spinning of cloth, as a last resort, will. Yet

the list of skills that the Wife proudly claims as women's seems short

indeed. Alison glorifies the only skills that she feels are uniquely

hers by attributing them to God. Her three talents have, in fact, been

left to women, as their property, by the masculine world.

If the Wife's participation in the cloth industry is problematic,

her activity within the institution of marriage is not. Alison's be-

havior as a wife reflects the conventions and expectations of four-

teenth-century marriage. Given the customs of her time, her interpre-

tation of marriage as a commercial transaction is not surprising.

Medieval marriage was, to a great extent, an economic venture in which

women were, essentially, acquisitions whose value existed in direct

proportion to the size of their dowries.[41] Within the context of mar-

riage, woman became, in effect, a coin, a symbol of a quantified amount

of stored wealth. The perception of marriage as a business enterprise

operated at all levels of medieval society. Because women from aris-

tocratic families could bring large amounts of wealth and real estate

---

41. Much of my information about the economics of medieval marriage comes from Carruther's article (full citation above); Eileen
Power's Medieval Women (full citation above); and Sylvia Thrupps's The
Merchant Class of Medieval London (Chicago: Univ. of Chicago Press,
1948). See also, F. R. H. Du Boulay's analysis of medieval attitudes
toward marriage in The Age of Ambition (London: Nelson, 1970).

to their marriages, their personal qualities were most often secondary
to the quantities and locations of their lands.[42] Although aristocratic ladies were often entrusted with the regulation of households
and lands during their husbands' absences, these lands (including the
acreage that the women had brought as dowry) were, by law, their husbands' possessions.[43] Material considerations were perhaps strongest
among the members of the aristocracy.[44] But, given its preoccupation
with the acquisition of material wealth and the social status attendant
upon it, the growing middle class was as eager as the aristocracy to
turn marriage into a paying proposition.[45]

The woman who entered marriage in the middle ages did not, however, surrender all rights to property. The "customs of the bourgeoisie"[46] (as distinct from the edicts of the Canon Law and the Common

---

42. Power, pp. 19 and 38. Of course, as Power points out,
courtly love and its "exaltation of the lady was the exclusive ideal
of a small aristocratic caste" (p. 27). But the precepts of courtly
love did not govern the aristocratic practices of medieval marriage
"which was so often a parental agreement, binding children in the interests of land" (p. 24). Courtly love, with its emphasis on the centrality of women and of women's power, may be seen, in part, as an
ethic of compensation, one which gave women and their selfhoods an importance deprived them by the economics of medieval marriage.

43. Ibid., p. 38.

44. Ibid., p. 19.

45. Thrupp, p. 29. Poor women suffered less from the commercial
cast of medieval marriage. Their economic importance in marriage took
a different, more vital form. According to Eileen Power, "As we
descend the social scale, we do not find the role of women declining.
On the contrary, her activity, if she was alone, her importance in the
life of the family if she was married, was all the greater for the
modesty, indeed exigency, of her income and possessions" (p. 53).

46. See Carruthers, p. 210.

Law) granted to the wife a third of her husband's total property (a half if the couple were childless) after his death.[47] Nor could her husband alienate this inheritance, known as the dower, without his wife's consent.[48] Although, at marriage, she surrendered her dowry to her husband for the duration of their life together, the wife, then, was not without material rights.[49] Yet she could regain control over her property only with the loss of her husband. Unlike the wife, however, the widow could independently manage her inherited property, if she remained unmarried long enough to exercise this right.[50] The Church's stipulation against remarriage that irritates Alison exerted little practical influence upon the marital customs of medieval society.[51] Widows (and especially childless widows) were valuable acquisitions because they could bring even greater wealth to their second (or third or fourth . . .) marriages than to their first. The enterprising young man, kin to Chaucer's Jankyn, would not eschew the wealthy, older widow who possessed the capital necessary to establish him in business and in society.[52] Yet, if women inherited property upon their husbands' deaths, it was expected that they would cede this property to

---

47. Power, p. 38; Thrupp, pp. 108-09; Thomas Reisner, "The Wife of Bath's Dower: A Legal Interpretation," MP (1973-1974), 301-02.

48. Power, p. 38.

49. Ibid.

50. Ibid.

51. Carruthers, p. 211; Thrupp, p. 106.

52. Thrupp, p. 197.

their new husbands at the time of remarriage.[53] Only the unmarried

woman and the widow could retain and manage possession of their own

property.[54]

The economics of medieval marriage have, then, left an imprint on

Alison as indelible as the birthmarks of Venus and Mars. Early in her

Prologue, the Wife of Bath informs her audience that she first entered

wedlock at the tender age of twelve (III. D, 4); Alison was precocious

even in an era that saw women married for the first time between the

ages of fourteen and seventeen.[55] She succinctly expresses her youth-

---

53. Power, p. 38.

54. That marriage was an economic undertaking is shown not only
by medieval marital customs and expectations. Etymologically, the word
economics refers to the workings of the household. In his article,
"Oikonomia: An Inquiry into Beginnings of Economic Thought and Language," Kylos, 11 (1958), pp. 29-54, Kurt Singer writes: ". . . the
word denotes activities of management, or administration, applied to
persons or goods belonging to an oikos, a term whose meaning varies
from house to family household, dwelling place or region, home land,
as well as property in general" (p. 30). Nicholas Oresme's translation
of Le Livre de Yconomique de Aristote demonstrates that this definition
of economics was known and operative in the fourteenth century. In the
introduction to his English language edition of Oresme's translation,
Albert Menut notes the increase, in the thirteenth and fourteenth centuries, of works, like Oresme's, on household economics and management
(p. 786). (All references to and citations from Oresme's translation
are taken from Menut's edition: Maistre Nicole Oresme: Le Livre de
Yconomique de Aristote, Transactions of the American Philosophical Society, New Series, Vol. 47.5 (Philadelphia, 1957.) Such works, of
course, dealt not only with the provisioning of the household, but also
with the relationship between husband and wife that would facilitate
the efficient regulation of domestic affairs (see Menut, p. 786). Not
surprisingly, woman was also subservient in this aspect of marital economics (p. 809). Although the wife should organize and regulate the
activities within the home itself, her power is not unqualified. She
must work according to the rules established by her husband (p. 826).
Doubtless, actual practice within the medieval household might have entailed more mutuality than Le Livre de Yconomique advises. But theory
does influence practice through its definition of standards, laws, and
conventions. It is specifically theory and its auctoritee against
which Alison argues in her quiting of the clerics.

55. Thrupp, p. 196. Carruthers puts the age somewhat higher, at

ful distaste for her old husbands: "'And yet in bacon hadde I nevere
delit'" (III. D, 418).[56] As Mary Carruthers writes: "The lesson that
Alison has learned is obvious: marriage is contracted for money
. . . ."[57] If marriage is a business enterprise, then Alison will
respect it as such so long as its power and profit are hers.

The Wife of Bath's modus operandi in the business of marriage
rests on a simple exchange. She will trade what she has and he wants
for what he has and she wants. In her marriages to the three husbands
who "'were goode men, and riche, and olde'" (III. D, 197), Alison
trades sex for wealth and property. She unabashedly confesses:

> "They had me yeven hir lond and hir tresoor;
> Me neded nat do lenger diligence
> To wynne hir love, or doon hem reverence.
> . . . .
> But sith I hadde hem hoolly in myn hond,
> And sith they hadde me yeven al hir lond,
> What sholde I taken keep hem for to plese,
> But it were for my profit and myn ese?"
> (III. D, 204-14)

Later in her Prologue, the Wife of Bath continues, with the same candor:

> "I wolde no lenger in the bed abyde,
> If that I felte his arm over my syde,
> Til he had maad his raunson unto me . . ."
> (III. D, 409-11)

If Alison's transformation of the marriage bed into a marketplace bears
disconcerting resemblances to the practices of the world's oldest profession, we must bear in mind the economic overtones of medieval marriage itself. The Wife of Bath has, in one sense, gotten her own back,

----

twenty (fn. 32, 221).

56. See Carruthers, p. 214.

57. Ibid.

both figuratively and financially. She denies her husbands the rights
that ecclesiastical and legal tradition would grant them to possess
her physically, spiritually, and economically:

> "Thou shalt nat bothe, thogh that thou were wood,
> Be maister of my body and of my good;
> That oon thou shalt forgo, maugree thyne yen."
> (III. D, 313-15)

In her marriages, then, the Wife of Bath engages in a revaluation
of convention similar in its methods and purposes to her revaluation
of clerical tradition at the beginning of her Prologue. More specifically, she transforms the conventions of medieval marriage by invert-
ing (and subverting) its prescribed power relationship. Her acts of
revaluation are fundamentally economic in more ways than one. Not only
does she turn a profit and increase her economic status through marriage. She also appropriates to herself the right to make conventions
that the very etymology of the word "economics" implied in the fourteenth century. In his Livre de Yconomique d'Aristote (a translation
into French of a treatise attributed to Aristotle), Nicholas Oresme
presents the following etymological definition of "economics." The
word, according to Oresme's translation, is

> . . . de ycon en grec, que est ymage ou signe; et de nomos,
> qu'est regle; et de ycos, qu'est science. Car par elle sait
> le principal de la maison faire signes et regles ou
> ordenances de gouverner sa famille et soy ou resgart de sa
> famille.
>
> (. . . from Greek ycon, meaning image or conventional sign;
> and from nomos, meaning rule or law; and from ycos, meaning
> science. For by means of economics, the master of the house
> is able to establish conventions and rules or ordinances for
> governing his family and himself in respect to his family.)[58]

---

58. Albert Menut's edition of Nicholas Oresme's translation, Le

The Wife of Bath, of course, appropriates economic power to herself by usurping her husbands' prerogative to manage their households--and her. But Alison also claims the "economic" right to govern herself, to make her own rules, to replace his conventions with her own. Economic power for the Wife of Bath entails her ability to make money, certainly. But it also represents her right to revalue and to formulate conventions like antifeminism and language, like money and marriage. By asserting her dominion over the ycon, the "image or conventional sign," Alison claims the right to revalue conventions in order to accommodate the reality of her experience. Moreover, Oresme's etymological definition of "economics" underlines the fundamentally economic nature of Chaucer's own literary enterprise. In his poetry, Chaucer, too, asserts his dominion over the ycon, as he appropriates language in order to establish the conventions through which he can organize the material of his art. This definition of "economics" clarifies the reasons for Chaucer's sympathetic attitude toward the Wife of Bath; her enterprises are, to a large extent, analogous to his. Both the Wife of Bath and Chaucer appropriate the ycon in order to transform it.

If the Wife of Bath sets out to revalue the conventions of medieval marriage, she succeeds, but not completely. As we have seen, medieval marriage turns woman into a possession which, like money, represents a fixed amount of land and wealth. The Wife of Bath is, however,

---

Livre de Yconomique de Aristote, p. 807-08. R. A. Shoaf cites this quotation in a different context, as the epigraph to his chapter, "The Merchant's Tale and the Economy of Marriage," in Dante, Chaucer, and the Currency of the Word: Money, images, and reference in late medieval poetry (forthcoming from Pilgrim Books, 1983).

aware of the status of woman as possession in her world. In her long
reproach to her old husbands, she says:

> "'Thou seist that oxen, asses, hors, and houndes,
> They been assayed at diverse stoundes;
> Bacyns, lavours, er that men hem bye,
> Spoones and stooles, and al swich housbondrye,
> And so been pottes, clothes, and array;
> But folk of wyves maken noon assay,
> Til they be wedded. . . .'"
>   (III. D, 285-91)

Even within this context, woman can prove to be a bad bargain. Alison's battle with her old husbands involves more than mere greed. In
her usurpation of their power and property, she attempts to reappropri-
ate herself from the marital economy into which she has been sold.
Yet, in order to possess herself (and to determine her own behavior and
worth), the Wife of Bath must bargain with the only goods that she, as
a woman, has: her sexual favors. She willingly sells sex for that
which seems to her more useful and thus more valuable, for property and
power and the independence that they will afford her. In the end, Alison wins her game only by using her sexuality as the currency that allows her to do business in marriage. At the same time that she succeeds in transforming the structure of marital power, she reinforces
the conventional status of woman as acquisition within marriage. The
possession of the coin has simply changed hands.

Alison, as we have seen, believes that her temperament is imprinted with the signs of Venus and Mars; it has been "coined," as it
were, by these astrological influences. In her description of her
first three marriages, however, we see another aspect of Alison's
"coining." The Wife of Bath and her sexuality become, in her marriages,
the currency minted, on the one hand, by her own need for self-deter-

mination and, on the other, by the masculine traditions that would
deny this need. If Alison's image is stamped on one side of the coin
of her personality, that of Jerome and his brothers is stamped on the
other. The Wife of Bath believes that, through domination in her marriages, she has won self-determination. Ironically, however, she allows herself to be bound by the very conventions that she attempts to
revalue. Alison has gained the power that belonged to her husbands,
but she has gained it by using the only methods she knows: the methods
that the masculine world has given her. It is obvious, however, that,
in Alison's opinion, she has paid a fair price for wealth and lands,
for the freedom to travel and to dress up and to visit her gossips.
She offers the wisdom of her experience to her audience:

> "And therfore every man this tale I telle,
> Wynne whoso may, for al is for to selle;
> With empty hand men may none haukes lure.
> For wynnyng wolde I al his lust endure . . ."
> (III. D, 413-16)

Interestingly enough, as the Wife turns herself, and specifically,
her sexuality, into a coin with which to purchase power, she herself
acquires certain traits which scholastic economic theory associated
with money. Alison demands the freedom to circulate without which
money does not fulfill its prescribed function. Moreover, she is not,
as she herself protests, to be hoarded away. She accuses her husband,
'"'I trowe thou woldest loke me in thy chiste!'"' (III. D, 317). In
Alison's opinion, women, like clothes and money, are useless if they
are locked up: '"'. . . we wol ben at oure large'"' (III. D, 322).
This attribution of money's characteristics to the Wife of Bath may
explain a mystery that has troubled scholars throughout the history of

Chaucer criticism. Although Alison willingly recounts the most inti-
mate details of her life, she never mentions any offspring from her
five marriages.[59] In light of the laws governing the dower, the absence of children would account for Alison's ability to amass large
amounts of wealth from her marriages. But, more significantly, money,
according to scholastic economic theory, is sterile. It cannot repro-
duce itself.[60] (The scholastics used this definition of money's sterility as the basis for their prohibition against usury.[61]) Centuries
elapsed before scholastic monetary theory acknowledged what practice
had long proven to be true: that money comes to money.[62]

In the Wife of Bath's world, wealth gives men power; by acquiring
her husbands' "'lond and tresoor,'" Alison usurps this power from them.

---

59. Mary Carruthers has this opinion of the Wife's children (or
lack thereof): ". . . we do not know whether or not the Wife has
children; we only know that she does not say so. . . . The 'problem'
of the Wife of Bath's children is of exactly the same sort as the most
famous of literary nonproblems: 'How many children had Lady Macbeth?'
and it deserves to be consigned to the wastebasket of critical inquiry
for the same reasons" (fn. 31, p. 221). By the same token, we could
consider any silence of the loquacious Wife as significant.

60. John T. Noonan, Jr., The Scholastic Analysis of Usury (Cambridge: Harvard Univ. Press, 1957), pp. 55-56.

61. Ibid., p. 56.

62. Joan Ferrante provides an illuminating reference in relation
to the idea of woman as coin in her book, Woman as Image in Medieval
Literature: From the Twelfth Century to Dante (New York: Columbia Univ.
Press, 1975): "The matrix of the woman, according to Guillaume de
Conches, is formed like a casket or vase, with a wide mouth at the
top, a round belly below, and a large neck in between. Inside the
surface is hairy in order to retain the seed, and it has cells imprinted like money with the human figure" (p. 7). In this light, Alison's progeny become the lands and wealth gained through her intercourse with her husbands. And in this light, too, money would come to
money.

But men also have another medium of exchange that the Wife covets: language. Language affords men power in the marketplace; they use it to name commercial value, to bargain, to set prices. As commerce flourished and trade increased, money was not the only convention that assumed a new importance and practicality. Lester Little writes of the growing merchant class:

> . . . they manipulated words, or in some instances they sought to manipulate people through the use of words. They argued, they kept records, they drew up contracts, they negotiated, they bought and sold, they hired and fired, they told stories and sang, they lectured, and they wrote books and letters. [63]

Language, then, is a convention invented and used by men for their own material profit. Through language, they can define values for themselves and the value of women.

Alison's bout with the antifeminists demonstrates her awareness of the linguistic power that men wield; she claims this power for herself in her quiting of them. Moreover, the Wife's chronicle of her marriages presents her long personal acquaintance with the power that language can provide. Alison entertains her audience with a long monologue that she levelled at her old husbands in order to gain their submission and their property. In her monologue, the Wife batters her husbands with accusations that they, allegedly, used to insult her. Her tirade begins with the dubious boast: "'For half so boldely kan ther no man/ Swere and lyen, as a womman kan'" (III. D, 227-28). And Alison concludes, with no inconsiderable satisfaction:

---

63. Lester K. Little, Religious Poverty and the Profit Economy in Medieval Europe (Ithaca: Cornell Univ. Press, 1978), p. 24.

> "Lordynges, right thus, as ye understonde,
> Baar I stifly myne olde housbondes on honde
> That thus they seyden in hir dronkenesse;
> And al was fals. . . ."
>   (III. D, 379-82)

The monologue is a testimony to the Wife's own ability to manipulate

language, to make and present fictions. It also establishes her talent

for using language as a medium of commercial exchange that guarantees

her profit. According to the Wife, she never loses in her verbal spar-

rings:

> ". . . by my trouthe, I quitte hem word for word.
> . . . .
> I ne owe hem nat a word that it nys quit.
> I broughte it so aboute by my wit
> That they moste yeve it up, as for the beste,
> Or elles hadde we nevere been in reste."
>   (III. D, 422-28)

Despite the Wife of Bath's verbal triumphs, despite the advantage

that Chaucer allows her to gain through her quick wit and even quicker

tongue, the content of her tirade against her husbands is puzzling.

The monologue is composed of the Wife's rebuttals to popular anti-

feminist condemnations of women, their appearance, their behavior,

their temperaments. Why does the Wife muster this arsenal of anti-

feminist condemnations in a speech intended to exemplify her own lin-

guistic abilities? And why, when many of these accusations describe

the Wife's own personality, does she include them here, risking self-

condemnation in her attempt at self-justification?

First, the monologue does permit Alison to answer these accusa-

tions. It allows her to express her anger at the injustice of con-

demning a wife for being anything other than a passive possession. In

her confrontation with the clerical tradition, Alison challenged the auctoritee of men who establish and justify antifeminism on the basis

of texts; in her monologue, she confronts the popular ramifications of

the clerical tradition. As Eileen Power wrote, "the period when the

urban classes were at the height of their prosperity and influence . . .

in the late thirteenth and the early fourteenth centuries, saw . . . a

resurgence . . . of a secular antifeminism as brutal as anything which

the Fathers of the Church had propounded."[64] Through her monologue,

then, Alison underlines the pervasiveness of antifeminism and the com-

pleteness of its condemnation of women. Whether the men are Saint

Jerome or middle class husbands, they evaluate women according to their

stereotypes. By exposing his readers, early in The Wife of Bath's

Prologue, to these two examples of antifeminist lore, Chaucer forces

them to confront the nature of antifeminism and to confront the fact

that all women within their experience do not conform to these conven-

tions. In other words, through his emphasis on antifeminism, Chaucer

brings his audience to an awareness of its profound limitations.

But the monologue displays more than Alison's ability to manipu-

late words. If the Wife of Bath gained control of her husbands' lands

and wealth, she has also usurped their language. By putting these

antifeminist accusations in her husbands' mouths before they themselves

could utter them, Alison has appropriated masculine conventions, the

conventions made by men for the purpose of classifying women. She thus

deprives her husbands of their linguistic power over her; she blunts

their own weapon. The words that would have been used against her,

---

64. Power, p. 11. Hope Weissman, "Antifeminism and Chaucer's
Characterization of Women," Geoffrey Chaucer, ed. George D. Economou
(New York: McGraw-Hill Book Co., 1975), p. 95.

that society has used against women, become hers to use to her own advantage. If the Wife adopted men's values by turning her marriage
into a profitable business transaction, if she adopted men's strategies
in her glossing of texts for her own purposes, she once again uses
men's conventions against them.[65] On a linguistic level, Alison's revenge is complete. As she herself says, she beats him to the punch:
"'Whoso that first to mille comth, first grynt;/ I pleyned first, so
was our werre ystynt'" (III. D, 389-90).

But beneath the profit motive that seems to be the Wife of Bath's
raison d'être and the primary cause of her usurpation of male language,
we can detect an emotional motive. By being the first to grind at the
mill, Alison also deflects the pain that these stereotypes can cause
even the "hardiest" of women. By silencing her husbands, she avoids
hearing herself stereotyped once again. The monologue contains accusations that fit the Wife closely: accusations about vanity and greed
and selfishness. But the monologue also contains generalizations
about all women that criticize more than women's love of finery or of
wandering. They also criticize women's love. According to the antifeminists whom the Wife cites, woman is the worst scourge ever to be
visited upon man. These lines end the Wife's monologue:

> "'Been ther none othere maner resemblances
> That ye may likne youre parables to,
> But if a sely wyf be oon of tho?
>   Thou liknest eek wommenes love to helle,
> To bareyne lond, ther water may nat dwelle.

---

65. For a similar analysis of the Wife's adoption and adaptation
of men's strategies, see Alfred David, The Strumpet Muse (Bloomington:
Indiana Univ. Press, 1976), pp. 145, 153; and David Aers, Chaucer,
Langland, and the Creative Imagination (London: Routledge and Kegan
Paul, 1980), p. 147.

> Thou liknest it also to wilde fyr;
> The moore it brenneth, the moore it hath desir
> To consume every thyng that brent wol be.
> Thou seyest, right as wormes shende a tree,
> Right so a wyf destroyeth hire housbonde;
> This knowe they that been to wyves bonde.'"
>
> (III. D, 368-78)

This is the opinion of women's love which, the antifeminists tell the Wife of Bath, all husbands possess. And, if they share this opinion of women and their love, why, the Wife's actions argue, do they deserve better than selfishness from her?

As the first three lines of this passage illustrate, men not only denigrate women's love. They use this love as the basis for their own metaphors and, in the process, they appropriate women as the signs constitutive of their own conventions. They make women into their ycons. As we have seen, by gaining her own domination over her husbands, their property, and their language, the Wife of Bath asserts her own dominion over the ycon, "the image or conventional sign." But, like the Wife's other efforts at defining her own power, this passage demonstrates the success as well as the limitations of her efforts. Although Alison uses these words to make her husbands miserable, they also express her own misery. When she appropriates the ycon as her own, just as when she reappropriates herself from men's possession, she only gains that which belonged to men in the first place. She can only repeat words that men have spoken. The Wife of Bath and Chaucer share similar concerns about the remaking of conventions and the individual's power over the sign. If Alison must use words, conventions, and strategies of gaining power invented by men before her, so must Chaucer. If each has received models for structuring responses to

experience, each is also restricted by these prior acts of image-mak-
ing. They are never free from conventions even as they try to recoin
them in their own images.

Because she is a woman, Alison has experienced the restrictions
of men's conventions in every aspect of her life. Despite the victori-
ous note on which she begins and ends this monologue, despite the
profit which her haggling brings her, we hear an undertone of pain and
loss amidst her boasts of her own cleverness:

> "For wynnyng wolde I al his lust endure,
> And make me a feyned appetit;
> And yet in bacon hadde I nevere delit;
> That made me evere I wolde him chide."
> (III. D, 416-20)

One can only imagine how unappealing these old husbands were if they
failed to arouse the lusty Wife of Bath. Despite her wynnyng, the
bacon was always there. Despite the material profit, there was always
an emotional and sexual loss: "'That made me evere I wolde him
chide.'" It is little wonder that this emotional loss made material
profit a necessary compensation for the Wife of Bath. And, when material gain was not sufficient, she had language, chiding, to ensure her
profit. If the institution of medieval marriage imprinted its stamp
upon Alison at an early age, it also provided her with an avenue of
escape, with a way of buying her right to self-determination. It
showed her that marriage was a business and that, if she were a coin,
she could also become a merchant in this exchange.

The Wife of Bath has gained a power in her marriages that is a
compensation for powerlessness in her world and for the emotional and
sexual losses in her marriages. The satisfaction that she takes in her

accomplishments is a testament to her resiliency. Alison can say that
"'. . . I have had my world as in my tyme'" (III. D, 473), for she has.
But she has gained possession of her world only through the methods
provided by her "'tyme.'" Alison has gained profit and power through
her own wit, but her profit has cost her more than she acknowledges.

Having transformed her first four marriages into profitable business ventures, Alison adopts commercial values as the paradigm for all
her values, personal and moral. Her evaluation of her own worth and
the worth of others, her ideas about exchange in relationships and
about the exchange that is communication, are determined by values deriving from the dynamics of the marketplace. Alison prefaces her account of her fifth marriage with an analysis of her attraction to
Jankyn, as if to explain what would appear to be an inconsistency in
her character: that she can love a man for himself and not for his
money. But even in this romantic moment, as the Wife tries to articulate the reasons why she loved the young Jankyn, her language cannot
escape the commercial idiom. In her analysis, she defines her values:

> "I trowe I loved hym best, for that he
> Was of his love daungerous to me.
> We wommen han, if that I shal nat lye,
> In this matere a queynte fantasye;
> Wayte what thyng we may nat lightly have,
> Therafter wol we crie al day and crave.
> Forbede us thyng, and that desiren we;
> Preesse on us faste, and thanne wol we fle.
> With daunger oute we al oure chaffare;
> Greet prees at market maketh deere ware,
> And to greet cheep is holde at litel prys;
> This knoweth every womman that is wys."
> (III. D, 513-24)

Alison presents her queynte fantasye (with pun intended, no doubt, by

both the wife and the poet) as representative of all women's idiosyn-
cratic, utterly feminine idea about what pleases them most. This
definition of women's personal preference derives, however, from modes
of valuation that are operative in the psychology of the marketplace.
The same principles governing international trade regulate Alison's
love life. Yet the mode of valuation that Alison claims as the province of her sex is a dangerous one, for both the merchant and the
lover.

If Alison defines personal, moral values according to the commercial ethic, it is appropriate to analyze her values in her own, that
is, in economic terms. The nature of medieval economic theory renders
the association of commercial and moral values more appropriate than
such an association may be in the late twentieth century. Because the
formulaters of economic theory were, by and large, the schoolmen, it
is not surprising that profit-making and smart business strategies were
not among their major economic concerns. Raymond De Roover writes:
"Chez les scolastiques . . . la théorie économique, ou ce qui en tenait
lieu, faisait partie intégrante de leur philosophie morale. À l'epoque
des scolastiques, la science économique n'était pas encore une science
autonome, elle faisait partie de la philosophie morale . . . ."[66] It
goes without saying that, if the scholastics, like their auctor Aristotle, saw economics as a subdivision of ethics, they would have moral
reservations about trade. Within the marketplace, one survived, to a

66. Raymond De Roover, La Pensée économique des scolastiques,
doctrines et méthodes (Montréal: Institut d'Etudes Mediévales, 1971),
pp. 18-19; Langholm, p. 5.

large extent, by one's wit; one made a profit by one's cunning. The

transactions of the marketplace could, quite obviously, tempt one to

avarice. In the Summa Theologiae, Aquinas followed Aristotle's example

in his condemnation of trade for the sake of profit (the only kind of

trade that the Wife of Bath has practiced throughout her marital

career). Aquinas wrote that such trade "juste vituperatur, quia,

quantum est de se, deservit cupiditati lucri, quae terminum nescit,

sed in infinitum tendit" ("is rightly open to criticism since, just in

itself, it feeds the acquisitive urge which knows no limit but tends

to increase to infinity"--ST, Q. 77, a. 4, pp. 228-29). But despite

their awareness of the injustice and profiteering to which trade could

lead, the scholastics, along with Aristotle, recognized the usefulness

of trade "propter necessitatem vitae" ("for the maintenance of life"--

ST, Q. 77, a. 4, pp. 226-27). For the scholastics, then, the commer-

cial exchange known as trade received its sole justification from mu-

tual human need (ST, Q. 77, a. 1, pp. 214-15). Yet, as the scholastics

were well aware, human need can become the prey of the unscrupulous.

It can be exploited by those concerned solely with their own profit.

Because of the injustice toward which trade could tend, the scholastics

established guidelines for fair business conduct and for the equitable

determination of prices. In the Summa, Aquinas bases these dicta on

Matthew vii. 12 (the Golden Rule): "Omnia quaecumque vultis ut faciant

vobis homines, et vos facite illis" ("So whatsoever you wish that men

would do to you, do so to them"--ST, Q. 77, a. 1, pp. 214-15). The

scholastic definition of fair exchange is founded upon reciprocity.

In the Ethics V. v, Aristotle cites reciprocity as the basis of, the reason for human community.

The scholastics established their rules for commercial conduct upon a reciprocal and just relationship between buyer and seller. As the passage describing her attraction to Jankyn shows, the Wife of Bath establishes value largely on the basis of supply and demand. The scholastics fully recognized the influence of fluctuating supply (_inopia_ and _copia_) on demand, and therefore, on price.[67] Nor did the scholastics condemn the fluctuation of price so long as it was not artificially regulated, for their own avaricious ends, by the merchants within the marketplace.[68] Only external forces operating upon the market (forces like rarity and climate) could legitimately cause prices to fluctuate. In the passage under discussion, however, the Wife of Bath ignores scholastic dicta concerning the establishment of prices. Her _queynte fantasye_ grants the individual the right to determine value; it makes the establishment of value purely subjective and personal. In her series of revaluations, the Wife of Bath has, of course, established value subjectively, in accordance with her own quest for self-determination.[69] Individuality and individual enterprise were the hallmarks of the growing middle class. For the bourgeoisie, social mobility depended upon the individual's energy and ability to define his own values in the marketplace and in society. But if a private

---

67. Raymond De Roover, _San Bernardino of Siena and Sant'Antonino of Florence_ (Boston: The Kress Library of Business and Economics, 1967), p. 21. Langholm, pp. 94-95, 126-28.

68. De Roover, p. 21.

69. See Aers, p. 88, for a similar interpretation of the self-centeredness of Alison's modes of valuation.

system of valuation expresses one's own desire for self-determination,
it does not necessarily indicate a moral attitude toward personal and
commercial exchange.

According to Alison, price is determined by the merchant on the
basis of his apprehension of the buyer's individual needs, tastes, and
desires. This mode of establishing value gave the merchant the opportunity to ignore the justum pretium. The scholastics defined the
justum pretium as the market price.[70] More specifically, it was the
price set by the community on the basis of its collective need and of
the item's virtuositas, its "objective utility."[71] According to Raymond De Roover, "the scholastics considered price determination as a
social process. Already Accursius (1182-1260), in his ordinary gloss
to the Roman Law, had modified the dictum, Res tantum valet quantum
vendi potest . . . by adding the . . . words sed communiter."[72] But
the Wife of Bath does not establish value according to the just price.
She believes that value is regulated by personal need and desire, by
individual taste.

In the last half of the thirteenth century, Peter John Olivi devised three criteria by which to determine value: "1) usefulness
(virtuositas); 2) scarcity (raritas); and 3) pleasurableness or desir-
ability (complacibilitas)."[73] As De Roover explains, the difference

---

70. De Roover, San Bernardino and Sant'Antonino, p. 20.

71. Ibid., p. 18. See also De Roover's article, "The Concept of
the Just Price: Theory and Economic Policy," Journal of Economic History, XVIII (1958), 420-21.

72. De Roover, San Bernardino and Sant'Antonino, p. 20.

73. Ibid., p. 19; Langholm, pp. 154-55.

between _virtuositas_ and _complacibilitas_ resides in the distinction
between objective and subjective utility.[74] For the Wife of Bath,
raritas is the very condition that determines _complacibilitas_; the
combination of these two factors increases, or rather, inflates value.
Under such market conditions the seller, aware of the buyer's personal
desires, may be tempted to ignore the just price and to demand, instead, a _pretium affectionis_, "a discriminatory price."[75] (_Pretium
affectionis_ is, of course, a rather appropriate phrase for describing
the cost paid by her old husbands for marriage to Alison.) The market
conditions that the Wife outlines allow the seller to think solely of
his own profit as he exploits another's inordinate desire for his rare
commodity. It was against such exploitation that scholastics warned
both buyers and merchants.

The Wife does not seem concerned that her mode of valuation may
be no more applauded by masculine moralists than her ideas about remarriage and marital sex. Nonetheless, this passage contains oversights of which Alison is not aware, oversights dangerous to the woman
who holds these values and dangerous in the economic and moral terms
developed by the scholastics. One of these oversights is immediately
evident. The Wife's first four marriages, as well as the concluding
lines of this passage, prove that her sex's _queynte fantasye_ does not
belong to women alone. Alison's old husbands also establish value according to this system. As she has boasted, they paid dearly--in more

---

74. _Ibid._, p. 18.

75. De Roover, "The Concept of Just Price," 426.

ways than one--for the sexual favors that the Wife withheld until she
received her pretium affectionis, their land and wealth. Alison has
a history of raising prices in direct proportion to her husbands desires and she knows that those desires grew with her resistance.
"'With daunger oute we al oure chaffare,'" says Alison in a statement
that translates the courtly love notion of daunger into her own commercial idiom. Women, therefore, can increase their own value by practicing daunger and by learning how to exploit individual desire. But the
Wife does not articulate the risk inherent in this system of values any
more clearly than she articulated the loss attendant upon the profit
made in marriage. The risk to women is the same in both cases. If
Alison, indeed, if all women, profit through such dealings, they also
become the chaffare which they sell.[76] Their perceptions of their own
worth are determined by the commercial mentality.

The system of values that the Wife of Bath outlines is also dangerous to women as buyers, for within this system, the customer risks
exploitation by the unscrupulous merchant. And Alison certainly suffers such exploitation at the beginning of her marriage to young
Jankyn. By becoming the buyer for the first time in her long career,
the Wife initially loses the supremacy that she was wont to command
when time was on her side. As buyer, Alison becomes the victim of the
system of values that she claims as her own. She pays too high a
price, materially and emotionally, to gain the love of the first husband whom she herself loves. She admits:

---

76. See Aers, p. 148.

> "... to hym yaf I al the lond and fee
> That evere was me yeven therbifoore,
> But afterward repented me ful soore."
> (III. D, 630-32)

This from the woman whose youth saw her obsessed with her own profit.

Alison has become the victim of her own system of values and time

would guarantee that she maintains this position unless her own values

change.

In the world of the Wife of Bath, all value, including her own,

derives from a conjunction of raritas and complacibilitas. Although

her inheritances make the Wife a valuable acquisition, time is fast

eroding the price that her sexuality can command on the marriage mar-

ket. In a moment of poignant self-awareness, the Wife of Bath says:

> "Unto this day it dooth myn herte boote
> That I have had my world as in my tyme.
> But age, allas! that al wole envenyme,
> Hath me biraft my beautee and my pith.
> Lat go, farewel! the devel go therwith!
> The flour is goon, ther is namoore to telle;
> The bren, as I best kan, now mooste I selle ..."
> (III. D, 472-78)

In order to free herself from a system of valuation in which she her-

self will become devalued with time, the Wife's own values must change.

Moreover, if this system produces profit in the marketplace, in human

relationships, it can only lead to frustration, to emotional bank-

ruptcy, as it were. The act of attainment entails the loss of value

if we want most what we cannot have. Alison's system of valuation does

not posit any lasting value, any permanent satisfaction, either mate-

rial or emotional.

The Wife of Bath's energetic resiliency, of course, protects her

from devastating loss. After the violent bout that left Jankyn's book and Alison's ear somewhat worse for the wear, she emerges, once again,

as the (self-proclaimed) victor, triumphant because she has gained

supremacy in her fifth marriage. In her explanation of her marital

bliss at the end of her Prologue, the Wife of Bath names maistrie as

the key to her success. Alison's Tale allows us to judge the accuracy

of her evaluation of her happiness.

Critics have called the tale an exemplum illustrating the thesis

of the sermon delivered in Alison's Prologue.[77] In addition, they

generally agree that the Tale, and, more specifically, the Loathly

Lady's well-timed metamorphosis, represent the Wife of Bath's own

wish-fulfillment fantasy.[78] In the Tale, through the power of lan-

guage, the aging but not aged Alison reverses the only force in God's

creation that she cannot badger into submission--the force of time.

Doubtless, the Wife of Bath would like to turn back the clock. Her

Tale, however, presents a wish-fulfillment fantasy more complex than

the personal desire for sexual rejuvenation. Transformation is central

to The Wife of Bath's Tale, with its scenes of magic and metamorphosis,

because this theme is closely related to, if not inseparable from the

theme of revaluation that pervades her Prologue. Moreover, at the same

77. See, for example, Bartlett J. Whiting's discussion of the
Tale in Sources and Analogues of Chaucer's Canterbury Tales, eds. W.
F. Bryan and Germaine Dempster (New York: Humanities Press, 1958), p.
223 and R. E. Kaske's article, "Chaucer's Marriage Group," Chaucer:
The Love Poet, eds. Jerome Mitchell and William Provost (Athens:
Univ. of Georgia Press, 1973), p. 51.

78. See Charles Muscatine, Poetry and Crisis in the Age of Chau-
cer (Notre Dame: Univ. of Notre Dame Press, 1972), p. 127 and Donald
Howard, The Idea of the Canterbury Tales (Berkeley: Univ. of California
Press, 1976), p. 253.

time that the Wife's Tale fulfills many of the wishes implicit in the quest for self-determination in her Prologue, it also indicates the transformation of Alison's own values.

The Wife of Bath's Tale, as Mary Curruthers is the most recent critic to note, is the story told by a woman that Alison imagines in her Prologue (III. D, 692-710). The Wife of Bath believes that, if women wrote stories, "'They wolde han writen of men moore wikkednesse/ Than al the mark of Adam may redresse'" (III. D, 696-97). But if Alison's Tale is intended to accomplish women's literary revenge, it is surprisingly mild. The Tale's answer to antifeminism transcends the vengeful vision of a world in which powerful women run roughshod over men; instead, it challenges the substance of antifeminism.

The concluding portion of The Wife of Bath's Prologue offers yet another catalogue of antifeminist wisdom, Jankyn's anthology of "'wikked wyves'" (III. D, 685). Although Jankyn's collection of condemnations is nothing new to the Wife, it is more painful to her, coming as it does from the man upon whom she bestowed her love and her property. For the first time, Alison is unable to turn antifeminist accusations to her own purposes, not, that is, until she has had enough. The Wife then delivers to antifeminism a final and decisive act of revaluation; she destroys the book that torments her.

Through its emphases and its language, Jankyn's book suggests the reasons motivating antifeminism, reasons significant to the shape that women's power assumes in the Wife's Tale. The book's exempla demonstrate that man's need to dominate woman derives as much from man's fear of her and of her otherness as it does from his belief in the evil

intrinsic to all womankind. Woman's otherness produces the generaliza-
tion accompanying antifeminism; it produces the need to control women,
to fix their meaning, by stereotyping and by reducing them to signs,
to tropes, to conventions. In Jankyn's catalogue, women are depicted
specifically as they are agents of loss. Because of them, men lose
strength, life, love, and dignity. Jankyn's catalogue of errant women
begins at the beginning: with the woman who brought the greatest of
all losses to man:

> "Of Eva first, that for hir wikkednesse
> Was al mankynde broght to wrecchednesse,
> For which that Jhesu Crist hymself was slayn,
> That boghte us with his herte blood agayn.
> Lo, heere expres of womman may ye fynde,
> That womman was the los of al mankynde."
> (III. D, 715-20; emphasis mine)

If woman caused the loss of grace, Eve's fall occasioned the most generous exchange relationship known to medieval Christianity. By becoming man, the Son of God was able to exchange his life for man's salva-
tion. If a man "'boghte us with his herte blood'" and if a woman
"'was the los of al mankynde,'" then woman is, indeed, a bad bargain,
and man is therefore able to use her as the symbol for all human imperfection. In a Prologue structured linguistically and conceptually by
the values of the commercial ethic, the emphases of Jankyn's catalogue
are significant. For a woman like Alison, obsessed with her own profit
and loss, the antifeminists' reiteration of the loss caused by woman
constantly reminds her of her own place in her world. For if men have
paid for the loss occasioned by Eve, women have paid twofold for their
mother's sin. Ironically, in the first marriage in which she contrib-
uted to her husband's material and emotional profit, her husband ex-

plicitly reminds her of the loss that women have brought to men. It
is little wonder that the catalogue concludes with Alison's articulation of personal pain at the loss occasioned her by antifeminism (III.
D, 786-87).

In her Tale, the Wife of Bath transforms the antifeminists' definition of woman as "'the los of al mankynde.'" From its first snide
reference to the friar as post-lapsarian incubus through the knight's
rape of the maiden and his ingratitude to the hag, the Tale portrays
man as the loss to womankind. Yet Alison spares her audience dia-
tribes against men. In the atmosphere of generosity pervading the
fairy tale, relatively little emphasis is given to the knight's crime.
The nature of his crime, a violation of woman's sexuality, is, of
course, significant within the context of the tale, but if the crime
is underplayed, it is because the tale's purpose is not vindication,
but education. The tale does not intend to punish men any more than
the queen intends to execute the young knight. Rather, the tale seeks
to enlighten men so that experience will be richer for both men and
women.

In the world of The Wife of Bath's Tale, women do not have to bargain for the power which they wield over themselves and over men and
they exercise their power generously. If Jankyn's book presents the
collective masculine fear of women's power and its consequences, The
Wife of Bath's Tale proves those fears baseless. Rather than incurring
loss to men, women in the tale grant men life. They redeem men by
educating them, by bringing them a respect for otherness, for women's
intrinsic worth. The tale demonstrates that, when women have power,

they, in fact, exercise it with more generosity and understanding than men have been wont to extend to women. Although it may seem incongruous for the Wife to deliver a fairy tale set "in th'olde dayes of the Kyng Arthour" (III. D. 857), that setting is thematically appropriate to her tale.[79] It locates the Wife's portrayal of women's power and authority within a context as poignant as it is illuminating, that is, within a context distanced temporally and socially from the fourteenth-century bourgeois world to which she herself belongs. Despite the Wife of Bath's revaluations of convention, the attainment of power comparable to that which the queen exercises can only occur within the world of magic and transformation of her fiction.

Alison's tale not only redefines the value of women. It also reintroduces the question of women's values at the same time that it presents a transformation in the Wife of Bath's system of valuation. Granted power to determine the young knight's fate, the queen sentences him with a quest appropraite to the nature of his crime: "'I graunte thee lyf, if thou kanst tellen me/ What thyng is it that wommen moost desiren'" (III. D, 903-04). At the end of his long and confusing quest, the knight receives his answer from the Loathly Lady: maistrie. Given the conclusion of The Wife of Bath's Prologue, the answer to the knight's quest is not surprising, for Alison has also attributed her happiness with Jankyn to this source:

> "He yaf me al the bridel in myn hond,
> To han governance of hous and lond,
> And of his tonge, and of his hond also;

---

79. See Bartlett J. Whiting's discussion of the sources for Alison's Tale in Sources and Analogues (full citation above).

And made hym brenne his book anon right tho."
(III. D, 813-16)

If, in her discussion of her own system of valuation, Alison has said,
"'Wayte what thyng we may nat lightly have,/ Therafter wol we crie al
day and crave'" (III. D, 517-18), the social traditions of the world
in which Alison bargained and Chaucer wrote make the answer maistrie
consistent with this formula for determining value. Maistrie is what
women desire and value most because, in the Wife's experience, women
want the maistrie (and I use "want" in both its meanings) that men
still control. Despite Alison's energetic quest for self-determination, her Prologue provides many examples of the power that men in her
world wield over women (as the young knight's crime exemplifies). Although Alison challenges the power of men and succeeds in appropriating
it to her own advantage, maistrie remains women's most coveted possession because the traditions and conventions of their world make it per-
petually inaccessible.

The Loathly Lady's answer is significant because it accommodates
the Wife's earlier formula for determining value. More important, in
relation to the ethical concerns of scholastic economic theory, this
answer presents the beginning of a change in the Wife's own attitude
toward valuation. In the Prologue, value was predicated not only upon
unattainability, but also upon personal preference, upon individual
taste. This subjective criterion for determining value occurs again
in the Tale. When the knight asks women what they most desire, women
respond with a confusing and daunting catalogue of their preferences.
Consensus becomes impossible because women translate his question into
personal terms. As the list grows to encompass many of the "thynges"

that the Wife has wanted and won in her Prologue ("richesse," "honour,"
"lust abedde"--to name but a few), Chaucer shows the futility of trying
to establish value on the basis of subjective interpretation.

Despite the diversity of individual responses, however, maistrie
is the answer uniting all women. The hag challenges the knight:

> "Lat se which is the proudeste of hem alle,
> That wereth on a coverchief or a calle,
> That dar seye nay of that I shal thee teche."
> (III. D, 1017-19)

When the knight delivers his answer, the queen's court accords him
unanimous approval:

> In al the court ne was ther wyf, ne mayde,
> Ne wydwe, that contraried that he sayde,
> But seyded he was worthy han his lyf . . .
> (III. D, 1043-45)

Maistrie has the highest value for all women of all social classes because women do not fully possess maistrie in the Wife's world. Their
consensus is a communal establishment of value based upon collective
need. Significantly, their consensus shows Alison's approach toward a
more equitable system of valuation than she had advocated in her
Prologue. The just price, the justum pretium, is founded upon such a
collective assessment of value. As Alison begins to transcend her preoccupation with subjective determination of value, she also moves
closer to the just exchange and the consequent self-transcendence that
occurs at the end of her Prologue and Tale.

The Wife of Bath's history and personality more than convince her
audience that she sincerely needs, wants, and values maistrie. Yet
Alison's answer becomes inadequate when she attributes her happiness
with Jankyn to the acquisition of maistrie. Throughout The Wife of

Bath's Prologue, Chaucer has shown us that maistrie is, at best, a
dubious value. When the Wife possesses maistrie, Alison is unhappy.
As the source of unhappiness throughout her Prologue, maistrie does
not provide an adequate explanation for the happiness that the Wife
and Jankyn, as well as the hag and the knight, enjoy. Throughout her
Prologue and Tale, the Wife of Bath has displayed an impressive, if
often irreverent, talent for redefinition and revaluation in order to
convince her audience that she both shapes her own life and determines
her own values. Ironically, however, despite her talent for revaluation, Alison fails to see that maistrie is not the source of her har-
monious relationship to Jankyn. Alison, her values, and her interpretation of her experience are trapped within the values of the commercial ethic and within her own socially conditioned desire for self-
determination.[80] The Wife of Bath is not aware that, in part, her
experience has redefined her own values.

On the basis of the information that Alison provides at the end
of her Prologue and Tale, Chaucer allows us to make a more accurate
interpretation of the Wife's values than the one that she herself
presents. According to Alison,

> ". . . whan that I hadde geten unto me,
> By maistrie, al the soveraynetee,
> And that he seyde, 'Myn owene trewe wyf,
> Do as thee lust the terme of al thy lyf;
> Keep thyn honour, and keep eek myn estaat'--
> After that day we hadden never debaat.
> God helpe me so, I was to hym as kynde
> As any wyf from Denmark unto Ynde,
> And also trewe, and so was he to me."
>   (III. D, 817-25)

---

80. Weissman, pp. 108-09.

Chaucer's text makes it clear that <u>maistrie</u> does not cause the Wife's happiness with Jankyn. <u>Maistrie</u> guarantees power and profit in a commercial exchange and, by extension, in Alison's first four marriages. In human relationships, however, <u>maistrie</u> can only breed a self-concern that is antithetical to love. As Alison's own words indicate, happiness comes to her and to the Loathly Lady because, if they have <u>maistrie</u> in their marriages, they also share that power with their husbands. For the first time in Alison's marital history (perhaps because of Jankyn's lovely legs or because of his amatory proficiency), she is in love, and she is kind. For this kindness, she receives kindness in return. The new component of the Wife's relationship with Jankyn is not <u>maistrie</u>, but her willingness to yield <u>maistrie</u> in the acknowledgment of another's needs. Alison has gained a possession, the happiness of a shared love, whose intrinsic worth is greater than that of power.

The scholastics, on the basis of Aristotle's teachings, designated mutual need as the origin of and justification for commercial exchange. The exchange that occurs at the end of both <u>The Wife of Bath's Prologue</u> and <u>Tale</u> is founded upon such an awareness of mutual need. It is a just exchange deriving not from the self-concern of <u>maistrie</u>, but from the self-transcendence of a generosity that approaches the Loathly Lady's definition of <u>gentillesse</u>.[81] As her own values become transformed, Alison exchanges the "'wo that is in mariage'" for the "'parfit joye'" (III. D, 1258) at the end of her <u>Prologue</u> and <u>Tale</u>. The values

---

81. Weissman offers a similar interpretation of the hag's sermon, p. 109. She does not, however, see the mutuality at the end of the tale as triumphant (p. 110).

that prevailed throughout her Prologue have changed. In the harmony
of marital truce with Jankyn, value is no longer regulated by supply
and demand, by inopia and copia. Nor is value determined by the
buyer's unsatisfied desire that the seller can turn to his own advantage. Instead, value is predicated upon the awareness of mutual need.
In this system of marital economics, each partner receives the justum
pretium: the love and respect and sense of self-determination that
one needs in return for the love and respect and awareness of another's
selfhood that one expends. The just exchange proves mutually profitable. Alison's happiness in her fifth marriage derives from reciprocity, from the just exchange and the subsequent satisfaction that
William Blake described so economically:

> What is it men in women do require
> The lineaments of Gratified Desire
> What is it women do in men require
> The lineaments of Gratified Desire.

But the Wife of Bath, who has established her life's experience
as her auctoritee, has never experienced an equitable exchange like
the one that she shares with Jankyn. This new experience qualifies
her previous system of values; it transforms her own revaluations.
Yet, because of her trust in her experience, Alison insists upon naming
her happiness as maistrie. Alison ends her Tale on the assertive and
energetic note that is synonymous with the Wife of Bath:

> . . . and Jhesu Crist us sende
> Housbondes meeke, yonge, and fressh abedde,
> And grace t'overbyde hem that we wedde;
> And eek I praye Jhesu shorte hir lyves
> That wol nat be governed by hir wyves;
> And olde and angry nygardes of dispence,
> God sende hem soone verray pestilence!
> (III. D, 1258-64)

In her own quest to revalue, the Wife of Bath fails at the moment of her greatest happiness because she fails to evaluate. Her failure and the reasons for that failure qualify the triumphant energy of her Prologue and the generous sentiment in her Tale. Alison errs and, in her erring, she fails to interpret the source of her happiness correctly. Caught within the values of the commercial ethic, Alison believes that these values are her own, that they constitute her queynte fantasye, that she has formulated them for herself in contradistinction to masculine conventions. In fact, while appropriating men's power, she has appropriated her values from the marketplace whose strategies are established by men. The Wife of Bath measures her own worth and her happiness with Jankyn according to this borrowed system of valuation. Even when she has established a just relationship based upon mutual need, the loquacious Alison lacks the words with which to name her new-found happiness.

Alison has argued for the importance of intrinsic worth and for the necessity of correlating signs with substance. She has argued for the importance of calling things by their proper names. Although she experiences the value of her happiness with Jankyn, she fails to name it properly by failing to name it according to its intrinsic worth. She settles instead for the name that the conventions of her own experience would give it. The teachings of the Wife of Bath's experience have themselves become conventions, the auctoritees according to which she measures value. Ironically, just as Alison adopts the methods of the clerics, she also suffers from their inability to perceive intrinsic worth outside the area of value that their own conventions have delineated. In the process, both the clerics and Alison end by devaluing because of the reductiveness of their own conventions. For the clerics, women are devalued as they are reduced to a symbol of human imperfection; for the Wife of Bath, reciprocity is devalued into maistrie, the metaphor for all that women value most.

The Wife of Bath's failure to name accurately the source of her happiness with Jankyn offers us a way of interpreting the deafness that ensued from her bout with antifeminism. D. W. Robertson has suggested that the Wife's deafness signifies her inability to hear the words of the Scriptures and the voice of God.[82] But Alison's character is, essentially, a voice, a voice with many modulations, bawdy and strident, energetic and assertive, sometimes loving and plaintive and introspective. Above all, Alison has the loud voice of one who cannot hear, not only what is spoken to her, but what she herself says. Alison is deaf to herself, to her own voice. She may have destroyed the substance of antifeminism (a destruction that she finishes in the redefinition of women in her Tale), but she does not hear what her own words would tell her: that she has not destroyed its methods. Even if Alison has played by the rules only to thwart them, she has played by them long enough for them to become her own. The Wife of Bath does not hear the transformation of value that her own words communicate. Nor does she hear her own misnaming of the intrinsic worth of the reciprocity that she has found with Jankyn. Yet, despite the reciprocity of her fifth marriage, the Wife also knows that her world still grants men maistrie.

_____

82. D. W. Robertson, Preface to Chaucer (Princeton: Princeton Univ. Press), p. 320.

Her Prologue begins with her bout with the clerics because men have power and language with which to establish values for themselves and for women. And her Tale ends with a cry for maistrie because the conventions of her world will continue to make it the thing that women most desire.

Chapter III

"'WE MAY CREAUNCE WHIL WE HAVE A NAME'": TAKING

IT ON FAITH IN THE SHIPMAN'S TALE

The Shipman's Tale is a fabliau about a merchant's wife who makes

love with a monk for profit while her husband is away on business and

then tries the same tactic on her husband when he returns. In this

tale, as many critics have observed, sex becomes a business,[1] business

replaces sex,[2] and we are left with "the reduction of all human values

to commercial ones."[3] The Wife of Bath, as we have seen, also presents

the ways in which sexuality becomes a form of currency. But, in the

Wife's Prologue, Chaucer explores the relationship between sex and

money and between sexual and material power more fully than he does in

the tale which, scholars believe, was originally assigned to Alison of

Bath.[4] The Shipman's Tale is a puzzling story both because of and in

_____

1. A. H. Silverman's essay, "Sex and Money in Chaucer's Shipman's
Tale," PQ, 32 (1953), 329-36, definitively established the relationship
between sex and money in this tale.

2. In his article, "The Quaint World of The Shipman's Tale,"
Studies in Short Fiction, 4 (1966-67), 181, Bernard S. Levy discusses
what he calls "the sexualization of commerce outside marriage" in this
tale.

3. E. Talbot Donaldson, Chaucer's Poetry: An Anthology for the
Modern Reader (New York: The Ronald Press Co., 1958), p. 931.

4. F. N. Robinson discusses the transference of this tale from
the Wife of Bath to the Shipman in his Explanatory Notes to The Works
of Geoffrey Chaucer, second edition (Boston: Houghton Mifflin Co.,
1957), p. 732. For the purposes of the analysis of The Shipman's Tale
in this chapter, I am reading the tale not as a work lent to the Shipman,

spite of its superficial similarities to aspects of The Wife of Bath's
Prologue. And it is also puzzling because the accurate observation
concerning its "reduction of all human values to commercial ones" is
not sufficiently specific, as we shall see, to explain its patterns of
moral devaluation.

In The Shipman's Tale, as this chapter will argue, Chaucer presents intention as the ethical determinant not only of commercial, but
also of personal and linguistic relationships. If good intention honors the value of contracts and of the language constituting them, false
intention ignores the terms of the contract just as (and at the same
time that) it uses language to hide motivation toward personal gain.
False intention betrays language as it deprives language of the ability
to express meaning clearly and honestly. In the process, the stable
value of language is threatened, for if language can be redefined to
suit individual purposes, it may ultimately prove to be arbitrary and
mutable. The shifting value of language and the question of its arbitrariness are at the heart of Chaucer's moral and artistic concerns in
The Shipman's Tale.

The details emphasized by the narrative reveal the aspects of the
tale that most interest the Shipman, and Chaucer. Although the tale is
a fabliau, it differs markedly from Chaucer's other productions in this
genre. For example, the setting of The Miller's Tale is richly ren-

---

but as a tale that shows the marks of the character presented in the
General Prologue. Chaucer's transference of this tale to the Shipman
was not, I believe, an arbitrary one. This tale, with its emphasis on
deceit and betrayal, is better suited to the Shipman than it would have
been to the Wife of Bath's concerns with the "olde daunce."

dered. The Miller painstakingly describes physiognomy and dress, his
characters' habits and the accoutrements of their daily lives. The
Reeve is also conscious of the physical details that constitute his
tale's setting. But although we know that the merchant in The Shipman's Tale is wealthy, that he entertains sumptuously, that his home is
more than comfortable, and that his wife is more than a little concerned with dress, the Shipman delivers this information, not through
detailed descriptions, but in declarative statements. Material wealth
as a symbol of "honour" or of social status does not interest the Shipman, who dismisses the benefits of conspicuous consumption early in his
tale:

> A wyf he hadde of excellent beautee;
> And compaignable and revelous was she,
> Which is a thyng that causeth more dispence
> Than worth is al the chiere and reverence
> That men hem doon at festes and at daunces.
> (VII. 3-7)[5]

Moreover, despite the relationship between sex and money in this tale,
sex seems as inconsequential to the Shipman as the prestige accruing
to material wealth. In the space of 434 lines, the tale presents two
sexual encounters, the consummation of the adulterous relationship between the monk and the wife and the energetic reunion of the merchant
and the same wife. Seven lines are given to the description of the
former, three to the latter. The titillation of the bed scenes, whether
they are illicit or otherwise, does not preoccupy the Shipman.[6]

----

5. All quotations from The Shipman's Tale are taken from the
second edition of F. N. Robinson's The Works of Geoffrey Chaucer and
will be cited by fragment and line number within the body of the text.

6. For a similar discussion of the emphases in the Shipman's nar-

Haste is an important element of the "bisinesse" of the merchant's household. With a briskness bordering on abruptness, the characters attend Mass and meals:[7]

> But hastily a messe was ther sayd,
> And spedily the tables were yleyd,
> And to the dyner faste they hem spedde . . . .
>   (VII. 251-53)

The merchant's business transactions in Bruges are conducted with as much dispatch (VII. 300-06) as the monk and the wife conduct their assignation. But if the Shipman underlines the perfunctory quality of these characters' habits, a similar economizing of time and words marks his narrative style. The Shipman does not linger over details. He repeatedly interrupts himself, breaking off one description to move onto the next. His tale is punctuated with phrases that convey this sense of abruptness: "Na moore of this as now, for it suffiseth" (VII. 52); "and there I lete hym dwelle" (VII. 306); "namoore of hym I seye" (VII. 324). Nor does the Shipman embellish his tale with carefully contrived figurative language. (When he does select a figure, he repeats it throughout the tale, regardless of its appropriateness to its context. Thus, when his relatively emotionless characters are happy, he repeatedly compares them to some form of jubilant bird [VII. 38, 51, 209, 369].) He does not waste the reader's time, or his own energy, on the intricacies of figurative language, unless, as we shall examine at length later, these figures are the puns that are a central element in

---

rative, see John C. McGalliard, "Characterization in Chaucer's Shipman's Tale," PQ, 54 (1975), 2 and 8.

7. See Janette Richardson, "The Facade of Bawdry: Image Patterns in Chaucer's Shipman's Tale," ELH, 32 (1965), 310.

his tale.

The Shipman's abruptness, of course, mirrors the haste with which his characters conduct themselves; economy in the expenditure of language is an appropriate stylistic device in a tale that begins with an admonition against unnecessary "dispence." But the artistic economy of The Shipman's Tale also reveals the preoccupations of the tale's narrator. The dispatch with which he treats ritual, sex, and setting allows him to dwell upon that aspect of the fabliau most interesting to him (and to Chaucer, in this tale). That aspect is, of course, the commercial one, for the Shipman is as staunch an adherent of the mercantile mentality as any of his characters. As critics have noted, the analogues do not offer the extended treatment of the merchant's character or of medieval financial transactions that we find in The Shipman's Tale.[8] Moreover, despite his relative lack of interest in description or rhetorical embellishment, the Shipman is careful to record dialogue.[9] In this tale, we come to know the characters' motivations and their individual interpretations of the mercantile mentality more through their words than through their actions. Chaucer and his narrator emphasize dialogue because their fundamental concerns in the tale focus on the ways in which business dealings are contracted.

The characteristics of these business dealings reveal the shape of the mercantile mentality in this tale at the same time that they deter-

---

8. See, for example, V. J. Scattergood's article, "The Originality of The Shipman's Tale," ChauR, 11 (1977), especially 212-13. Scattergood also notes the Shipman's significant omission of certain details, such as proper names, in this tale.

9. See McGalliard on dialogue, 2 and 5.

mine the ways in which moral values are debased. The Wife of Bath's
commercial activities involved the direct sale of her sexual favors to
her husbands. By bargaining with language, Alison received the best
price for her goods and she was paid directly in land, money, gifts, or
privileges. In The Shipman's Tale, the financial dealings are not simple sales transactions. When the merchant wishes to purchase his
"chaffare" at Bruges, he does not pay in ready cash for his merchan-
dise. Rather, he makes a "chevyssaunce" (VII. 329). When the wife
needs a hundred francs to subsidize her clothing allowance, she does
not turn to her husband (although the tale never gives us any reason
to believe that he would have denied her the sum). Instead, she asks
the monk, Don John, for a loan. Don John does not grant the loan from
his own funds. He, in turn, asks the merchant for the hundred francs
that will gain him the sexual repayment promised by the merchant's
wife. These three loans, the ways in which they are contracted, and
the ways in which they are repaid form the basis of the commercial
transactions in the tale. That the financial exchanges are credit
transactions rather than sales or gifts provides the mechanism for the
plot's intricate dénouement and for the duping of the merchant which is
the Shipman's major interest in the tale.[10] But the credit transactions are more than plot devices; they provide the key to the thematic
and ethical concerns of The Shipman's Tale. Moreover, by associating
his characters to each other through credit relationships, Chaucer presents yet another consequence of the commercial ethic in this tale:

_____

10. Silverman, 334, makes this point about the Shipman's interest
in the merchant's fate.

the devaluation of language when it is misused in the name of personal

profit. Through an examination of the workings of and attitudes toward

credit in the late Middle Ages, we can more fully understand the nature

of this moral and linguistic devaluation.

Because the merchant's "chevyssaunce" is the only credit transac-

tion in the tale used for specifically professional purposes, we can

use it as a touchstone by which to assess the loans of the monk and the

wife. The Shipman describes this "chevyssaunce," its execution, and

its mode of repayment at length:

> This marchant, whan that ended was the faire,
> To Seint-Denys, he gan for to repaire,
> And with his wyf he maketh feeste and cheere,
> And telleth hire that chaffare is so deere
> That nedes moste he make a chevyssaunce;
> For he was bounden in a reconyssaunce
> To paye twenty thousand sheeld anon.
> For which this marchant is to Parys gon
> To borwe of certein freendes that he hadde
> A certeyn frankes; and somme with him he ladde.
> (VII. 325-34)

And the Shipman informs us about the resolution of the deal:

> This marchant, which that was ful war and wys,
> Creanced hath, and payd eek in Parys
> To certeyn Lumbardes, redy in hir hond,
> The somme of gold, and gat of hem his bond . . . .
> (VII. 365-68)

Considering the General Prologue's description of the Shipman's profes-

sional involvement in overseas trade, his familiarity with the techni-

calities of medieval finance is not surprising.[11] What is interesting,

_____

11. The Shipman might very well have been familiar, too, with a
partnership known as the foenus nauticum, a credit transaction popular
among shipowners. John T. Noonan describes this contract in The
Scholastic Analysis of Usury (Cambridge: Harvard Univ. Press, 1957):
"In this contract, money or goods were loaned to a shipowner, the creditor assuming the risks of his debtor while the money or goods were

however, is that the Shipman, who offers only the essential details

concerning his characters' material and emotional existences, devotes

fourteen lines to an explanation of the dynamics of the merchant's

loan.

In fact, the Shipman provides enough information to allow us to

identify the merchant's credit transaction and the obligations under

which it placed him. The nature of this loan is central to Chaucer's

moral and artistic questions in this tale. In a recent article, Ken-

neth Cahn goes far toward defining the mechanism of the merchant's

trade in Bruges.[12] As Cahn points out, the merchant's credit transac-

tion is not a simple loan or _mutuum_.[13] Rather, it is a species of

---

actually at sea. If . . . the property were lost, the debtor will not
be liable in any way to return the loan. Once the voyage is completed,
however, the borrower trades at his own risk, and if he loses the loan
through commercial misfortune, he must still repay the lender. The
Roman Law permits the creditor to charge twice the legal rate of interest for the time he actually runs the risk of the sea. This extra
charge is described as 'the price of peril'. . . . The _foenus nauticum_
is, in fact, half a loan, half a partnership. The Roman law . . .
treats it strictly as a kind of licit usury; and the canonists and
scholastics follow the sharp distinction between it as a loan, and the
normal partnership" (pp. 134-35).

12. Kenneth S. Cahn's article, "Chaucer's Merchants and the
Foreign Exchange: An Introduction to Medieval Finance," _SAC_, 2 (1980),
pp. 81-119, presents an impressive effort to define the activities of
Chaucer's merchants in the context of contemporary financial practices.
I am indebted to Cahn's discussion of the merchant's credit transaction
in _The Shipman's Tale_ in my own analysis of his financial dealings and
I am also indebted to the bibliography that his article provides. Cahn,
however, does not apply the data that he has gathered to the tale in
order to offer an interpretation of it. Consequently, my own discussion of the merchant's transaction will focus on the moral aspects of
his loan.

13. Cahn, 95. For further discussion of the mechanism of the
merchant's exchange, see three works by Raymond DeRoover: "What is Dry
Exchange: A Contribution to the Study of English Mercantilism," _Jour-
nal of Political Economics_, 52 (1944), 250-66; _L'Évolution de la Lettre_

foreign exchange known as "merchants' exchange." Such a transaction, called a cambium per litteras, employed bills of exchange and required both a change of place and a change of currency. Cahn cites the change in the names of currency as textual evidence for the identification of the loan in The Shipman's Tale.[14] While in Bruges, the merchant borrows twenty thousand shields to cover his expenses there. He then repays the debt of twenty thousand shields in Paris by using the equivalent amount of francs. These francs are converted into shields by foreign exchange and then transferred to Bruges, the site of the original debt, in order to resolve the merchant's obligations there. Raymond DeRoover clarifies what seems to us, in an age of charge cards and paper money, to be a rather unwieldy mode of finance:

> Au moyen âge, la lettre de change était réellement une lettre «de change», ou en d'autres termes, une cédule qui servait à constater et executer le contrat de change. Ce dernier peut se définir comme une convention par laquelle le «donneur» ou datore, fournissait une somme d'argent au «preneur» ou prenditore, et recevait en échange un engagement payable à terme (opération de crédit), mais en un autre lieu et en un autre monnaie (opération de change). Tout contrat de change engendrait donc une opération de change et un opération de crédit, toutes deux intimément liées. Il s'ensuit que la lettre de change . . . était à la fois un instrument de transfert et un instrument de crédit.[15]

To summarize, the merchant, lacking funds in Bruges, took shields on credit there, used foreign exchange to convert francs to shields in Paris, and thereby acquitted himself of his debt.

---

de Change, XIVe-XVIIIe siècles (Paris: Librairie Armand Colin, 1953); and "The Scholastics, Usury, and Foreign Exchange," Business History Review, 41 (1967), 257-71.

14. Cahn, 86-87.

15. De Roover, L'Evolution de la Lettre de Change, p. 43.

Chaucer's tale also tells us that, in this transaction, the merchant was "bounden in a reconyssaunce" (VII. 330). The "bond" (VII.
368) which the merchant resolved in Paris was a common document, useful
because it provided "a full record of the transaction and a relatively
full summary of the details and stipulations involved in it."[16] Although a recognitio could be synonymous with a bond, a recognisance
named a more stringent series of obligations than the bond. According
to M. M. Postan, a "full legal recognisance" was a "more formal acknowledgement of the obligation by the debtor before a judicial tribunal."[17]
It is not clear from Chaucer's text whether the merchant's "reconyssaunce" is the more informal bond or the "full legal recognisance."
In either case, the inclusion of this term in the account of the merchant's financial transactions makes it clear that his loan carried
well-defined obligations. And the merchant must fulfill these obligations in order to ensure the success of his business venture.

With characteristic haste, the merchant heads to Paris to honor
the obligations under which his credit transaction has placed him.
The merchant is not only diligent in counting his profits; he is also
conscientious in resolving his debts. To all appearances, the merchant
conducts himself with integrity in his business affairs. If, however,
we are to use the merchant's "chevyssaunce" as a touchstone by which to
judge the other loans in the tale, we must examine the morality of the
financial agreement into which he entered. It is common knowledge that

---

16. M. M. Postan, "Private Financial Instruments in Medieval England," Medieval Trade and Finance (Cambridge: Cambridge Univ. Press,
1973), pp. 29-30.

17. Postan, p. 35.

a strict canonist and scholastic prohibition against usury existed throughout the Middle Ages. While a chronicle of the development of usury theory is unnecessary here, we should attempt to place the merchant's use of foreign exchange within the context of traditional medieval suspicions about loans and credit transactions.[18] Among medieval economic theorists, a consensus existed concerning the definition of usury: "Usury was any excess whatsoever above the principal of a _mutuum_, or loan, exacted by reason of the loan itself, either according to contract or without previous agreement."[19] But opinion was not quite so unanimous concerning which financial transactions brought with them the taint of usury.[20] Because they recognized that credit and loans were necessary in order to facilitate trade, the scholastics permitted money to be loaned or invested under certain circumstances, such as in the formation of partnerships. This concession came despite scholastic awareness that any credit contract could hide a usurious loan behind a legitimate name.[21]

By the time of Sant'Antonino and San Bernardino, the merchant's

---

18. For a comprehensive study of the evolution of usury theory, see John T. Noonan's book, The Scholastic Analysis of Usury (full citation above).

19. De Roover, "The Scholastics, Usury, and Foreign Exchange," 258. For further discussion, see Noonan, p. 31.

20. See De Roover's, "The Scholastics, Usury, and Foreign Exchange," 260-61, for a brief exposition of the contradictions that could be found not only between individual scholastic thinkers, but within the work of one man.

21. Ibid., 260, 268.

exchange was not considered "usurious unless misused to conceal a loan."[22] But, as De Roover points out, the possibility of such misuse provided the scholastics with ample grounds for controversy over the transaction's licitness: "The exchange contract itself was an ambiguous kind of contract, since it usually involved an advance of funds in one place to be repaid _later_ in a different place and usually in a different currency. By definition, an exchange transaction was thus inextricably tied to a credit transaction."[23] The factor diminishing the ambiguity surrounding the licitness of foreign exchange was risk. Because it lessened the probability of anticipated profit, the amount of risk inherent in any credit transaction or partnership increased that transaction's legitimacy in scholastic opinion.[24] De Roover writes: "Exchange rates being fickle, then as now, medieval banking was speculative because profits were uncertain and unpredictable. . . . After all, usury was a _certain_ gain on a loan."[25] It would seem, then, that in his use of foreign exchange, the merchant had not participated in a usurious credit transaction, either as debtor or creditor. The important consideration regarding the merchant's use of foreign exchange is that, according to scholastic opinion, he had employed as

---

22. Ibid., 268; also, Cahn, 95.

23. De Roover, "The Scholastics, Usury, and Foreign Exchange," 265. See also, Noonan, p. 184 and p. 190 for a summary of the ambiguity surrounding foreign exchange and of the vestigial scholastic hostility toward it.

24. De Roover, "The Scholastics, Usury, and Foreign Exchange," 267; also, De Roover, "What is Dry Exchange?" 258.

25. De Roover, "The Scholastics, Usury, and Foreign Exchange," 267.

licit a credit transaction as he could. He had acted with probity and

he had fulfilled the obligations under which he was bound.[26]

For the scholastics, intention was as important a criterion as
risk in their assessment of the licitness of a credit transaction. The
intention to make a profit on a loan constituted usury. Moreover, intention, especially as it became translated into preoccupation with
profit, was central in their judgment of a merchant's morality. Intention is, however, difficult to determine. When we try to estimate
human intention, we often enter a realm of equivocation similar to
that which the schoolmen entered when they tried to determine the justice of mercantile profits. In order to evaluate the morality of the
merchant's business transactions in The Shipman's Tale, we must place
them within the context of scholastic analysis of mercantile activity.
This context illustrates the difficulty of assessing intention and of
formulating judgments of character on the basis of it.

---

26. Scattergood, 218, underlines the merchant's honesty. There
remains, of course, the possibility that the merchant was the victim
of usury, because he repays his bond to "certeyn Lumbardes" (VII. 367).
The Lombards had a reputation for international usury (see Noonan, pp.
63-64). Yet, as Aquinas points out, the man who is the victim of usury
does not suffer the same culpability as the usurer: "Ita etiam in
proposito dicendum est quod nullo modo licet inducere aliquem ad
mutuandum sub usuris; licet tamen ab eo qui hoc paratus est facere et
usuras exercet mutuum accipere sub usuris propter aliquod bonum, quod
est subventio suae necessitatis vel alterius" ("Applying this to the
case in question, then, it is never right to induce another to lend
at interest, although it is permissible to accept a loan from somebody
who is prepared to make such a loan and so is already in this business,
if the object is the doing of some good in the shape of relieving one's
own or another's need"), Summa Theologiae, Q. 78, a.4, pp. 250-51.
Throughout this chapter, I refer to the edition and translation of the
Summa prepared by Blackfriars (London: Eyre and Spottiswoode; New York:
McGraw-Hill Book Company). Within the text of this chapter, quotations
from the Summa will be cited by question, article, and page number.

As we have seen, the scholastics looked askance at mercantile activity. Following their auctor Aristotle, the scholastics believed that there were, essentially, two types of commerce: one commendable because it provided for the needs of the community and one condemnable because it satisfied the merchant's overwhelming desire for profit.[27] The scholastics regarded as sinful all those business practices that served to inflate price or to ensure inordinate profit at another's expense.[28] By the late fourteenth century, however, economic theorists were well aware that profit was an incentive to the necessary social institution of trade. Profit was therefore considered a legitimate commercial concern so long as merchants "did not seek gain for the sake of gain but as a just reward for their exertion."[29] According to De Roover, "To be justified, profits should be moderate and directed towards a laudable end, such as the support of one's family according to social status, the relief of the poor, or the welfare of the community, lest there be a lack of vital supplies."[30]

Thus, despite justified suspicion of commercial motivation, to be a merchant in Chaucer's time was not, in itself, a passport to sin. In

---

27. Aristotle, The Politics, ed. and trans. H. Rackham, Loeb Library (Cambridge: Harvard Univer. Press, 1959), I. iii, pp. 31-51. See also, Raymond De Roover, San Bernardino of Siena and Sant' Antonino of Florence: The Two Great Economic Thinkers of the Middle Ages (Boston: The Kress Library of Business and Economics, 1967), p. 10.

28. See De Roover, San Bernardino and Sant' Antonino, pp. 11-12.

29. Ibid., p. 10.

30. Ibid., p. 14.

his discussion of the fourteenth-century Regula mercatorum, a "hand-
book devoted exclusively to the moral concerns of merchants,"[31] Lester
Little writes: "The book's very existence announces flatly that there
is such a thing as a Christian morality for merchants, indeed that
there is a religious life for merchants. There had been a time when
vita religiosa was a technical term, referring to a level of spiritual
worthiness reserved exclusively for those who vowed to live according
to a rule, the Rule for Monks."[32] Don John, of course, demonstrates
that the Rule for Monks was not incapable of being broken and we can
make the same assumption about the Rule for Merchants. But has the merchant in The Shipman's Tale taken his place in the new ranks of the
worthy merchants? What are the intentions with which he conducts his
business?

San Bernardino presents four criterion for assessing a merchant's
virtue: "diligence or efficiency (industria), responsibility
(solicitudo), labor (labores), and willingness to assume risks
(pericula)."[33] The merchant in The Shipman's Tale manifests these
traits. As we have seen, he wastes no time in honoring the debt that
he has contracted. His self-seclusion in his counting house and his
frugal habits in Bruges are testament to his industria, solicitudo, and
labores. His speech to his wife manifests his consciousness of the
pericula that he must confront in his attempt to earn his livelihood:

---

31. Lester K. Little, Religious Poverty and the Profit Economy in
Medieval Europe (Ithaca: Cornell Univ. Press, 1978), p. 195.

32. Little, p. 195.

33. De Roover, San Bernardino and Sant' Antonino, p. 13.

> "Wyf," quod this man, "litel kanstow devyne
> The curious bisynesse that we have.
> For of us chapmen, also God me save,
> And by that lord that clepid is Seint Yve,
> Scarsly amonges twelve tweye shul thryve
> Continuelly, lastynge unto oure age.
> . . . .
> And therfore have I greet necessitee
> Upon this queynte world t'avyse me;
> For everemoore we moote stonde in drede
> Of hap and fortune in oure chapmanhede."
> (VII. 224-38)

The scholastics considered the speculative nature of medieval trade as justification for profit, just as they considered the speculative nature of an investment in partnership as justification for the investor's compensation. Moreover, it is interesting to note that, even if the merchant's activities in this tale do not require overseas travel, piracy was one of the factors contributing to the riskiness of commercial life.[34] The Shipman's General Prologue portrait more than suggests his connection with piratical activities (I. A, 398-99).

The merchant in The Shipman's Tale, then, seems to fit the scholastics' qualifications for the ethical businessman.[35] The credit transaction in which he engages is, for all intents and purposes, a legitimate one. None of his business dealings appear calculated to defraud colleagues or customers. Moreover, as many critics have observed, there is evidence in the tale that the merchant (despite his wife's protestations to the contrary) is a gracious host, a generous if

34. See M. M. Postan's discussion of piracy in his chapter, "The Trade of Medieval Europe: The North," in The Cambridge Economic History of Europe, eds. M. M. Postan and E. E. Rich, II (Cambridge, Eng.: Cambridge Univ. Press, 1952), 141-43.

35. For critics who comment upon similar laudable traits in the merchant, see Scattergood, 220; Silverman, 332; Richardson, 312; and McGalliard 13 and 15-16.

not profligate husband, a good friend, a not altogether incompetent
bedfellow. Yet, despite this portrait of the merchant's honesty, it
is difficult to gauge his intentions. He seems too concerned with his
business transactions and with the affairs of his counting house. Is
his concern predicated entirely upon the insecurity of mercantile life
and the uncertainty of fortune? Or does his preoccupation with profit
cause him to exaggerate the degree of risk that he confronts? Moreover, business affairs seem always to be on the merchant's mind, whether
he is granting Don John a loan or visiting his wife upon his return
from Bruges or paying the monk a call in Paris.[36] His unintentional
double entendre, "'But o thyng is, ye knowe it wel ynogh,/ Of chapmen,
that hir moneie is hir plough'" (VII. 287-88), is not only an infelici-
tous description of the function that his hundred francs will play in
the monk's hands. It also suggests his belief in money's fertility, a
belief condemned by the scholastics in their attempt to formulate a
consistent theory prohibiting usury.[37] If the merchant is more ethical
than his wife and his friend, how good is he? Despite his integrity,
he does not reveal many qualities that would make him an exemplary
Christian.[38] Yet, despite his worldliness, he seems to be free from

------

36. David H. Abraham, in his article, "Cosyn and Cosynage: Pun
and Structure in The Shipman's Tale," ChauR, 11 (1977), 324, sees the
mention by the merchant of the loan at this juncture of the tale as an
example of the merchant's own deceptiveness. It seems just as likely
that his mention of the loan derives from his own preoccupation with
the transaction at hand.

37. For a brief discussion of money's alleged sterility, see De
Roover's "The Scholastics, Usury, and Foreign Exchange," 259-60.

38. See Richardson's discussion, 311-12, of the merchant's flaws.

the failings that would traditionally consign a merchant to hell.[39]
If it is difficult to interpret the merchant's intention and the extent
of his morality, it is because Chaucer deliberately made him an ambiguous character to serve his own ethical and artistic purposes in this
tale. Like the credit transaction that he employs, the merchant appears to be ethical although he himself may be hiding his intentions.
The most moral member of the triangle in The Shipman's Tale is also
most successful at keeping his "'estaat in pryvetee'" (VII. 232).

   If the intentions motivating the merchant's complex credit transaction are not entirely clear, the financial dealings of the monk and the
wife do not pose similar problems. In their credit transactions, one
friend asks another for a loan, a practice that has probably existed
as long as there has been anything to lend. These loans are granted
without legal stipulations and without designated dates of repayment.
The mechanism of these credit agreements is not, in itself, illicit.
Yet these informal transactions demonstrate the importance of intention
in determining a loan's legitimacy. Because the intentions motivating
the credit transactions of the wife and the monk are blatantly immoral,
these intentions undermine whatever licitness may have resided in their
loans. The merchant is the only character who acts with integrity in
relation to these informal transactions. Although he informs Don John
of the importance of capital to his business, he readily grants the
monk the loan (thereby making the wife's request to Don John appear all
the more suspicious). The merchant tells the monk:

---

   39. Also, see Scattergood on this point, 220.

> "O cosyn myn, Daun John,
> Now sikerly this is a smal requeste.
> My gold is youres, whan that it yow leste,
> And nat oonly my gold, but my chaffare.
> Take what yow list, God shilde that ye spare.
> . . . .
> Paye it agayn whan it lith in youre ese;
> After my myght ful fayn wolde I yow plese."
>   (VII. 281-92)

The merchant does not mention interest; it is clear that he grants the loan because of his affection for the monk.[40] The monk, of course, borrows the money in bad faith. Not only does he have no intention of repaying the merchant: he will use the loan in order to purchase the merchant's wife.

The credit transaction between the monk and the wife is even more unethical, because it is not graced by the good intention of the creditor. To begin, it is doubtful that the agreement between the monk and the wife is actually a loan. The wife will not take a loan if she can sell herself and Don John readily changes his role from creditor to purchaser.[41] In the space of four lines, the wife's business transaction degenerates from the request for a loan to the hope of acquiring turpe lucrum, a "gain accruing from any illicit contract or from sinful and unlawful activities prohibited by either divine or human law or by both, such as prostitution, monopoly, gambling, tournaments, histrionics, simony, and the like."[42] Moreover, if we continue to regard Don John as a creditor, his loan to the wife assumes overtones of usury.

----

40. Ibid., 216; on this point, see also McGalliard, 15-16.

41. Scattergood, 218.

42. De Roover, "The Scholastics, Usury, and Foreign Exchange," 263.

When he catches his would-be debtor by the flanks, Luke's injunction
(taken as the basis of the usury prohibition), "Lend freely, hoping
nothing thereby" (6:35),[43] is probably the farthest thing from his
mind.

Although the merchant is concerned with profit, he conducts his
business with integrity. The other characters, equally concerned with
profit (material or sexual, which for them amounts to the same thing),
cannot claim the same integrity in their ventures. In this light, we
can see more clearly why the observation that "all human values [are
reduced] to commercial ones" in this tale is not sufficiently specific.
For what, specifically, are commercial values? If we define such
values as the concern for profit, then we can say that commercial interests regulate the behavior of all the characters in The Shipman's
Tale. But, as we have seen, there are both right ways and wrong ways
of gaining profit, just as there are both right and wrong reasons for
being concerned with it. Commerical interests, as they are represented
by the merchant, can produce a mentality that honors obligations and
contracts. As represented by the wife and the monk, these interests
entail the inordinate desire for gain, at any ethical cost, against
which economic theorists warned. In this tale, Chaucer shows that,
despite its obvious limitations, the mercantile mentality can exhibit
redeeming qualities. And he also demonstrates that one need not be a
merchant in order to engage in the fraud and deceit conventionally as-

---

43. I take this quotation from John T. Noonan's The Scholastic
Analysis of Usury, p. 20. Noonan cites the verse from Luke and discusses its significance as the cornerstone of the usury theory.

sociated with this profession.

The Shipman's interest, as we have said, focuses on the financial transactions that can be used to ensure profit. But the Shipman presents the formation of the illicit relationship between the monk and the wife in much greater detail than he allows to the merchant's legitimate "chevyssaunce." He is more attracted to the abuses of credit and to the trickery and deceit that can accompany it than he is to a study of credit as a viable means of conducting business. This preoccupation with deceit is not surprising coming from the character who views a "nyce conscience" (I. A, 398) as an expendable commodity. His own unscrupulous business practices (his thievery and his piracy) explain the scorn that his tale communicates for the merchant's adherence to obligations.[44] It is the Shipman's personal translation of the mercantile mentality that invests his tale and shapes its attitude toward ethical value (or the lack thereof). The Shipman is obsessed with modes of deception and betrayal and his obsession has more far-reaching consequences than the commercialization of human values. Deception employed in the name of profit destroys value. It is the way in which this destruction proceeds and its implications for human and artistic relationships that interests Chaucer in The Shipman's Tale.

In her prologue, the Wife of Bath presents a world in which marital relationships have become commercial exchanges. The Wife's world

---

44. Jill Mann, in her discussion of the Shipman, notes the association of shipmen with fraud, theft, and murder in estates literature: Chaucer and Medieval Estates Satire: The Literature of Social Classes and the General Prologue to the Canterbury Tales (Cambridge, Eng.: Cambridge Univ. Press, 1973), pp. 170-71.

is a marketplace in which women hawk their wares and sell them to the highest bidder. But by using the paradigm of commercial relationships in The Wife of Bath's Prologue and Tale, Chaucer also shows the transformation that can ensue if one approaches a more just assessment of the relationship between buyer and seller and of the determination of value. At the end of her Prologue and Tale, the Wife of Bath advocates (albeit unwittingly) a mode of human and commercial exchange founded not upon domination, but upon reciprocity. As critics have noted, no change of values occurs in The Shipman's Tale.[45] The possibility of enlightenment, such as Chaucer explored in The Wife of Bath's Prologue and Tale, is outside the purview of The Shipman's Tale. If credit transactions interest the Shipman because they allow him to reveal deceit and trickery, they interest Chaucer because they allow him another occasion for constructing an analogy between commercial practices and the dynamics of human relationships in general. By focusing on credit transactions and their implications, Chaucer studies the formation of all human relationships and the ways in which those relationships can be robbed of emotional and ethical value.

The etymology of the word credit reveals the basis of ideal credit transactions as well as of ideal human relationships. Credit derives from credere, 'to believe.' As Kurt Heinzelman has observed, ". . . belief is, in fact, the real meaning of credit."[46] The same etymological connection between belief and credit exists in Middle English.

---

45. Scattergood, p. 226; Richardson, pp. 312-13.

46. Kurt Heinzelman, The Economics of the Imagination (Amherst: Univ. of Massachusetts Press, 1980), p. 130.

<u>Creaunce</u> also derives from <u>credere</u>; as a verb, <u>creaunce</u> means 'to bor-
row on credit'; as a noun, it means 'belief' or 'creed.'[47] It is the
necessary presence of faith (and the consequences of its absence) not
only in financial transactions, but in all human relationships, which
interests Chaucer in this tale. Moreover, the amount of faith invested
in a credit relationship is synonymous with the nature of the intention
with which the transaction is made. Self-serving, profit-seeking intention destroys the faith that should inhere in any credit transaction.
Honest intention determines the financial success as well as the moral
legitimacy of the merchant's "chevyssaunce." Similarly, his faith in
Don John (however misplaced) relieves his personal loan to the monk of
any suspicion of usury. The successful workings of credit transactions
involve the reciprocal exchange of good faith. Along with his money,
the creditor extends to the debtor the faith that the latter will not
default on the loan. But the debtor also extends faith to his creditor, the faith that he will not be exploited by the terms of the loan.
Of course, for the medieval creditor, judicial safeguards like the
recognisance existed to discourage the debtor from defaulting. And the
usury prohibition theoretically kept the creditor from defrauding his
debtor. But such legal safeguards did not exist in the case of the informal loans between friends that we find in this tale. In such in-

---

47. My information on the etymology of <u>creaunce</u> and on the similarities of meaning between <u>creaunce</u> as noun and <u>creaunce</u> as verb
comes from <u>A Chaucer Glossary</u>, eds. Davis, Gray, Ingham, and Wallace-
Hadrill (Oxford: The Clarendon Press, 1979). In addition, <u>The Oxford
English Dictionary</u> lists 'reputation' under the meanings of <u>creance</u>
(n.) and 'to pledge oneself, vow, plight one's troth,' under the meanings of <u>creance</u> (v.).

stances, the presence of the trust, belief, and faith inherent in the word "credit" (as well as in the concept of friendship) becomes even more important in protecting the contracting parties from loss. Needless to say, this trust is betrayed by the self-serving intentions of the monk and the wife. The otherwise astute merchant suffers the greatest losses in the tale as he is defrauded of his hundred francs and betrayed by his wife and his friend. They prove to be better businessmen than the conscientious merchant himself, better because they have succeeded in attaining maximum profit at minimum risk.

The contract between the monk and the wife demonstrates the thoroughness of deceit and betrayal in this tale and the ways in which deceit operates. The contract also reveals that, in the presence of false intention, honor ceases to exist even among thieves. As the monk and the wife begin their mutual confessions, they promise secrecy to each other concerning their words, their loan, and the alleged love that binds them together. The monk says:

> ". . . and therfore telleth me
> Al youre anoy, for it shal been secree.
> . . . . .
> Ne shal I of no conseil yow biwreye."
> (VII. 129-33)

And the wife repeats his words in her promise to maintain their secrecy: "'Ne shal I nevere, for to goon to helle,/ Biwreye a word of thyng that ye me telle'" (VII. 137-38). But the merchant is not the only one whom this pair deceives. At the first opportunity, when the merchant visits the monk, and later, when the merchant confronts his wife, the two break their bond as quickly as they made it.[48] Neither

---

48. See Richardson, 311.

the monk nor the wife intend to honor the terms of their agreement if they can do so only at their own risk. The wife opens the way to this breach of faith even before she makes her contract with the monk. She begins her confession to Don John with declarations that life with the merchant is torment to her. Given the amount of information about the merchant that we have at this point in the tale, we begin to suspect her veracity. Augustine wrote that "Nemo enim mentiens in eo quod mentitur servat fidem; nam hoc utique uult, ut cui mentitur fidem sibi habeat, quam tamen ei mentiendo non servat" (". . . no one who lies keeps faith concerning that about which he lies. For he wishes that the person to whom he lies should have that faith in him which he does not himself keep when he lies").[49] But the characters who betray the merchant cannot be expected to behave more honorably with each other. Despite their declarations of love, it is likely that neither believes that their contract derives from affection. Although the wife wants money and the monk wants sex, they maintain the pretense of love. Adultery itself is debased into prostitution by their bad faith.

In the exchange of their false vows of love and secrecy, the monk and the wife liberally embellish their promises with oaths.[50] Oaths

---

49. Augustine, De Doctrina Chriatiana, ed. Joseph Martin, Corpus Christianorum Series Latina, 32: I. xxxvi. 40. Throughout this chapter, I quote from Martin's edition and from D. W. Robertson, Jr.'s translation, On Christian Doctrine (New York: Bobbs-Merrill Co., Inc., 1958). This passage is found on p. 30 of the translation. Quotations from De Doctrina Christiana will be cited by section number within the body of the text. Page numbers after these citations refer to Robinson's translation.

50. Many critics have noted the habitual swearing of the characters in The Shipman's Tale. See Abraham, 322 and Paul S. Schneider, "'Taillynge Ynough': The Function of Money in The Shipman's Tale,"

are, in and of themselves, peculiar linguistic phenomenon. They are words used to increase our audience's perception of our truthfulness. Aquinas wrote that "juramentum ad confirmationem ordinatur" ("an oath is taken for the purpose of confirmation"--ST, Q. 89, a. 1, pp. 204-05). And he continued: "Juramentum autem quaeritur ad subveniendum alicui defectui, quo scilicet unus homo alteri discredit" ("An oath is required to remedy a weakness, namely, one man's lack of belief in another"--ST, Q. 89, a. 5, pp. 214-15). Oaths are words used to reinforce language as if we shared a common suspicion of the mendacity of language and of each other. We rely on oaths to give our language value because we fear that talk, in itself, is cheap. When we want to use language and to be believed, we swear by someone or something whose existence and value we perceive as existing outside the structures of language, at the same time that we are reducing the objects of our oaths to words. By using oaths, we hope to attract to ourselves the value of the object by which we swear and, in so doing, to give ourselves and our language credibility. Oaths are, then, a kind of linguistic collateral that testifies to the presence of faith behind our words at the same time that they ask others to invest their faith in the words we have spoken.

The oaths sworn by the monk and the wife are open to suspicion because their actions demonstrate that they value things outside themselves only insofar as those things satisfy their own desires. Their

_____

ChauR, 11 (1977), 205. For a different interpretation of swearing from the one presented in this chapter, see George R. Keiser, "Language and Meaning in Chaucer's Shipman's Tale," ChauR, 12 (1977), 147-49.

oaths, used to accomplish their mutual deception, are ironic in light
of the tale's subsequent events. The monk declares his secrecy by
swearing, "'. . . on my porthors here I make an ooth'" (VII. 131), when
his willingness to enter an adulterous relationship with the wife demonstrates how highly he values his "'porthors,'" symbol of the monastic
life to which he has vowed fidelity and celibacy. The wife prefaces
her vow of secrecy to Don John with the words , "'Ne shal I nevere, for
to goon to helle'" (VII. 137), when her desire for the hundred francs
makes it obvious that she fears the loss of her "arraye" more than she
fears the pains of hell.[51] The wife's closing oath seals her contract
as well as her fate. She tells Don John:

> "For at a certeyn day I wol yow paye,
> And doon to yow what plesance and service
> That I may doon, right as yow list devise.
> And but I do, God take on my vengeance
> As foul as evere hadde Genylon of France."
> (VII. 190-94)

The wife swears by the arch-traitor of medieval epic as she makes the
promise to betray her husband that she will readily betray. False
oaths were, of course, condemned in the Middle Ages. According to
Aquinas, "si quis juret se facturum aliquod peccatum, et peccavit
jurando et peccat juramentum sevando" ("if a man swears to do something
sinful, he sins in swearing and in keeping the oath"--ST, Q. 89, a. 7,
ad. 2, pp. 222-23). And Quintillian discusses the abuse of oaths in
terms appropriate to our discussion of faith and betrayal: "Nec
meretur fidem qui sententiolae gratia iurat" ("the advocate who drags
in an oath merely for the sake of some trivial rhetorical effect, does

---

51. See Richardson's comments on the monk and the wife, 311.

not deserve much credit."[52] We cannot extend much credit to the oaths

of the monk and the wife. Rather than emphasizing the truth behind and

therefore the value of their words, these oaths end by revealing the

nature of the swearers and the bankruptcy of language motivated by

false intention. For the monk and the wife, the oaths accomplish a

rhetorical inflation with which they hope to hide their motives. For

Chaucer, these oaths represent the linguistic devaluation prevalent

throughout this tale because there is no faith behind the language to

make it good. When the monk bids the wife, "'Gooth now, and beeth as

trewe as I shal be'" (VII. 207), the wife obeys him by matching his bad

faith with her own. The monk's injunction assumes an irony that even

the self-consciously ironic monk does not anticipate.

In this tale, oaths are not the only linguistic formulations de-

valued by false intention. The monk and the wife succeed in breaking

nearly all the contracts and vows under which they bind themselves.[53]

In her adulterous relationship with Don John, the wife betrays her mar-

riage vows to the merchant. By fornicating with the wife, the monk

breaks his vows of celebacy to his order and ruptures the alliance of

cosynage that he has voluntarily sworn to the merchant. That these

multiple betrayals constitute breaches of contract is central to

Chaucer's ethical and artistic preoccupations in this tale. The assump-

tion underlying medieval (as well as modern) contracts is that they are

---

52. Quintillian, Institutio Oratoria, trans. H. E. Butler, Loeb
Library, III (New York: G. P. Putnam's Sons, 1921), IX. ii. 98, p. 437.
All quotations from the Institutio Oratoria will refer to this edition
and will be cited by section and page number within the text.

53. For critics who have discussed the breaking of vows in The
Shipman's Tale, see Richardson, 210-11, Keiser, 147-49.

made to hold. But, in the Middle Ages, a moral as well as financial
imperative demanded that contracts be honored. According to Gabriel
Le Bras,

> The canonists taught that simple contracts were binding in
> themselves. . . . Whether he is on oath or not, a Chris-
> tian's word must be kept. . . . This belief had the twofold
> merit of binding men by their declared intentions, without
> any formal obligation, and at the same time of facilitating
> commercial operations under the ultimate protection of the
> confessor and the ecclesiastical authority.[54]

If oaths and contracts carried with them a well-defined moral obligation, vows were surrounded by a greater solemnity and sanctity because
they were made not to men, but to God.[55]

   In The Shipman's Tale, Chaucer demonstrates that credit agreements
are betrayed because of the absence of the faith that should bind the
characters to each other. Through his emphasis on dialogue, on the
words exchanged between characters, Chaucer makes it clear that all
relationships in this tale, both personal and professional, are founded
upon contracts, vows, and oaths. Consequently, these relationships can
be construed as credit associations (whether or not they involve a
monetary transaction). If the number and variety of these relationships (marital, mercantile, ecclesiastical, and fraternal) can be reduced to credit associations, it is because Chaucer underlines their
common denominator. Through his use of dialogue, he shows us that all
human relationships manifest themselves linguistically, for language,

---

54. Gabriel Le Bras, "Conceptions of Economy and Society," in
Cambridge Economic History of Europe, eds. M. M. Postan, E. E. Rich,
and Edwar Miller, III (Cambridge, Eng.: Cambridge Univ. Press, 1963),
561.

55. Aquinas, ST, Q. 89, a. 5, ad. 1 and Q. 88, "de voto."

as Aquinas understood, is the only means we have to communicate relationship. Aquinas wrote: "Sed promissio quae ab homine fit homini non
potest fieri nisi per verba vel quaecumque exteriora signa" ("A promise
cannot be made by one man to another unless words or some other external signs are used"--ST, Q. 88, a. 5, pp. 160-61). And because all relationships rely upon language, they become, by nature, credit relationships. Language is the only means available to us for establishing
our credit, our characters, our believability. When we use language to
express ourselves to others, we are asking them to invest their faith
in us, when all we have to offer them as collateral is our language.
In this tale the monk and the wife use language to betray relationships.
They use language falsely, to suggest that a good intention exists
where there is none present. In so doing, they violate the credit that
should exist in all human relationships. But when the wife declares
that she will never "'biwreye a word of thyng that ye me telle'" (VII.
138), the formulation of her false promise underlines the fact that, in
this tale, language itself is both "betrayed" and "exposed" (the two
related meanings of "biwreye"). Because of the false purposes with
which it is used, language is betrayed, robbed of its ability to communicate meaning. But the tale also reveals that language, too, has
the capacity to betray.

   The different attitudes toward intention distinguishing the merchant from the monk and the wife influence not only their perceptions
of relationship, but also their perceptions and use of language. Two
statements from the tale encapsulate these conflicting attitudes toward
language. The merchant tells the monk: "'We may creaunce whil we have

a name;/ But goldlees for to be, it is no game'" (VII. 289-90). The

wife, on the other hand, finding herself betrayed by her monk-lover

and accountable to her husband for a hundred francs, says: "'Marie, I

deffie the false monk, daun John!/ I kepe nat of his tokenes never a

deel . . .'" (VII. 402-03).[56]

The merchant contends, with a certainty born of his pragmatism,

that his "name," his reputation, must be founded upon gold, as well as

upon integrity and honesty, in order for him to acquire the credit

necessary to conduct his business. He must establish a reserve of

credibility in order to operate without a reserve of ready cash. In

his credit transactions, the merchant offers his "name" as collateral,

as a sign that he is to be trusted. One's "credit" is, of course,

synonymous with one's good reputation, with one's believability; one

cannot get credit of the monetary kind without credit of the moral

kind. There must be a reputation of honesty and of the capacity to

produce gold in order to validate one's "name." The merchant's state-

ment presents an assessment of language similar to that implied in The

Wife of Bath's Tale by the hag's redefinition of gentillesse. As we

have seen, the hag's discussion of the intrinsic worth necessary to be

designated gentil is analogous to Oresme's belief in the intrinsic

value of the coin. If Oresme argued that the coin should contain the

fixed and stable amount of value designated by its name and if the hag

believes that the word gentil should consistently name intrinsic worth,

---

56. According to A Chaucer Glossary, tokenes in the wife's speech
means 'ready cash,' although the word can also mean 'signs, tokens.'
The word carries the latter, generalized meaning in the monk's remark
to the merchant at VII. 359. We should keep both the general and the
particular meaning in mind when examining the wife's statement.

we find a similar perception of the value of the word in the merchant's speech. He believes that a "name" must signify a fixed amount of integrity. Given the merchant's profession, this integrity, this creditability is virtually synonymous with the amount of gold for which the possessor of the "name" can be trusted. In short, the merchant believes that there must be gold behind the name, that the name must signify a fixed amount of moral and financial worth. Chaucer here makes clear the analogy between money and language, between the word and the coin, that we discussed in relation to The Wife of Bath's Prologue and Tale.

The wife's dismissal of Don John's "'tokenes'" underlines the lack of faith that either she or the monk is willing to bring to any relationship. But her statement also reveals both the lack of faith that she is willing to invest in her language and her consequent lack of faith in the creditability of language. Because she is not willing to invest her language with stable meaning, the wife does not entertain the possibility that there should be gold behind the name, that language itself possesses intrinsic value. This lack of belief in language's intrinsic value explains why Chaucer gave this tale to the Shipman rather than to the Wife of Bath. For the merchant's wife, "'tokenes'" are arbitrary signs, used for her own convenience, and as such, they can be devalued at her whim. Consequently, the wife readily violates the contracts and the vows that she has made. The wife's attitude toward language is antithetical and thus fundamentally threatening to the view of the world and of his own professional place within it that the merchant expresses to her in the counting house. The world, as the merchant perceives it, is full of the "'drede/ of hap and fortune'" (VII. 237-38). Consequently, there must be some certainties that he can rely on, even if he must create them for himself. And one of these certainties is his "name." Because his world is plagued by the arbitrariness of fortune, he must be able to rely upon the stability of the sign, whether that sign is the word or the coin or the system of signs constituting his credit contracts.

Nowhere in this tale does Chaucer explore the issue of the reliability and the credibility of language more fully than in his use of the puns that structure his narrative. Despite a good deal of controversy concerning the frequency of puns in Chaucer's work in general and in The Shipman's Tale in particular, the past two decades of Chaucer scholarship have demonstrated that punning occurs in relation to the words cosyn and cosynage, and taille and taillynge.[57] The way in which puns function explains the difficulty that twentieth-century readers experience in trying to determine whether a fourteenth-century word is actually a pun. Punning requires a similarity of sounds shared by two words that possess different meanings. As Bernard Levy has observed, ". . . punning reduces words to literal sounds."[58] But, appropriately enough for this tale, puns may also be considered a form

---

57. For works on Chaucer's puns, see Paull Baum's important article, "Chaucer's Puns," PMLA, 71 (1956), 225-46; Ruth M. Fisher's "'Cosyn' and 'Cosynage': Complicated Punning in Chaucer's 'Shipman's Tale,'" Notes and Queries, CCX (1965), 168-70; and David Abraham's article, cited above, as well as Silverman, 330 and 335. For an example of the directions that controversy about Chaucer's puns can assume, see Claude Jones, "Chaucer's Taillynge Ynough," MLN, 52 (1937), 570 and Robert A. Caldwell, "Chaucer's Taillynge Ynough, Canterbury Tales B² 1624," MLN 55 (1940), 262-65.

58. Levy, p. 210.

of verbal trickery for they operate by initially confusing the reader

or, as Aristotle wrote, by "misleading the hearer beforehand."[59] Puns

trick the reader into believing that the word on which the pun is made

has only one meaning until he becomes aware, from the context, that

another meaning is intended.

Although, as we have seen, the Shipman generally eschews figura-

tive language, he has a predilection for puns. Given his interest in

deceptive relationships, it is not surprising that the Shipman chooses

figures that rely on linguistic trickery for their effectiveness. In

addition, puns constitute not only verbal trickery, but also, as Freud

observed, a kind of verbal economizing that reduces the number of words

expended by using one word to express two meanings.[60] Economy of ex-

pression is, as we have noted, a significant characteristic of the

Shipman's own narrative style. Moreover, the pun not only permits this

verbal economizing; as Freud also noted, there is a profit from the

pleasure that the pun provides: "The pleasure of the wit . . . appears

greater the more remote and foreign the two series of ideas which be-

come related through the same words are to each other. . . . (p. 713).

The pun's trickery and its ability to reduce the expenditure of lan-

guage while producing the profit of pleasure make it an appropriate

rhetorical strategy for the Shipman. Undoubtedly, Chaucer too is inter-

---

59. Aristotle, The Art of Rhetoric, trans. J. H. Freese, Loeb Library (Cambridge: Harvard Univ. Press, 1959), III. xi. 6, p. 409. All
other quotations from The Art of Rhetoric will be cited by section and
page number within the text.

60. Sigmund Freud, "Wit and Its Relation to the Unconscious," The
Basic Writings of Sigmund Freud, trans. and ed., A. A. Brill (New York:
The Modern Library, 1938), pp. 652, 655, 712-13. All other quotations
from Freud's essay will be cited by page number within the text.

ested in the entertainment and the pleasure that the pun can afford
his audience. But the puns in this tale raise issues that transcend
the Shipman's desire to deceive and/or amuse his audience. In a tale
that explores the formation and devaluation of credit relationships,
Chaucer is concerned with the nature of the linguistic relationships
that puns create.

The central pun in The Shipman's Tale is, of course, the pun on
cosyn and cosynage, words that, on the one hand, can denote closely-
knit relationships, and, on the other, deceptiveness and duping. In
a recent article, David Abraham establishes the pun's significance as
a structuring device in Chaucer's tale.[61] Abraham traces the way in
which the recurrences of the words establish the pun's double meaning
and organize the tale's narrative:

> Just as much as the humorous effect of the tale is derived
> from this persistent interplay of relationship and decep-
> tion, the structure of The Shipman's Tale can be seen to
> depend upon the way in which the primary and secondary
> meanings of the puns on cosyn and cosynage in the first
> part are balanced with the reversed primary and secondary
> meanings in the second part . . . .[62]

As Abraham points out, the pun on cosynage actually defines the modus
operandi of puns in general: ". . . cosyn and cosynage are what I
would call archetypal puns--that is, they are puns which, in use, define their own function. The puns in The Shipman's Tale do, structur-
ally, what they mean, semantically. The medium literally is the mes-

---

61. I am indebted to David Abraham's article, "Cosyn and Cosynage:
Pun and Structure in The Shipman's Tale," for its careful presentation
of the repetition of the puns throughout the tale and for its perceptions about the workings of puns.

62. Abraham, p. 325.

sage--they relate and deceive."[63]   Abraham's perceptive analysis of
punning and its operations in this tale does not include an interpretation of the moral and linguistic implications of punning. It is in relation to the tale's ethical and artistic concerns that I would like to
elaborate some of Abraham's observations.

Because the Shipman applauds deception, he delights in puns and
specifically in the pun on cosyn and cosynage that names deception and
relationship in one breath. Of course, Chaucer's moral and artistic
interests in punning escape the Shipman. The pun on cosynage bril-
liantly underlines the tale's concern with the betrayal of relationships through deceit. But, through the repetition of this pun, Chaucer
also presents the disconcerting revelation that language itself can be
arbitrary and deceptive. The pun initially implies that the conventional relationship between signifier and signified is being communicated. By revealing that another meaning is intended and possible, the
pun also shows that we have been tricked. The pun questions our assumption that a stable and necessary relationship exists between the
signifier and the signified. It confronts us with the arbitrariness
of language. The pun, then, is a figure that deliberately creates artificial, or, more specifically, unconventional relationships. In
other words, it constructs relationships for which the conventional
correlation of signifier and signified does not provide. But a pun
may also be considered as an original coining in which one uses language freely and creatively in order to present relationships that had

63. Ibid., p. 326.

not previously existed within the realm of linguistic conventions.
Such an interpretation of the pun has its dangers. If the pun can be
considered as an act of original coining, as an act representing our
freedom to play with language, it can also be viewed as a linguistic
counterfeit whose surface fails to present and represent the meaning,
the value that convention has assigned to this surface.[64] In other
words, the pun can threaten our assumption that there is gold behind
the name, that a word has a fixed referent, a stable and necessary intrinsic value.

Abraham has noted that the structure of the pun on cosynage mirrors the structure of the tale. What is more, the mode of constructing
a pun is also analogous to the mode of constructing the relationship
between the monk and the merchant to which the pun on cosynage gives
its name. The monk and the merchant begin their relationship as
friends. On the monk's initiative, however, the relationship is
strengthened through their vows of cosynage.

> And for as muchel as this goode man,
> And eek this monk, of which that I bigan,
> Were bothe two yborn in o village,
> The monk hym claymeth as for cosynage;
> And he agayn, he seith nat ones nay,
> . . . .
> And ech of hem gan oother for t'assure
> Of bretherhede, whil that hir lyf may dure.
>   (VII. 33-42)

As in the relationship contracted between the monk and the wife, this

---

64. Stewart Justman also makes this observation about puns as
counterfeits in his article, "Literal and Symbolic in The Canterbury
Tales," ChauR, 14 (1980). Justman writes: ". . . a counterfeit is
a copy of the 'letter' in the wrong 'spirit.' . . . puns, irony, and
impersonation all involve counterfeiting in this sense" (204).

bond of cosynage is constructed from and through vows. It is defined
by an act in which Don John "claymeth" the merchant as a cosyn, in
other words, by an act in which the monk names the merchant cosyn.
Through this act of naming, the monk creates a relationship that had
not previously existed. He creates, as it were, an artificial or unconventional relationship by strengthening the tie between them from
one of friendship to one whose name implies consanguinity.[65] If the
monk and the merchant were actually cosyns, they would be related by
blood, that is, there would be a natural relationship between them. As
their relationship stands after this act of renaming, it is founded
only upon the artifice of language. Their cosynage is a credit relationship that will repay its participants with the anticipated affection and loyalty only if there is the gold of good intention behind the
name (since, in fact, there is not blood).

We quickly learn that, in constructing this artificial bond, the
monk says one thing and means another. His initial intention, like the
initial intention of the pun that names this new relationship, is to
deceive. The monk constructed this relationship in bad faith, if not
to profit from the merchant's hospitality, then to profit sexually from
closer acquaintance with his wife. In other words, his claiming the
merchant in cosynage creates an artificial relationship for the purposes of deception. In a speech that combines the abuse of oaths with
the renunciation of cosynage, the monk reveals how little he values

65. Although "cosynage" can be used to designate any relationship
of a particularly close nature (see the MED), according to A Chaucer
Glossary, the word usually refers to relationships of blood in Chaucer's works.

vows and language:

> "Nay," quod this monk, "by God and seint Martyn,
> He is na moore cosyn unto me
> Than is this leef that hangeth on the tree!
> I clepe hym so, by seint Denys of Fraunce,
> To have the moore cause of aqueyntaunce
> Of yow, which I have loved specially
> Aboven alle wommen, sikerly.
> This swere I yow on my professioun."
>   (VII. 148-55)

The presentation, early in this tale, of the formation and degeneration
of the monk's relationship with the merchant warns us to be wary of the
promises and acts of naming that are our only proof of a relationship's
existence. Interestingly enough, Don John, the namer of relationships,
is the only character in the tale who has a proper name. Yet this name
serves to divorce him even further from the ecclesiastical vocation
that he has betrayed. The other characters in the tale are named only
by their roles, by their professions; they are simply "the merchant"
and "the wife." Their names connote relationship, the wife's to her
husband, the merchant's to his trade. By the end of the tale, the
adulterous woman is wife to the merchant in name alone and, because of
his own betrayal of relationships, the monk has transformed cosynage
into a pun meaning deception. The merchant is the only character who
lives up to his name. Ironically, however, his consciousness of his
name and his "name" causes him to neglect his other relationships to
his own undoing.

Chaucer's puns on cosyn and cosynage also underline his artistic
preoccupations in The Shipman's Tale, preoccupations that are similar
to his ethical concerns in this tale. Chaucer's presentation of the
nature and operation of credit relationships allow him, as we have

seen, to explore the workings of language. But if an author is to use
puns effectively, he must engage in what is, essentially, a credit relationship with his audience. Like a credit transaction, the linguistic transaction that occurs when one uses puns relies upon intention
and risk. Because of the initial deception that the pun produces, the
author risks having his audience miss his point. In other words, he
risks the failure to communicate meaning. On the other hand, without
this risk, there would be no legitimate pun. Paull Baum wrote: "Unless the context is such as to permit a doubt, there is no ambiguity
and no pun. . . . In the true pun, however, there is first a recognition of two or more possibilities, and a rapid balancing between them;
then the pleasure of finding that either will fit."[66]

Yet if a pun cannot exist without the presence of ambiguity,
neither can it exist if it is obscure, if its intention is not apparent. Aristotle may have stated the obvious when he said of puns and
jokes that they are "only agreeable to one who understands the point"
(AR, III. xi. 7, p. 411). But the importance of making intention clear
is central to the successful working of puns (as well as to the success
of all figurative language and all credit contracts). In using a pun,
an author extends credit to his audience, for he places in them the
faith that they will repay him with their understanding, with their
comprehension of his intention. But in his relationship to his audience, the author is also a debtor; he owes them the clarification of
his intention. Of course, any artistic (like any mercantile) venture

---

66. Baum, 227.

runs the risk of loss, of failure. But just as Chaucer studies credit relationships in this tale in order to emphasize the importance of intention and risk in all human relationships, he underlines the magnitude of his own artistic risk and the importance of the just representation of intention through the use of a rhetorical strategy like the pun, which relies, for its success, on the audience's apprehension of the artist's purpose.

Chaucer further emphasizes the issue of intention through the use of irony, another rhetorical strategy which, like the pun, operates deceptively by saying one thing and meaning another. Critics have long sought to determine the nature of Chaucerian irony and my discussion is, by no means, intended to provide a comprehensive study of Chaucer's use of irony throughout The Canterbury Tales. Irony pervades The Shipman's Tale and the chief target of the Shipman's irony is the unwitting merchant. His ironic characterization of the merchant is apparent in the tale's second line, when the Shipman describes the merchant as "riche . . . for which men held hym wys" (VII. 2). Irony, as we have seen, occurs in the dialogue between the monk and the wife, for they will betray the very oaths by which they swear. Moreover, as many critics have noted, irony is implicit in the parallelism of incidents within the tale, as for example, when the monk and the wife consummate their business deal at the same time that the merchant is scurrying around Bruges.[67] The merchant's closing request to his adulterous wife for honesty is as ironic as the professed truth of her reply. It is

---

67. See, especially, Levy's discussion of this parallelism, 214-16.

difficult to overlook the Shipman's irony or to miss his intentions.
He mocks the merchant and his scrupulous attention to his business and
to the letter of his contracts. Moreover, the Shipman uses his other
characters and their actions in order to enhance his mockery of the
merchant. Delighting in deceit, the Shipman uses irony for the same
reason he uses puns, in order to perform an act of linguistic trickery.
But what is the target of Chaucer's irony? Because Chaucer does
not share the Shipman's delight in the betrayal of relationships, what
is the target of his irony? What are his intentions?

As Donald Howard observes, Chaucerian irony often involves the
narrator's unwitting exposure of a truth about himself: "The irony is
that the tales reveal something about the teller--they tell a tale of
their own which the teller does not intend. The circumstance is like
that of the fabliau: the paradigm of the 'trickster tricked' is applied to the storyteller . . . ."[68] As we have seen, the Wife of Bath
reveals more about herself, her values, and the changes which those
values undergo than she herself recognizes or acknowledges. But the
Shipman is a more difficult character to assess than the Wife of Bath.
He has few inhibitions about revealing the unsavory aspects of his
character; as the crimes in his General Prologue portrait show, he
feels that he has nothing to hide.[69] He revels in his characters' deceptiveness and their abilities to make a riskless profit because these
values and these tactics have been his own. Although Chaucer ironi-

---

68. Donald Howard, The Idea of The Canterbury Tales (Berkeley:
Univ. of California Press, 1976), p. 123.

69. Mann, pp. 170-71.

cally reveals the bankruptcy of his narrator's values, the Shipman intends that his values should be bankrupt. It is difficult to determine
the target of Chaucer's irony in this tale, aside from the obvious one
of condemning the exposition of values that blatantly contradict the
Christian ethic. In fact, it is as difficult to determine the target
of Chaucer's ironic intention as it is to determine his attitude toward
the merchant or the merchant's own intention. Again, I believe that
Chaucer has obscured his intention deliberately because that is one of
the thematic concerns of his tale: the difficulty of assessing intention and of locating the meaning behind the sign.

That intention is central to the successful use of irony is emphasized by two very different writers. According to Quintillian's definition of ironia,

> In eo vero genere, quo contraria ostenduntur, ironia est;
> illusionem vocant. Quae aut pronuntiatione intelligitur
> aut persona aut rei natura; nam, si qua earum verbis
> dissentit, apparet diversam esse orationi voluntatem.

> (. . . that class of allegory in which the meaning is con-
> trary to that suggested by the words, involves an element
> of irony, or, as our rhetoricians call it, illusio. This
> is made evident to the understanding either by the delivery,
> the character of the speaker or the nature of the subject.
> For if any of these three is out of keeping with the words,
> it at once becomes clear that the intention of the speaker
> is other than what he actually says.--IO. viii. vi. 54, pp.
> 332-33)

Freud's definition of irony is similar to that of Quintillian, but
Freud adds an important caveat relevant to our discussion of intention:
". . . ironic expressions are particularly subject to the danger of being misunderstood" (p. 757). These two quotations clarify the workings
of irony in The Shipman's Tale as well as the reasons for Chaucer's
preoccupation with irony. First, it becomes obvious that the central

puns on cosyn and cosynage are essentially ironic, for they transform
the words' conventional meanings into their antonyms: a relationship
of affection becomes one of treachery. Second, because of "the dangers
of being misunderstood," the writer who uses irony must be certain that
his intention is clear. Again, in the presence of irony, a credit relationship similar to that governing the use of the pun must exist between the writer and his audience. But, in the case of irony, this
credit relationship is a peculiar one. It depends, of course, upon a
type of cosynage, upon a close bond of understanding between writer and
audience. Yet the successful workings of irony also depend upon the
other type of cosynage that emerges in this tale, upon a complicity between author and audience. As the author directs his irony toward his
character(s), he and the audience watch an act of deception; they watch
the character(s) being duped. Together, the author and the audience
share a vision that is more enlightened, more ethical than the one
which the character(s) or the narrator manifests. If the Shipman enlists our complicity as he dupes the merchant, Chaucer enlists our complicity as he reveals the value of the merchant's integrity (a value
that the Shipman scorns) as well as the limitations of the Shipman's
unethical vision.

But there is another aspect of irony that pertains to Chaucer's
thematic concerns in this tale. Augustine illustrates his definition
of irony with a telling, although commonplace example: "Sed ironia
pronuntiatione indicat, quid uelit intellegi, ut cum dicimus homini
mala facienti, 'res bonas facis'" ("Now irony indicates by inflection
what it wishes to be understood, as when we say to a man who is doing

evil, 'You are doing well'"--DDC, III. xxix. 41, p. 103). Although,
theoretically, irony is only required to say the opposite of what is
meant, the ironic statement generally follows the outline of Augustine's example. In its definition of irony, The Oxford English Dictionary underlines irony's perjorative tendency: irony is a figure
"usually taking the form of sarcasm or ridicule in which laudatory expressions are used to imply condemnation or contempt."[70] Thus, the
word or formulation used ostensibly to praise is meant to deride. As
with the pun, the surface of the ironic formulation, its signifier,
does not correlate with its conventionally established signified. In
other words, because of ironic intention, the word ascribing value ends
by performing an act of devaluation. In this way, irony, like the
false oaths and the puns in this tale, involves a literary counterfeiting,[71] in which the author, because of his own intention, recoins the
word to suit his purposes. But the recoining entailed by irony makes
even more explicit the devaluation involved in literary counterfeiting.
Irony deliberately names value, names gold when, and because, no gold
exists behind the name. The use of irony throughout this tale is
thematically appropriate. Because of the breaches of their vows, the
wife and the monk become false representations of the roles that their
names assign. We can see why the Latin rhetoricians called irony
illusio, for these counterfeit characters give only the illusion of
fulfilling the roles designated by their names.

---

70. My information on the perjorative tendency of irony comes
from the OED, compact edition, p. 484.

71. See Justman, 204.

From our discussions of betrayal and credit, of puns and irony,
it is evident that The Shipman's Tale is profoundly organized according
to narrative, thematic, stylistic, and linguistic interconnections.
One way in which we have defined the common denominator of these structures is through emphasis on the tension between credit and betrayal.
The tale's emphasis upon change, or, more specifically, upon transformations, provides another way of defining this common denominator. In
The Wife of Bath's Prologue and Tale, the theme of transformation, sym-
bolized by the hag's metamorphosis, is presented through the changes of
value that Alison's redefinition of convention produces. In the end,
as we noted, the Wife of Bath's values also experience a transformation,
one which she herself never names. Although no transformation of
vision, no progress toward enlightenment occurs in The Shipman's Tale,
it too contains changes: changes of relationship among the three
characters (even the merchant feels that his relationship with Don John
has changed after he mentions the loan); changes of faith; changes in
currency; and changes in the meaning of language. I would like to
focus on the latter two transformations and the similarities between
them.

As we have seen, the merchant's loan is a species of foreign exchange involving a change in the name of currency and a change of place.
Although, ostensibly, only the name, and not the value of the money
borrowed, has changed in this transaction (the twenty thousand shields
should translate into an equivalent number of francs), the fluctuation
of exchange rates, as well as any interest hidden in the exchange, suggests that not only the name on the coin, but also the value of the

money, has changed in the course of the transaction. The scholastics

condoned foreign exchange because it facilitated business and because

they accepted the supposition that only the names of the coins, and

not their value, had changed. They called foreign exchange permutatio

praesentis pecuniae cum absenti.[72]

In order to clarify the connection between Chaucer's interest in

the merchant's credit exchange and his artistic interests in this tale,

we must look at Quintillian's definition of metaphor or, in Latin,

translatio:

> Copiam quoque sermonis auget permutando aut mutuando quae
> non habet, quodque est difficillimum, praestat ne ulli rei
> nomen deesse videatur. Transfertur ergo nomen aut verbum
> ex eo loco in quo proprium est, in eum in quo aut proprium
> deest aut translatum proprio melius est.
>
> ([The metaphor] adds to the copiousness of language by the
> interchange of words and by borrowing, and finally succeeds
> in accomplishing the supremely difficult task of providing
> a name for everything. A noun or a verb is transferred
> from the place to which it properly belongs to another
> where there is either no literal term or the transferred
> is better than the literal.--IO, VIII. vi. 4, pp. 302-03)

We need only substitute the appropriate economic terms for the literary

terms in Quintillian's definition of metaphor in order to obtain a

definition of the merchant's credit transaction, of his permutatio.[73]

(Of course, in the light of Quintillian's definition, the merchant's

enterprise closely resembles that in which Chaucer, an experienced bor-

rower from texts, would have engaged in his works of translation.

---

72. De Roover, "What is Dry Exchange?" p. 265.

73. I am also indebted to R. A. Shoaf's discussion of "proprium"
and of the question of literal language in his chapter, "The Wife of
Bath and the Mediation of 'Privitee,'" Dante, Chaucer, and the Currency
of the Word: Money, images, and reference in late medieval poetry

Translating a work from one language [or coinage] into another, Chaucer could have hoped that the value of the original would have remained stable, that nothing had been "lost in the translation," as it were. Or he could have hoped to make a profit in the translation by embellishing the original to his own purpose, by glossing it with his own originality.[74]) By demonstrating through his own tropes the connection between taking loans and making metaphors, Quintillian underlines the connection between economics and language and the centrality of nominal change to both systems. Moreover, in the making of figurative language, we not only change names; we also change values. Quintillian's statement that the metaphor is _melius_ than the literal term suggests this change of value. In the merchant's credit transaction as in the artist's use of metaphor, value is added; copiousness is increased.

A good artist relies on the linguistic borrowings of metaphor as surely as a good businessman relies on credit transactions to ensure the success of his enterprise. Puns and irony, the salient rhetorical devices in The Shipman's Tale, are of course, forms of metaphor, because they too require a transference of the word "from the place in which it properly belongs." Yet if metaphors are supposed to increase value, the rhetorical devices that Chaucer selects in this tale underline the series of devaluations and betrayals at the center of the tale's thematic concerns. He uses puns and irony because they can be

---

(forthcoming from Pilgrim Books, 1983).

74. R. A. Shoaf offers a fuller discussion of Chaucer's relation to his translated texts in "Notes Towards Chaucer's Poetics of Translation," SAC, 1 (1979), 55-66.

likened to counterfeits which do not offer the value promised by their names. But if puns and irony are, in effect, linguistic counterfeits, then, the tale implies, all figures are counterfeits because, by definition, they assign names that are not "proper"; they increase value by a change of name. The value of money is mutable because, by changing the name on the coin, we can change its value. As The Shipman's Tale shows, the value of words is mutable for the same reason.

Chaucer underlines the impermanence of language in the tale's final scene, as the wife offers her husband the same business arrangement that she had contracted with Don John. Should she fail to repay the merchant, he can become her creditor:

> "Ye han mo slakkere dettours than am I!
> For I wol paye yow wel and redily
> Fro day to day, and if so be I faille,
> I am youre wyf; score it upon my taille,
> And I shal paye as soone as ever I may."
> (VII. 413-17)

The wife's marital and linguistic duplicity is embodied in the mode of credit that she suggests to her husband in her sexual pun: "'. . . score it upon my taille'" (VII. 416).[75] The pun and her reasons for choosing it as well as Chaucer's reasons for assigning it to her are significant. When she tells her husband that he can keep track of her debts by scoring them upon her taille, she suggests, in reality, a form of marital prostitution rather than a bona fide credit relationship. Moreover, the taille is no more reliable as a mode of recording credit than the wife herself. The taille, of course, was a piece of wood upon

---

75. In addition to the Jones and Caldwell debate on the pun on taillynge, see Silverman, 330 and 335; also Abraham, 326.

which incised notches formed a record of debts.[76] In his discussion

of the bond, M. M. Postan notes that, by the late fourteenth century,

the bond had replaced the tally because the former offered a written,

and therefore more reliable, account of the terms of the credit trans-

action.[77] Postan provides an interesting footnote on the tally's un-

reliability:

> In Common Law, even a sealed tally did not attain the full
> legal conclusiveness of a bond. . . . In the words of C. J.
> Beresford, Eyre of Kent (1313-1314), Vol. II (5.5), p. 58,
> 'a tally is not a pure deed as is a writing, for what has
> been inscribed on a tally can be shaved off and something
> different from what was there before can then be put in its
> place at the will of the custodian of the tally, without
> anyone being able to detect it, which is not the case with
> a writing.'[78]

Because the inscriptions on the tally can be changed, the tally, as a

means of recording credit, is as unreliable as the signs constituting

language have proven to be in this tale. Because they can be erased,

the notches on the tally can be as impermanent as language itself; the

value designated by the notches can be eradicated by bad faith as

easily as the meaning behind the signs constituting language can be

eradicated by false intention.

As we have seen, The Shipman's Tale presents two attitudes toward

language: that of the Shipman and his two traitors, who play with lan-

guage, but who are also interested in language's ability to betray; and

---

76. M. M. Postan, "Private Financial Instruments in Medieval
England," p. 29. See also Carl Stephenson, "The Origin and Nature of
the Taille," in Mediaeval Institutions Selected Essays (Ithaca: Cornell
Univ. Press, 1967) for a complete discussion of the taille (especially
pp. 92-93).

77. Postan, pp. 29-30.

78. Ibid., fn. 11, pp. 32-33.

that of the merchant, who believes in the value of contracts and in the existence of gold behind the name. Which attitude toward language does Chaucer espouse? He, like the Shipman, manipulates language and engages his audience in a complicity similar to the Shipman's as he ironically reveals his characters' flaws. But if Chaucer shares the Shipman's attitude toward language, he, as poet, risks becoming the "trickster tricked," the manipulator of language who is betrayed by the duplicity and the unreliability of his own medium. Moreover, it is clear that Chaucer has ethical and artistic qualms about the Shipman's use of language and about the devaluation of language and relationship that occurs when the monk and the wife consider oaths and vows as no more than arbitrary signs to be debased for their own purposes. In The Wife of Bath's Prologue and Tale, Chaucer argued that words, like coins, should name intrinsic value and that any redefinition of convention should attempt to align that convention with intrinsic worth. Yet Chaucer's own manipulation of language weakens his similarity to the merchant, who believes that words must have stable referents. Despite the moral attractiveness of the belief in the inherent value of signs, Chaucer underlines the dangers of such a belief. Although the merchant is financially astute, although he spends hours in his counting house pondering "'this queynte world'" (VII. 236), he is duped by his trust in signs, by his trust in appearances. And I believe that Chaucer is self-conscious about the possibility of his own identification with the merchant. The merchant hides his intentions because he believes that, for his own advantage and success, he should "'kepen oure estaat in pryvetee'" (VII. 232). His guarding of his own intention does not undermine his belief in the value of honesty or integrity; rather, to him, it represents something akin to "worldly wisdom." And Chaucer also guards his intention for his own advantage, in order to engage the reader in the interpretation of his work. If Chaucer has moral reservations about being aligned with the Shipman and his traitors, he is also wary of being associated with the merchant, of studying the world from the security of the counting house, of making his own nearsighted reckonings, and of believing that he can interpret the world because he has an awareness of the fortune and risk governing the world's affairs. If Chaucer does not want to be the trickster, neither does he want to be the tricked.

In The Shipman's Tale, Chaucer's own rhetorical strategies, his use of the duplicity of language for his own artistic profit, call into question his belief in the possibility of language's stability and reliability. Augustine had written:

> Sicuti cum loquimur, ut id, quod animo gerimus, in audientis animum per aures carneas inlabatur, fit sonus uerbum quod corde gestamus, et locutio uocatur, nec tamen in eundem sonum cogitatio nostra conuertitur, sed apud manens integra, formam uocis qua se insinuet auribus, sine aliqua labe suae mutationis adsumit . . . .

> (In order that what we are thinking may reach the mind of the listener through fleshly ears, that which we have in mind is expressed through words and is called speech. But our thought is not transformed into sounds; it remains entire in itself and assumes the form of words by means of which it may reach the ears without suffering any deterioration in itself.--DDC, I. xiii, p. 14)

Augustine's statement manifests a faith in the integrity of language, in the stability of language, that Chaucer's use of language in this tale undercuts. First, our thoughts are not always communicated in speech; rather, as this tale so often demonstrates, speech can serve

to mask our thoughts. When, early in the tale, the monk expresses concern for the exhaustion caused by the wife's nocturnal labors, his reaction to his own words shows the completeness with which language, at
least, can guard our pryvetee: "And with that word he lough ful
murily,/ And of his owene thought he wax al reed" (VII. 110-11).
Thought does not always translate itself into words. Moreover, Chaucer's use of puns, figures that reduce words to sounds, shows our
ability to perceive words only as sounds. It is when we perceive words
only as configurations of sounds that they assume an arbitrariness un-
dermining Augustine's belief in language's stable referentiality.

In The Shipman's Tale, language seldom represents intention. In
other words, because language itself is betrayed, it does not often
"biwreye," that is, expose, intention. The consummation of the adulterous relationship between the wife and the monk is significant because it shows these two characters honoring their oaths by fulfilling
their promises. Chaucer takes due note of the occasion, as, for once,
they make their language good:

> And shortly to the point right for to gon,
> This faire wyf acorded with daun John
> That for thise hundred frankes he sholde al nyght
> Have hire in his armes bolt upright;
> And this acord parfourned was in dede.
> (VII. 313-17; emphasis mine)

The matching of the word to the deed and the frequent failure to accomplish this correlation is relevant to Chaucer's concerns about the
arbitrariness of language in this tale. Yet Chaucer's choice of words
in the last line of this passage in conjunction with his punning on
cosyn and cosynage has resonances that echo back to the General Prologue and to the pilgrim-narrator's preoccupation with the veracity of

his reporting of The Canterbury Tales.

In the General Prologue, the pilgrim-narrator offers his apology

for the forthcoming indelicacy of some of the Tales:

> Whoso shal telle a tale after a man,
> He moot reherce as ny as evere he kan
> Everich a word, if it be in his charge,
> Al speke he never so rudeliche and large,
> Or ellis he moot telle his tale untrewe,
> Or feyne thyng, or fynde wordes newe.
> He may nat spare, althogh he were his brother;
> He moot as wel seye o word as another.
> Crist spak hymself ful brode in hooly writ,
> And wel ye woot no vileynye is it.
> Eek Plato seith, whoso that kan hym rede,
> That wordes moote be cosyn to the dede.
>   (I. A, 731-42; emphasis mine)

As the pilgrim-narrator's allusion to Plato makes clear, the belief

that words should be appropriate to their topics, to their contexts,

is hardly new. The belief finds its way from Plato, through rhetorical

and philosophical treatises,[79] to the Roman de la Rose, in which we

find the following statement attributed to Sallust:

> "si n'est ce pas chose legiere,
> ainz est mout fort de grant maniere
> metre bien les fez en escrit;
> car quiconques las chose escrit,
> se du voir ne nous velt ambler,
> li diz doit le fet resambler;
> car les voiz aus choses voisines
> doivent estre a leur fez cousines."

> (". . . still it is not any easy thing to set down deeds in
> writing; it requires great strength of technique, for if any-
> one writes something without wishing to rob you of its truth,
> then what he says must resemble the deed. Words that are
> neighbors to things must be cousins to their deeds.")[80]

---

79. As Robinson's notes to the General Prologue point out, we
find a similar observation on the relationship of the word to the deed
in The Consolation of Philosophy, iii, pr. 12.

80. Jean de Meun, Le Roman de la Rose, ed. Félix Lecoy (Paris:
Librairie Honore Champion, 1965), 15155-62. The English translation
is by Charles Dahlberg, The Romance of the Rose (Princeton: Princeton

The statement "words should be cousins to deeds" implies that they, in fact, can be cousins to deeds, that a right relationship can exist between the phenomenon described and the language used to describe it. In other words, the belief that words should reflect substance implies a concomitant belief in the stable correlation between signifier and signified. Because a rhetorical transgression occurs if we fail to assign topics their proper formulations, then language cannot, in fact, be arbitrary. Language, then, has the capacity to reflect extralinguistic reality accurately, truthfully; because of this capacity, the word must possess intrinsic value. There is, ideally, the right word for the right thing and it is the duty of the user of language to find this word, to construct this right relationship "or ellis he moot telle his tale untrewe."

But, as we have seen, the way in which the characters in The Shipman's Tale use language, as well as Chaucer's own manipulation of it, calls into question a belief in language's stable referentiality. In this light, the punning on cosyn and cosynage provides us with another way of reading Chaucer's General Prologue statement concerning the relationship of the word to the deed. Aquinas wrote: "Dicendum quod ad fidelitatem hominis pertinet ut solvat id quod promisit. Unde secundum Augustinum, fides dicitur ex hoc quod fiunt dicta" ("Human fidelity demands that one keep promises, as Augustine says, one is called faithful because his deeds agree with his words"--ST, Q. 88, a. 3, pp. 166-67). Chaucer asks if we can take language on faith with any more certainty

---

Univ. Press, 1971), p. 258.

than we can trust the vows of fidelity, the professions of relationship made to us by others. The word, rather than naming the deed or the intention, can, in fact, conceal. Because of its capacity to present a meaning other than its surface would signify, the word can fail to name the deed accurately. The desire to guard "pryvetee," to mask intention, can result in the presentation of words other than the appropriate ones. The Shipman's Tale has shown us that we cannot trust signs, that they can cozen us as surely as they cozen the trusting merchant. Through the Shipman, Chaucer warns us, early in the tale, that signs are untrustworthy for "Swiche salutaciouns and contenaunces/ Passen as dooth a shadwe upon the wal" (VII. 8-9). These lines not only articulate the Shipman's own attitude toward the transitoriness and thus the arbitrariness of language. They also present Chaucer's own fear that the Shipman might be right.[81]

Of course, as a Christian, Chaucer would have understood that all things of this world, including his own language, are unstable and mutable. Edmund Reiss writes, in terms appropriate to the Platonic overtones of the lines in question:

> Just as elements in this mutable world are but signs of eternal realities, so these transient things are necessarily imperfect as well as inadequate in providing a full understanding of the realities they reflect. The human art that depicts man and creation are thus an imperfect reflection of what is already an imperfect reflection. . . . to depict man, to write of his striving and loving, may be considered de facto an ironic act.[82]

---

81. Richardson, 310 and Keiser 147, are among the critics who gloss these lines as Chaucer's Christian admonition against the worldly values that the tale's characters and their narrator embrace.

82. Edmund Reiss, "Chaucer and Medieval Irony," SAC, 1 (1979), 69.

But for a medieval writer, the issue of the stability of the sign and of language's referentiality would have profound metaphysical repercussions that would extend beyond a concern with the permanence of his own art or the reliability of the medium of which that art is composed. If systems of signs are revealed as arbitrary and unstable, then man is left without the certainty of where to place his faith. If the world is a system of divinely designated signs, a question arises concerning their mutability and duplicity, concerning the trustworthiness of any signs.

The tale that has been structured by puns ends with a tour de force of punning as the Shipman says: "Thus endeth now my tale, and God us sende/ Taillynge ynough unto oure lyves ende" (VII. 433-34). In this triple punning on credit, intercourse, and storytelling,[83] we can hear Chaucer's voice behind the blasphemous prayer of his narrator. The Shipman asks for an abundance of the false credit and of the sexual compensation that can accrue to one's own profit and pleasure if one thinks only of one's own desires; he also requests more tales that exalt this self-centered profit-seeking. For the Shipman, "ynough" is never "ynough."

We hear another wish from Chaucer. As the poet asks God to send credit and storytelling, the pun that he uses points to the inextricable connection between them, as well as to the reasons why faith is necessary to his art. The pun on taillynge underlines the faith that we must invest in Chaucer's stories themselves, and in his intention, the

---

83. Abraham, 326.

faith that the author is not trying to trick us (or if he is, that his trickery will lead to our enlightenment, to our discovery of the gold behind the name). In the use of this pun, Chaucer asks for credit for his art after he has presented a tale that would shake our faith in people and in the language that they speak. At the same time, he asks if we can ever have enough faith in the words that we use. His question is, in itself, ambiguous and Chaucer does not give us the answer in this tale. He does suggest, however, that we should have just enough faith in language to use it properly and just enough faith to realize that it can be misused.

If Chaucer's tale has a moral, it implies that, when we use language, we must do so with an ethical and social committment to our words and to their meanings. Language, like money, was invented to facilitate human exchange. Social usage alone legitimizes money and language and grants them whatever claim they may have to stability, to immutability. When language is defined only in accordance with personal intention and for the sake of personal gain, the result is a linguistic piracy that the Shipman could well understand and condone, a linguistic piracy that appropriates public institutions for private ends at the expense of human exchange. Interestingly enough, Chaucer offers this prayer for the credibility of language and storytelling before he presents The Prioress's Tale, the tale told by the character whose General Prologue portrait is a testament to the multivalency of signs. The slogan on the Prioress's broach, "Amor vincit omnia," should confirm our faith in the power of human emotion rightly directed and in the power of divine love to rescue us from the crises of faith into which the mutability of this world might plunge us. But, given

the nature of the woman who wears the broach and the nature of signs,

we doubt that it does.

Chapter IV

CHAUCER AND THE "'SLIDYNGE SCIENCE'": VALUE AND ITS

ALCHEMICAL TRANSFORMATION IN THE CANON'S YEOMAN'S

PROLOGUE AND TALE

In The Canon's Yeoman's Prologue and Tale, Chaucer presents, for

the last time in the Canterbury sequence, a study of the desire for

profit and its influence upon ethical values and human relationships.

The tale's "Secunda Pars" describes a premeditated confidence game

designed, like Alison's badgering of her old husbands and the business

contract between Don John and the wife, to promote personal profit.

Like The Wife of Bath's Prologue and The Shipman's Tale, the "Secunda

Pars" underlines the importance of language, its persuasiveness, and

its duplicity to the acquisition of profit, at the same time that it

reveals the moral bankruptcy behind the deceptive use of language. In

fact, this last of The Canterbury Tales to treat the desire for mate-

rial profit may be read as an example of the commercial mentality gone

mad. The alchemical enterprise, were it successful, would produce un-

limited profit, unlimited return on a minimum investment. It would

endow its practitioners with the Midas-touch. The Canon's Yeoman, as

he introduces his master to the pilgrims, says:

>   ". . . al this ground on which we been ridyng,
>   Til that we come to Caunterbury toun,
>   He koude al clene turne it up-so-doun,

And pave it al of silver and of gold."[1]

This ability to transmute base metal into gold and silver would constitute a form of wish-fulfillment for many of the Canterbury pilgrims and for the characters in their tales: for the young Wife of Bath, for the Merchant and January, for the Physician, the Shipman, and the commercially astute Harry Bailley who shows a marked interest in the Canon's enterprise. The acquisition of the Philosopher's Stone would end the quest for riskless profit that has motivated many of the Canterbury characters.

But the presentation of alchemy in The Canon's Yeoman's Prologue and Tale is more complex than an emphasis on its commercial profitability would suggest. At the heart of the alchemical enterprise is the desire to increase value through a process of transmutation that would turn base metals into gold. Because alchemy attempts to revalue the elements of the material world, it provides an appropriate culmination for Chaucer's interest in value and its transformation throughout The Canterbury Tales. Chaucer's depictions of the quest for profit, for the increase of material value that is the essence of profit present his concern with the ethical values associated with commercial relationships. But Chaucer also uses commercial relationships to figure the artistic and ethical problems posed by his own poetic enterprise. The Wife of Bath's Prologue and Tale allow Chaucer to present his case

---

1. The Canon's Yeoman's Prologue, VIII. G, 623-26. All quotations from The Canterbury Tales in this chapter refer to F. N. Robinson's The Works of Geoffrey Chaucer, second edition (Boston: Houghton Mifflin, 1957), and will be cited by fragment and line number within the body of the text.

for the redefinition and revaluation of prior literary conventions;
through the credit relationships of the monk and the wife, The Shipman's Tale explores the question of language's reliability.

In The Canon's Yeoman's Prologue and Tale, Chaucer not only discusses the influence of potential profit upon the individual's perception of his world. Alchemy is an appropriate enterprise for Chaucer
to study at the end of a work that has been concerned with ambivalence
and with the instability of economic, ethical, and linguistic value.
For alchemy is a science which confronts its practitioners with ambivalence, that is, with the possibility that one substance can have
several different valuations. Alchemy looks at lead and sees beneath
its surface the possibility of gold. In its effort to transform intrinsic worth, alchemy removes the possibility of stable referentiality. Lead should signify lead, but, through alchemical intervention,
lead may also signify gold. Alchemy thus provides an extended metaphor
for the intellectual, artistic, and moral concerns of Chaucer's literary quest as he nears the end of the Canterbury pilgrimage and of his
own artistic career.[2]

---

2. Like many scholars and critics, I read The Canon's Yeoman's
Prologue and Tale as late productions in Chaucer's literary career.
The textual evidence (the reference to Boughton-under-Blee, for example) shows that The Prologue and Tale belong late in the Canterbury
sequence. Moreover, the style of The Canon's Yeoman's Prologue and
Tale, as E. Talbot Donaldson has pointed out, also indicates that they
came late in Chaucer's career: "As Chaucer approached the end of his
literary activity his interests apparently became increasingly dramatic, a tendency that is itself dramatized by this disruption of the sym-
metry of the original plan," Chaucer's Poetry: An Anthology for the
Modern Reader (New York: The Ronald Press Co., 1958), p. 945. See also
Edgar H. Duncan, "The Literature of Alchemy and Chaucer's Canon's

The interruption of the Canon and his Yeoman into the established Canterbury group serves Chaucer's dramatic and poetic purposes.[3]
It recalls the structural and spiritual framework of the pilgrimage itself, whose goal has often been obscured by the subjects of the pilgrim's tales. As Paul Taylor points out, in The Canon's Yeoman's Prologue, "[w]e have the first direct reference to the direction and goal
of the pilgrimage with the mention of Canterbury (VIII, 624) since the
General Prologue."[4] By interrupting the plan of his tales, Chaucer
makes us more aware of his art, its scope, and its purpose. Moreover,
by allowing the Canon and his Yeoman to disrupt the pilgrimage, Chaucer

---

Yeoman's Tale: Framework, Theme, and Character," Speculum, 43 (1968),
634, for a similar opinion about the lateness of The Canon's Yeoman's
Prologue and Tale.

   3. The textual problems within The Canon's Yeoman's Prologue and
Tale have caused considerable critical controversy while producing
several different readings of the poem. In "The Literature of Alchemy
and Chaucer's Canon's Yeoman's Tale," Edgar Duncan summarizes the results of investigations into these textual problems (such as the presence of two canons and the Yeoman's address to the canons), 633-34.
Albert E. Hartung's article, "'Pars Secunda' and the Development of The
Canon's Yeoman's Tale," ChauR, 12 (1977), 111-28, offers a detailed
discussion of these textual problems. See also Charles Muscatine,
Chaucer and the French Tradition: A Study in Style and Meaning (Berkeley: Univ. of California Press, 1973), p. 214. It is, of course, impossible to determine whether the Yeoman's performance was an after-
thought which Chaucer inserted into The Tales or whether it was part of
Chaucer's original plan. After reviewing the textual problems presented by The Canon's Yeoman's Prologue and Tale, I am not convinced
that the unit does not operate as a coherent poetic whole. My reading
of The Canon's Yeoman's Prologue and Tale is based on the assumption
that we can read it as such a coherent whole.

   4. Paul B. Taylor, "The Canon's Yeoman's Breath: Emanations of a
Metaphor," ES, 60 (1979), 382. Taylor also writes: "His entire performance brings the significance of the procession to Canterbury as a
rehearsal of the soul's progress toward God back to the surface of the
pilgrim's attention. With his and his Canon's arrival, we are jolted
out of a conceptual and back into a perceptual setting, and this for
the first time since the Pardoner's laconic reference to the 'ale-

also calls attention to them. Their sudden approach and their di-
shevelled appearance accentuate their status as curiosities among the
Canterbury pilgrims. The Canon and his Yeoman are unknown quantities
that must be explained and interpreted before they can be integrated
into the plan of the pilgrimage. The Yeoman's hints about the nature
of his master's craft and the mystery surrounding the Canon's flight
virtually demand that the Yeoman's contribution to the story-telling
competition (of whose terms, of course, he is unaware) explain his art
and his hostility toward his master. The Yeoman's *Tale* attempts to
provide such an explanation as he tries to integrate himself into the
company of pilgrims.[5]

In response to Harry Bailley's questions, the Canon's Yeoman delivers a confession as professionally detailed and as personally revealing as those of the Wife of Bath and the Pardoner.[6] He describes
the experiments in their laboratory and his participation in them; he
presents the alchemical elements and the failure of their occupation;
he stresses the hostility toward his master that he manifested in his
Prologue. But while the Canon's Yeoman's confession answers some questions, it raises others which he does not address in either part of

---

stake,'" 381-82.

5. A. V. C. Schmidt comments on the Yeoman as an outsider in
his introduction to his edition of The General Prologue to The Canterbury Tales and The Canon's Yeoman's Prologue and Tale (London: Univ. of
London Press, 1974), p. 38. Traugott Lawler also examines the relationship of the newcomers to the Canterbury pilgrims in The One and The
Many in The Canterbury Tales (Hamden: Archon Books, 1980), p. 126.

6. Lawrence V. Ryan discusses the similarities between the Wife
of Bath, the Pardoner, and the Canon's Yeoman in "The Canon's Yeoman's
Desperate Confession," ChauR, 8 (1974), 306-07. See also Lawler, p. 42.

his _Tale_. He does not reveal why he and his Canon accosted the pilgrims. He does not explicitly define his Canon's motives, or his own,
a definition that would allow an assessment of the morality of their
enterprise. Most important, however, is the question, raised throughout the _Tale_ itself, concerning his own ability to abandon the
"slidynge science" which he has pursued for seven years. Some critics
have suggested that the Yeoman finds among the Canterbury pilgrims the
human fellowship from which his craft has excluded him.[7] But other
critics, unconvinced by the Yeoman's repeated cursing of alchemy and
his Canon, have wondered if he will reach the shrine at Canterbury.[8]
That both possibilities are likely at the end of The Canon's Yeoman's
Tale demonstrates the Yeoman's profound ambivalence toward alchemy, an
ambivalence central to the appropriateness of alchemy as a metaphor for
Chaucer's own art.

The tone and structure of The Canon's Yeoman's Tale are determined
by the Yeoman's disillusionment with alchemy and with his Canon. The
"Prima Pars" of his _Tale_, a chronicle of the failure occasioned by the
quest for the Philosopher's Stone, begins with the Yeoman's articulation of loss:

> Al that I hadde I have lost therby,
> And, God woot, so hath many mo than I.
> Ther I was wont to be right fressh and gay
> Of clothyng and of oother good array,

---

7. For critics who have discussed the Yeoman's need for the fellowship on the pilgrimage, see Lawler, p. 144 and Ryan, 306.

8. See, for example, Donaldson, _Chaucer's Poetry_, p. 946 and R.
M. Lumiansky, _Of Sondry Folk_ (Austin: Univ. of Texas Press, 1955), p.
231.

Now may I were an hose upon myn heed;
And wher my colour was bothe fressh and reed,
Now is it wan and of a leden hewe --
Whoso it useth, soore shal he rewe! --
And of my swynk yet blered is myn ye.
Lo! which avantage is to multiplie!
                    (VIII. G, 722-31)

In these lines, the tension between the ideal and idealized goal of

alchemy and the reality of its effect upon the Yeoman is manifest in

the ironic attitude toward his craft that he self-consciously adopts

throughout his Tale. "Multiplication," the alchemical process that

should have increased his wealth, has instead produced poverty.[9] More-

over, as the Canon's Yeoman himself acknowledges, seven years of effort

have adversely transformed him, not only financially, but also physi-

cally.[10] His "colour" has become a "leden hewe," a transformation in-

verting the progression of colors preliminary to the attainment of the

Philosopher's Stone (see also lines 1095-1100).[11] The Canon's Yeoman's

---

9. Edgar H. Duncan describes the process of "multiplicacioun"
upon which Chaucer and the Yeoman play ironically throughout the Prologue and Tale: ". . . while no alchemical treatise that I have read
refers to the entire alchemical process in such words [i.e., as "multiplicacioun"], multiplicatio does have a specialized signification in
the literature: It designates the operation or series of operations by
means of which the transmuting elixer, after it had been prepared, was
supposed to be tremendously increased in strength and efficacy. With
this meaning, it figures prominently in the Rosarium of Arnold of Villa
Nova...," "The Literature of Alchemy and Chaucer's Canon's Yeoman,"
635. Joseph E. Grennen discusses the irony surrounding the term in the
Yeoman's Tale in "The Canon's Yeoman and the Cosmic Furnace: Language
and Meaning in the 'Canon's Yeoman's Tale,'" Criticism, 4 (1962), 227.

10. An observation of the irony of the Yeoman's physical transformation is almost universal in the criticism of the Yeoman's Prologue
and Tale. See, for example, Donaldson, p. 946; Ryan, 305; and Judith
Scherer Herz, "The Canon's Yeoman's Prologue and Tale," MP, 58 (1961),
232.

11. Joseph E. Grennen in "Chaucer's Characterization of the Canon
and his Yeoman," JHI, 25 (1964), 279-80, remarks on the inversion of

transmutation into an element of his craft indicates the completeness
of his committment to the "sligynge science." In his quest to transform the value of the material world around him, the Yeoman has, as he
knows, been transmuted into the dross of the alchemical process. The
reiteration of failure and frustration throughout the "Prima Pars" of
the Yeoman's Tale justify his hostility towards his craft and toward
the master whom he served.

    In this tale, whose position in the Canterbury sequence evokes
endings, the Canon's Yeoman himself points to the end of his association with alchemy. Yet, in his detailed presentation of the effects of
alchemy on his material and emotional existence, the Yeoman neglects to
reveal his reasons for undertaking the quest for the Philosopher's
Stone. The Yeoman's emphases in the "Prima Pars" do, however, suggest
his motives. He repeatedly mourns the material loss--the loss of
money, clothing, and good looks--that he has suffered during his apprenticeship. (The Yeoman takes up this lament at lines 722-45, 782-
83, 830-37, 882-83 and, at the end of his Tale, at lines 1402-05). The
questionable sympathy that he extends to the priest in the "Secunda
Pars" of his Tale also suggest his motives. Significantly, the articulation of initial motivation, absent from the personal chronicle of
the "Prima Pars," occurs in the fiction of the "Secunda Pars."[12] Al-

---

the color progression in relation to the Yeoman's physical transformation. Paul Taylor summarizes the alchemical process: "The transformation of the Yeoman is the exact opposite of the desired result of the
blowing. Alchemy attempts the conversion of lead to a red colour, for
the change of lead's black and white to red is the sequence signalling
the change from death to life in metal" (385).

    12. See Ralph G. Baldwin, "The Yeoman's Canon: A Conjecture,"
JEGP, 61 (1962), 236-37.

though the Yeoman's apostrophe to the priest--"With coveitise anon thou shalt be blent!" (VIII. G, 1078)--acknowledges the latter's ava- rice, he calls the priest "o sely innocent" (VIII. G, 1076).[13] His attitude toward the greedy priest and his repeated references to his own loss of material goods imply that a similar covetousness initially attracted him to alchemy. But the Yeoman can admit neither to himself nor to his new-found audience the reasons for his present debasement. If he must assume the loss, he will not also assume the blame for his association with alchemy.

Yet as the intense emotionalism of the "Prima Pars" indicates, the Yeoman's initial motives have themselves been transformed into a full-blown obsession. Within the psychological framework of this ob- session, the desire for wealth, like wealth itself, is absorbed in the desire for the emotional and intellectual gratification that success would afford.[14] If the Yeoman (or his Canon) were driven only by the desire to amass material wealth, he would have renounced the alchemical quest before he had lost all the wealth that he was seeking. Moreover, if material profit remained his only motivation, the Yeoman could have turned, with or without his master's assistance, to a confidence game similar to the second canon's. It is unlikely that the "Secunda Pars" presents ruses practiced by the Yeoman and his Canon.[15] If they had

---

13. See Ryan's discussion of the Yeoman's relationship to the priest, 304. Also, Lumiansky, pp. 228-29.

14. Donaldson has pointed out this characteristic of the Canon's Yeoman's portrait, p. 946, as does Robert Burlin, Chaucerian Fiction (Princeton: Princeton Univ. Press, 1977), p. 176.

15. See, for example, Baldwin, 237.

performed such (markedly successful) deceptions, they would not need
to live in the indigence that the Yeoman, in his Prologue (VIII. G,
657-62), describes to the Host.[16]

An initial desire for worldly wealth has become, for the Yeoman,
an obsession from which he has yet to extricate himself. The Canon's
Yeoman's Prologue and Tale demonstrate a profound ambivalence toward
alchemy that contradicts the Yeoman's repeated condemnations of it.
Although his Tale is filled with warnings to his audience and acknowl-
edgments of the personal cost of alchemy, although he has wasted seven
years in the laboratory, he ends his Prologue with a statement that
echoes throughout his Tale:

> "And yet, for al my smert and al my grief,
> For al my sorwe, labour, and meschief,
> I koude nevere leve it in no wise."
> (VIII. G, 712-14)

It might be argued that, by the end of his Tale, the Yeoman has di-
vorced himself from alchemy.[17] But a linguistic acknowledgment of
failure does not necessarily entail a psychological acceptance of it;
his final acknowledgment of futility does not proclaim his cure. Moreover, the content and structure of the two parts of his Tale subvert
the condemnation of his art that he too loudly proclaims.

---

16. Baldwin hypothesizes that the Canon and his Yeoman ride up
in haste because they have just accomplished a deception similar to
the one in the "Secunda Pars" (242). Interestingly, however, the
Yeoman, who has no difficulty naming the elements of his master's craft
in the "Prima Pars" does not know the components of the second canon's
"poudre" (VIII. G, 1148-51).

17. Bruce L. Grenberg, in "The Canon's Yeoman's Tale: Boethian
Wisdom and the Alchemists," ChauR, 1 (1966) believes that the Yeoman
has experienced regeneration, 53-54.

The words that the Canon's Yeoman chooses to name alchemy attest to his ambivalence. He refers to alchemy as an "art" (lines 716 and 1424) in contexts indicating that the word should be read as "skill" or "trade" rather than as "artfulness" or "deception." The Yeoman also calls alchemy a "science" (680; 732), that is, an enterprise founded upon learning and wisdom. Each designation of alchemy as a "science" is qualified by the use of "slit" (682) or "slidynge" (732) in order to express the Yeoman's perception of alchemy's elusiveness. Yet, in these contexts, alchemy emerges as a respected and respectable enterprise whose intellectual rigor makes it inaccessible to the Yeoman and his Canon. The Yeoman uses "science" pejoratively only once; in the "Secunda Pars," the second canon, as he swindles the priest, calls his bogus alchemy a "'crafty science'" (1253). In this instance, the negative connotation of "science" derives from its ironic context. The Yeoman's ambivalence becomes more apparent in his repeated use of "subtilitee" and "craft," words whose connotations range from "skill, cleverness, trade, art" to "guile, deception, trick, cunning."[18] When the Canon's Yeoman labels the second canon's confidence game a "subtilitee" or "craft," the ironic context underlines the word's negative connotation. Yet, even in the "Secunda Pars," these words carry an ambiguous meaning. For example, the second canon tells the priest that he will teach him "'This noble craft and this subtilitee'" (VIII. G, 1247). Although the Yeoman intends an ironic exposure of the second

---

18. My information on the words "art," "craft," "science," and "subtilitee" is taken from A Chaucer Glossary, compiled by Douglas Gray, Norman Davis, Patricia Ingham, and Anne Wallace-Hadrill (Oxford: The Clarendon Press, 1979).

canon's treachery, the irony would be lost if the words connoted only
guile and deceit. Moreover, when the Yeoman designates alchemy, as he
has experienced it, with the words "craft" and "subtilitee," we are
meant, I believe, to read the words without their pejorative connotations. In his descriptions of their futile efforts, the Yeoman calls
alchemy "oure craft" (at lines 785 and 865, for example); there is no
reason to read "craft" as "guile" in these contexts. At the end of
the tale, the Yeoman again calls alchemy a "craft" (1395), this time in
relation to the philosophers who are the custodians of alchemical
secrets. I examine this point at length because the words that the
Yeoman chooses to name his enterprise underline the ambivalence of his
attitude toward it. Moreover, Chaucer selects words to describe alchemy whose ambiguous meanings are transformed by the contexts in which
they appear. If alchemy is a metaphor for Chaucer's own art, it is
significant that the words naming "art" can also designate "cunning"
and "deceit."

In response to the Host's invitation to reveal the secrets of his
trade, the Canon's Yeoman apologizes for his ignorance:

> "Now wolde God my wit myghte suffise
> To tellen al that longeth to that art!
> But nathelees yow wol I tellen part.
> . . . .
> Swich thyng as that I knowe, I wol declare."
> (VIII. G, 715-19)

But despite his recurrent emphasis upon his limited intelligence, the
Yeoman's catalogues of elements and procedures occupy over a hundred
lines (755-861) of the "Prima Pars." These catalogues prove that seven
years with the Canon have not left the Yeoman ignorant of alchemy. If
his apprenticeship has consumed his material wealth, it has left him

with considerable information about his science.[19]   Yet, midway through

his catalogues, the Yeoman offers another apology for his intellectual

limitations:

> Ther is also ful many another thyng
> That is unto oure craft apertenyng.
> Though I by ordre hem nat reherce kan,
> By cause that I am a lewed man . . .
> (VIII. G, 784-87)

The elements in the Canon's Yeoman's catalogues are not logically ord-

dered; they spew forth as chaotically as the mixture bursts from the

crucible at the end of the "Prima Pars." Nonetheless, despite the

Yeoman's apologies for the disorder and for his "lewednesse," these

hundred lines of his Tale reflect an organization imposed on his mate-

rial by his ambivalence toward his art.[20]

---

19. Some critics accept the Yeoman's admission of his own ignor-
ance. See Muscatine, p. 217 and John Webster Spargo, "The Canon's
Yeoman's Prologue and Tale," Sources and Analogues of Chaucer's Canterbury Tales, ed. W. F. Bryan and Germaine Dempster (New York: Humanities
Press, 1958), p. 688. Other critics, however, do not find the Yeoman
as ignorant as he himself claims. See, for example, Grenberg, 74;
Taylor, 384; and Donald Howard, The Idea of the Canterbury Tales
(Berkeley: Univ. of California Press, 1976), p. 296. In her article
"Vincent of Beauvais and Chaucer's Knowledge of Alchemy," SP, 41
(1944), 371-89, Pauline Aiken acknowledges both that the Yeoman shows
an impressive acquaintance with alchemical techniques and that he makes
some mistakes. Aiken attributes these mistakes not so much to the
Yeoman as to Chaucer, who may have misunderstood some of the material
in the sources which he consulted "in order to introduce local color
and to give greater realism to the personality of the Yeoman" (373).

20. Many critics have discussed the Yeoman's ambivalence and,
while my argument about this aspect of the Yeoman's character resembles previous discussions at various points, there has been no full
treatment of his ambivalence or its relationship to Chaucer's attitudes
toward his own art. Lumiansky's discussion includes observations about
the Yeoman's ambivalence and his unwillingness to assume responsibility
for his actions, Of Sondry Folk, pp. 231-33. Burlin also analyzes the
Yeoman's desire to blame external forces for his failure, the strategies adopted to accomplish this blaming, and the intellectual pride
that emerges in his Tale, Chaucerian Fiction, pp. 176-79. Donald

Throughout the Yeoman's listing of elements and procedures, alchemical catalogues alternate with articulations of loss and disap-
pointment.[21] These alternations culminate with his lament over the
ultimate cause of their failure: the elusiveness of the Philosopher's
Stone. Traugott Lawler writes: "As he speaks of groping and failure,
the Yeoman seems himself to be groping for a way to get hold of his
narrative and descriptive material"; and Lawler goes on to compare the
Yeoman's narrative to "the alchemist's jumbled and groping attempt to
transmute his intractable materiality."[22] In addition, the catalogues
represent the Yeoman's "groping attempt" to resolve his own ambivalence. Within the hundred lines, five interruptions of the catalogues
express the loss occasioned by and the futility of alchemy (at lines
769-70, 773, 777-83, 830-51, and 860-61).[23] The balanced length of the
passages presenting, on the one hand, the materials of alchemy and, on
the other, its failures, indicates the conflict transpiring within the

---

Howard discusses the way in which the Yeoman's ambivalence structures
his Tale and forms his attitude toward the Canon in The Idea of The
Canterbury Tales, pp. 294-96. In his article, "The Canon's Yeoman's
Prologue and Tale: An Interpretation," PQ, 46 (1967), 1-17, John Gardner finds ambivalence throughout The Canon's Yeoman's Tale, but he believes that the Yeoman "will now pursue the right without hesitation"
(14).

21. Howard, p. 294.

22. Lawler, p. 135.

23. Muscatine presents a list of the Canon's Yeoman's articulations of failure throughout the "Prima Pars" (p. 218), but his interpretation of the Yeoman is different from the one I have presented
here. Muscatine finds the catalogue "dully repetitive," an indication
that the Yeoman is a "simple, unlearned soul" (p. 217). He does say,
however, that ". . . this insistent chorus voices a frustration beyond
that of a mere mechanical failure. It registers a failure of vision.
It says that dealing with matter as matter has no end, that is, no

Yeoman at the same time that he describes their practices. At the beginning and at the end of his catalogues, the alternations occur at
short intervals. In the middle of his presentation, however, after his
apology for his ignorance, the Yeoman delivers a long list of vessels,
instruments, and materials whose finale is his translation of the allegorical names of the elements. This display of his own erudition
ends, however, with the Yeoman's lengthy repudiation of alchemy and of
the learning that must accompany it. But even this long repudiation
does not rupture the Canon's Yeoman's attachment to his craft and to
its materials. He interrupts himself in order to offer more information: "Yet forgat I to maken rehersaille/ Of watres corosif . . ."
(VIII. G, 852-53).

The alternations of the catalogues of elements with repudiations
of alchemy reflect the Canon's Yeoman's vascillation between two conflicting systems of value: the value of alchemy, of its temptation,
and of its promised rewards as set against the value of life free from
this obsession and its futility. His need to resolve his indecision
provokes the Yeoman's repeated condemnations of the art. He must use
language to distance himself from alchemy, to try to effect the transformation of his own ambivalence. When the Yeoman is in the midst of
a verbal recreation of the world in which he has lived for seven years,
he must remind himself that he has left his craft and his master. At
these points, he interrupts himself with another condemnation. The
alternations reflect a consciousness that is trying, without success,

---

teleology" (p. 218).

to resolve its ambivalence, to determine its relationship to the polarities of hope and frustration which have characterized its experience.[24] It is no wonder that, at the end of this psychomachia, rendered in the particularities of the world that he is leaving, the Yeoman says: ". . . as for the beste,/ Of alle thise names now wol I me reste" (VIII. G, 858-60). But the exhaustion of the conflict does not prevent him from his concluding lament over the Philosopher's Stone's elusiveness.

In the Canon's Yeoman's confession, Chaucer presents a study of character as complex as any of his portraits in The Canterbury Tales. Like the Wife of Bath and the Pardoner, the Canon's Yeoman reveals information about his character in the context of a description of his professional practices. Although, in all three cases, the professional revelations do not reflect well upon personal ethics, all three demonstrate a pride in their work and, especially, in their learning. For these characters, pride in learning (even if the value of that learning is questionable), like concern for personal profit, exists to compensate for loss. The Wife of Bath has received her knowledge of the antifeminist tradition the hard way. She wields these texts, as she wields language and seeks profit, in order to compensate for her lack of power and self-determination. Similarly, the Pardoner misuses his learning and his language in the name of monetary gain in order to compensate for his own wants: the want of fertility, of sexual creativity.

---

24. Lawler remarks that the conjunction of failure and hope constitute, for the Yeoman, "the challenge and the ineluctable attraction of alchemy" (p. 135).

The Canon's Yeoman, at the same time that he repudiates the craft that has wasted his time, his money, and his health, displays his intellectual wares before his audience as proudly as either the Wife of Bath or the Pardoner. Pride in his learning is significant in the apprentice who has made us aware, because he has so often been made aware, of the limitations of his knowledge. Even the Yeoman's repudiation of the learning necessary to practice alchemy manifests an undercurrent of pride; he knows enough about the arcane science to know what he rejects:

> Ascaunce that craft is so light to leere?
> Nay, nay, God woot, al be he monk or frere,
> Preest or chanoun, or any oother wyght,
> Though he sitte at his book bothe day and nyght
> In lernyng of this elvysshe nyce loore,
> Al is in veyn, and parde! muchel moore.
> To lerne a lewed man this subtiltee --
> Fy! spek nat therof, for it wol nat bee;
> And konne he letterure, or konne he noon,
> As in effect, he shal fynd it al oon.
> (VIII. G, 838-47)

This statement, intended to demonstrate the futility of the alchemical quest, ends by proving to the Canon what he needs to know: that even the most learned fail.[25] For, unlike the Wife of Bath and the Pardoner, the Canon and his Yeoman, despite their learning, have not attained professional success. The Canon's Yeoman's list of elements, instruments, and procedures, his display of learning, is all that he has left. It must compensate for the material and emotional expendi-

---

25. Even Petrus Bonus, in his *Pretiosa Margarita Novella*, admitted that he had never succeeded in achieving the goal of alchemy. See Lynn Thorndike, *A History of Magic and Experimental Science*, Vol. III (New York: Columbia Univ. Press, 1934), pp. 151-52.

tures of the last seven years, as well as for his shame at his physical
transformation. If the Yeoman has paid as dearly for his erudition as
the Wife of Bath, his learning is still costly to him. It reminds him
of alchemy and its temptation. It reminds him that the Philosopher's
Stone still exists to be created from the elements around him. And his
learning also reminds him of its limitations. All that the Yeoman has
left is his learning and the language with which to display that learning. But, because his language itself is fraught with ambivalence, it
fails to transform that ambivalence into a resolution to leave alchemy.

The Yeoman's ambivalence necessarily extends to his Canon. His
presentation of his master reverberates with hostility toward the man
whose wisdom has seemed to promise the success of alchemy itself. The
Yeoman begins his exposure of the Canon with an ambiguous comment on
the scope and purpose of the Canon's intelligence:

> "He is to wys, in feith, as I bileeve.
> That that is overdoon, it wol nat preeve
> Aright, as clerkes seyn; it is a vice.
> Therfore in that I holde hym lewed and nyce.
> For whan a man hath over-greet a wit,
> Ful oft hym happeth to mysusen it.
> So dooth my lord, and that me greveth soore . . ."
> (VIII. G, 644-49)

These lines are as self-contradictory as the Yeoman's attitude toward
alchemy. His backhanded compliment to his master's wisdom is undermined by the Yeoman's observation that too much wisdom constitutes ignorance. It is difficult to determine the reasons for the Yeoman's
mockery of his Canon's intelligence or the sincerity of his sympathy
toward the master whom he will soon abandon and curse. Moreover, because of the contradictions in his presentation of the Canon, it is

difficult to determine if the Yeoman comprehends the nature and goals

of the alchemy which his master practices.

In order to discuss the Canon and the Yeoman's attitude toward

him, I would like to consider the spectrum of fourteenth-century al-

chemical practices, for the morality of the alchemist can be inter-

preted from the kind of alchemy he pursued. Moreover, the ambivalence

pervading the Yeoman's presentation of alchemy not only reflects his

own state of mind. It also mirrors the ambivalence surrounding alchemy

and alchemists during the late Middle Ages. The Canon's Yeoman's Tale

demonstrates both Chaucer's knowledge of alchemy and his awareness of

the various forms that alchemy could assume.[26]

While the scope of this chapter does not require an outline of

the development of alchemy, it is necessary to place Chaucer's treat-

ment of it within the context of contemporary practices and attitudes.[27]

---

26. Chaucer's knowledge of alchemy has been debated, but schol-
arly consensus believes that Chaucer, while probably no adept, certainly knew and used the literature of alchemy in The Canon's Yeoman's
Prologue and Tale. For discussions of Chaucer's familiarity with al-
chemy, see Dorothée Metlitzki, "The Code of Chaucer's 'Secree of
Secrees': Arabic Alchemical Terminology in The Canon's Yeoman's Tale,"
Archiv Für Das Studium Der Neueren Sprachen und Literaturen, 207
(1970), 260-76; Pauline Aiken, "Vincent of Beauvais and Chaucer's
Knowledge of Alchemy," 371-89; Edgar H. Duncan, "The Literature of Al-
chemy and Chaucer's Canon's Yeoman's Tale," 633-56; and John Webster
Spargo, "The Canon's Yeoman's Prologue and Tale," in Sources and
Analogues, pp. 685-90.

27. My discussion of alchemy, here and later in this chapter,
derives primarily from histories of alchemy written in English. Among
the most helpful are Arthur John Hopkins, Alchemy: Child of Greek
Philosophy (New York: Columbia Univ. Press, 1934); Eric J. Holmyard,
Alchemy (Baltimore: Penguin Books, 1957); Serge Hutin, A History of
Alchemy, trans. Tamara Alferoff (New York: Walker and Co., 1962); and
Jacques Sadoul, Le grand art de l'alchimie (Paris: Editions Albin
Michel, 1973). Lynn Thorndike's A History of Magic and Experimental
Science (Vol. II, New York: The Macmillan Co., 1929; Vols. III and IV,

During the first half of the fourteenth century, alchemy was sufficiently popular (especially among ecclesiastics) for Pope John XXII to
condemn it. Holmyard writes: ". . . it seems that so much alchemical
or counterfeit gold was being coined or otherwise circulated in France
that John XXII felt compelled to issue a decretal against such practices."[28] The decretal, entitled "De Crimine Falsi," underlines the
falsity of alchemists, their purposes, and their results and it pre-
scribes restitution as punishment for lay alchemists and excommunica-
tion for ecclesiastical practitioners.[29] According to Lynn Thorndike,
the decretal "should not be taken too seriously as an evidence of complete skepticism as to the possibility of transmutation. Indeed, its
implications that the alchemists were able to pass off their product
as coinage is almost an indiscreet admission that they were attaining
a measure of success."[30]

The Pope's decretal, of course, neither curtailed the practice of
alchemy nor the composition of alchemical treatises in England and on
the Continent.[31] Moreover, the much cited Plea Rolls from Edward III's

---

New York: Columbia Univ. Press, 1934) traces the development and transmission of medieval alchemy. I have not consulted works on alchemy in
German, but the footnotes in Dorothée Metlitzki's article, "The Code of
Chaucer's 'Secree of Secrees,'" provide references to German sources
related to the conclusion of The Canon's Yeoman's Tale.

28. Holmyard, p. 145. See also Thorndike, Vol. III, pp. 31-32.

29. Despite his decretal, the pope himself may have been interested in alchemy. Thorndike writes: "In 1330 the pope gave money to
his physician, Gaufré Isnard, bishop of Cavaillan, for an alembic to
make aqua ardens (alcohol) and 'for a certain secret work' for himself
which sounds very much like an elixir of life, if not an attempt to
make gold" (Vol. III, p. 34).

30. Thorndike, Vol. III, pp. 33-34.
31. See Thorndike, Vol. III, pp. 48ff. for a discussion of con-

reign testify that the kind of alchemy condemned by John XXII was still alive and well in England in 1374. Edgar Duncan recounts the now famous incident of Canon William Shuchirch:

> . . . when William de Brumley, a chaplain of Harmandsworth, was apprehended with four counterfeit gold pieces in his possession, he claimed to have made them by the art of alchemy per doctrinam of William Shuchirch, the said canon of Windsor. . . . He [de Brumley] had taken the pieces to Gautron, keeper of the king's money in the Tower, and offered to sell them if they appeared of any value. Two separate juries, on one of which a goldsmith sat, valued the pieces at 35 shillings. Had they been pure gold, the jurors affirmed, the pieces would have been worth . . . 86 shillings and 8 pence. Chaplain de Brumley was released, after warning, under bond; and the records are thenceforth silent regarding Canon Shuchirch.[32]

Duncan describes an incident documented in the Close Rolls of Richard II for 1393, that involves a monk of the Priory of St. James and follows the same outline as the Shuchirch episode.[33] I cite these examples to demonstrate the fraud with which alchemy was often associated in Chaucer's time (a fraud which the papal prohibition had failed to eradicate). The apocryphal story that, at Edward III's bidding, Raymond Lull produced twenty-two tons of alchemical gold from which the king proceeded to mint rose nobles shows the acknowledged appeal of alchemy in high places.[34] As Albert Hartung has pointed out, the royal

---

temporary refutations of Pope John XXII's decretal. See also Holmyard, pp. 146-48 on John Dastin's letters to the pope on behalf of alchemy. Thorndike, Vol. III, p. 97, discusses the growth of alchemical literature during the first half of the fourteenth century.

32. Duncan, pp. 633-34. It is this incident that, as Duncan points out, led Manly to conjecture that The Canon's Yeoman's Tale is Chaucer's own complaint against an alchemical duping that he had taken (specifically at Canon Shuchirch's hands). See also, Hartung, 120.

33. Duncan, 634.

34. Holmyard, pp. 124-25, recounts this story in detail. Rose

interest in alchemy was sparked by the shortage of gold and the consequent need for mintable species.[35] Thus, despite the papal prohibition
and the prosecution of counterfeiters, the practice of alchemy did not
constitute a felony in England until 1403.[36] Legally, at least, the
enterprise of the Canon and his Yeoman would not have been considered
a crime.[37]

The disreputable incarnation of alchemy made it attractive, of
course, to those concerned with amassing personal gain and mintable
gold. That aspect of alchemy which constituted a respected intellectual, scientific, and spiritual pursuit is less easy to summarize. Alchemists were called "philosophres" and alchemy, "philosophie" (as it
is in The Canon's Yeoman's Tale), because influential thinkers within
the Greek, Arabic, and scholastic intellectual traditions addressed
the questions and possibilities posed by transmutation, often with conflicting results.[38] Although many, like Avicenna, denied the possibility of transmuting base metals into authentic gold, as many others
were convinced that transmutation was not only possible, but had been
accomplished.[39] The ambivalence surrounding alchemy derived not only

-----

nobles, it should be noted, were not minted before 1465.

35. Hartung, 121.

36. Duncan, 634.

37. Although the Canon and his Yeoman are not committing a felony
by practicing alchemy, there is the question of whether the Canon is in
apostasy in relation to his order. Marie Hamilton discusses this issue
in her article, "The Clerical Status of Chaucer's Alchemist," Speculum,
16 (1941), 103-08.

38. Hutin, p. 13.

39. Holmyard discusses Avicenna's attitude toward alchemy, pp.
92-93. Avicenna credited alchemists with the ability to make imita-

from the distinction between alchemy as an intellectual pursuit and
alchemy (or, more specifically, pseudo-alchemy) as a commercial enterprise that could produce fraud and counterfeiting. Medieval thinkers
were also ambivalent about alchemy's goals. The dispute about the possibility of transmutation was so entrenched that, when Petrus Bonus
wrote his Pretiosa Margarita Novella, he presented arguments both for
and against the possibility (concluding that, despite his own failures,
transmutation was possible).[40]

The ambivalence surrounding alchemy was compounded by the diversity of motives among its practitioners. Alchemists themselves represented a broad socio-economic spectrum ". . . from kings, popes, and
emperors to minor clergy, parish clerks, smiths, dyers, and tinkers."[41]
Their motives ranged as widely. John Read's survey of alchemists and
their purposes presents categories to accommodate the cast of alchemists in The Canon's Yeoman's Tale:

> At one end of the spectrum came the mercenary impostors or
> charlatans, using a pretended knowledge of the "Divine Art"
> as a means of extracting gold of a strictly non-alchemical
> origin from the money bags of credulous patrons; at the
> other, the devotees of a mystical alchemy . . . murmured
> prayers commingling the Christian mystery of the Trinity
> with the alchemical mystery of the triune stone. Between
> these extremes there came the simple uninformed puffers . . .
> sustained in their arduous and never ending operations by a
> vivid faith in the possibility of transmutation . . . beyond
> these . . . were ranged philosophers, like Albertus Magnus
> and Roger Bacon, who sought to peer beyond the experimental

---

tions of gold, but he did not believe that the alchemists could change
the essences of metals through transmutation.

40. Thorndike, Vol. III, pp. 151ff.

41. Holmyard, p. 13.

veil in their search for an all-embracing cosmical scheme.[42]

As this classification of alchemy and alchemists makes clear, alchemy is an ambivalent, in fact, a multivalent pursuit whose own value becomes redefined according to the context in which it is studied or practiced. For alchemy was not only pursued for a variety of motives; it elicited a variety of evaluations from those who addressed themselves to its problems.

The ambivalence toward alchemists in general and the Yeoman's ambivalence toward his Canon in particular make it difficult to determine the Canon's character or his motives. Predictably, critical assessment of the Canon covers the spectrum outlined by Read in the passage quoted above. Some critics see the Canon as a cheat and a fraud, as one and the same with the canon of the "Secunda Pars."[43] In some analyses, the second canon becomes the devil himself (or if not Satan, at least one of his right-hand men).[44] Critics who are more generous to the Canon credit him with delusion rather than with diabolical intent.[45] Because of his repeated failures, no critic has ventured to find in the Canon the adept devoted to alchemy as a spiritual pursuit.

---

42.   John Read, The Alchemist in Life, Literature, and Art (London: Thomas Nelson and Sons, Ltd., 1947), pp. 23-24.

43.   For examples of those critics who are not convinced of the Canon's honesty, see Gardner, 8 and Donaldson, p. 946.

44.   Gardner, 9.

45.   For critics who discuss the Canon's delusion, see Holmyard, p. 173 and Lawler, pp. 131ff. Read sees the Canon as both deluded and a charlatan, 31-39. John Reidy, in "Chaucer's Canon and The Unity of The Canon's Yeoman's Tale," PMLA, 80 (1965), 31-37, presents a sympathetic attitude toward the Canon and his delusion, but finds in the "Secunda Pars" a forecast of the deceptive ways into which the Canon's bad fortune will lead him.

But that the Canon is not a successful adept does not make him a
charlatan. As both Traugott Lawler and John Reidy have pointed out,
the poverty of the Canon and his Yeoman does not necessarily mean that
they plan to snare the pilgrims in a confidence game similar to the
second canon's.[46] The second canon's practice is tantamount to theft
and the Yeoman specifically underlines the premeditation that produces
his confidence game:

> And understondeth that this false gyn
> Was nat maad ther, but it was maad bifore;
> And othere thynges I shal tellen moore
> Herafterward, whiche that he with hym broghte.
> Er he cam there, hym to bigile he thoghte . . .
> (VIII. G, 1165-69)

In the Prologue and in the "Prima Pars" of his Tale, the Yeoman does
refer to their own need to rely on others for financial support. Yet
he consistently uses the word "borwe" (at lines 674 and 735) to describe their financial transactions with those whose aid they must en-
list in order to fund their enterprise. In the context of a patronage
system, the wealthy could provide alchemists with resources that allowed them to continue their search for the Philosopher's Stone.[47] Of

----

46. Reidy, 32; Lawler, p. 131. In the sympathy which it extends
to the Canon, my own discussion of his character resembles those of
Reidy and of Lawler in many respects. My discussion, like Lawler's
(pp. 131ff.), underlines the differences between the first and the
second canons. See, also, Burlin's discussion of the Yeoman's relationship to his Canon, which suggests that, although the Yeoman does
not understand "the psychological and moral obscurities of his master's
behavior" (p. 178), he is willing to blame his Canon, through the
figure of the second canon, for his own involvement with alchemy (pp.
177-78).

47. That such a patronage system existed is clear from Pope John
XXII's request to his physician (see footnote #30) and from the apocryphal story concerning Edward III and Raymond Lull. That such a system existed and could have pernicious consequences is implied in a

course, in order to persuade a patron to loan money, the Canon and
his Yeoman must claim a success that they have not, in reality, enjoyed. The Yeoman himself underlines their misrepresentation of their
success: "'For evere we lakken oure conclusioun./ To muchel folk we
doon illusioun'" (VIII. G, 672-73). The acquisition of financial support on these grounds can, of course, be construed as fraud, but the
desire and need to borrow money in the hope of finally achieving success does not constitute premeditated theft. As Lawler argues, ". . .
he [the Canon] attracts others to his work because he needs their
money, and to that extent victimizes them; but they become his associates rather than his victims."[48] According to many critics, the
Canon's actions in the Prologue to the Yeoman's Tale augment his sus-
piciousness. But interestingly, it is the pilgrim-narrator, not the
Yeoman, who attributes guilt to the Canon (VIII. G, 686-89). The
"sorwe and shame" (VIII. G, 702) with which the Canon rides away may be
caused as much by sorrow and shame at repeated failure as by guilt at
his repeated fleecings of gullible patrons.[49]

To argue against the identification of the Yeoman's Canon with
the canon of the "Secunda Pars" does not, however, define the Canon's

---

treatise entitled "The Secret Treasure of Operations of Nature," as-
cribed to Arnold of Villanova. The treatise, "in the form of a dialogue between master and disciple," warns the disciple that, to be an
alchemist, one "must have enough money for two years' expenses at
least, [and] must on no account put oneself under the power of any
prince or magnate . . ." (Thorndike, Vol. III, pp. 74-75).

48. Lawler, p. 131.

49. Reidy, 35-36.

own intentions. While there is no direct evidence in the <u>Tale</u> to classify the Yeoman's Canon with the adepts, the practitioners of esoteric alchemy, neither is there reason to reduce him, as many critics have, to a "puffer," an ignorant blunderer.[50] It is more likely that, of the two, the Yeoman is the puffer or "bellowsblower." (This is, as he tells us, his function in the laboratory--lines 755; 923-24.[51]) Moreover, despite his frequent disparagements of his master's skill, the Yeoman often notes the Canon's learning, a learning reflected in his own alchemical catalogues. From the portrait of him presented by his disillusioned apprentice, the Canon emerges as a learned man, familiar with alchemical treatises, and aware, from his reading, that he must accept failure until he receives the divine inspiration which his Yeoman discusses at the end of the <u>Tale</u>.

The Yeoman's ambivalence toward his master is apparent throughout the scene in the laboratory.[52] The Canon, as this description of him shows, seems to have accepted failure as an occupational hazard. His reaction to the eruption in the laboratory is more complacent than that of his associates, for, amidst the conflicting opinions about the cause of their failure, the Canon's voice remains determined and encouraging:

> "What," quod my lord, "ther is namoore to doone;
> Of thise perils I wol be war eftsoone.
> I am right siker that the pot was crased.
> Be as be may, be ye no thyng amased;

---

50. Reidy, 34; Read, pp. 31-32. Both critics see the Canon as a blunderer, who may be familiar with alchemical texts, but who does not know what he is doing.

51. Read, p. 33.

52. See Lawler, p. 134.

>   As usage is, lat swepe the floor as swithe,
>   Plukke up youre hertes, and beeth glad and blithe."
>   (VIII. G, 932-37)

And the Canon's patience in the face of the failure that he confronts,

yet once again, continues as he interrupts the wrangling of his assoc-

iates, no novices in the alchemical pursuit:

>   "Pees!" quod my lord, "the nexte tyme I wol fonde
>   To bryngen oure craft al in another plite,
>   And but I do, sires, lat me han the wite.
>   Ther was defaute in somwhat, wel I woot."
>   (VIII. G, 951-54)

Of course, the Canon's speech may be intended to encourage his associ-

ates' investments in his experiments. But, if the Canon will risk

failure in the presence of his patrons, he is not indulging in the

second canon's sleight-of-hand, that is meant always to succeed. Sig-

nificantly the Canon is willing to assume responsibility for the acci-

dent and he will take the blame if they fail again. His words belong

to a man who has, as the Yeoman admits, forsaken worldly goods (VIII.

G, 879-82) and devoted himself to learning his art, with full awareness

that he must await divine inspiration before he can succeed.[53] It is

important to note that this description of the Canon's patience and

encouragement is offered by the Yeoman who has cursed and abandoned

his master.

Repeatedly, throughout the "Prima Pars" of his Tale, the Yeoman,

---

53. As John Reidy has noted, the Canon manifests many characteristics prescribed for alchemical adepts. Reidy writes that "[a]lche-
mists set for themselves a high standard of conduct" (33) and he continues, "[f]rom what we see of him in his laboratory he [the Canon]
exhibits several of the required virtues, being patient, long-suffer-
ing, and gentle . . ." (35).

directly or indirectly, acknowledges the Canon's learning. Although

the following passage documents the Canon's failure, it also reflects

the Yeoman's pride in the skill and wisdom of the man whom he calls

"my lord" even as he damns him:

> Er that the pot be on the fir ydo,
> Of metals with a certeyn quantitee,
> My lord hem trempreth, and no man but he --
> Now he is goon, I dar seyn boldely --
> For as men seyn, he kan doon craftily.
> Algate I woot wel he hath swich a name,
> And yet ful ofte he renneth in a blame.
> And wite ye how? ful ofte it happeth so,
> The pot tobroketh, and farewel, al is go!
>   (VIII. G, 899-907)

As he moves from his master's reputation to his failure the Yeoman

demonstrates the confusion in his own attitude toward his master. Yet,

in the end, the Yeoman shares neither his master's skill nor his pa-

tience. Although he has been seduced by the temptation of alchemy, the

Yeoman's committment to their craft is not so unambivalent as his mas-

ter's. Nor does he share the Canon's goals; his own are directed

toward the material and intellectual gratification of converting the

elements of the world around him.

The Canon's learning has not been sufficient to bring the Yeoman

the success. In fact, according to the Yeoman, no amount of learning,

whether it derives from the Canon or from alchemical literature, de-

livers the success that it promises. If the elements themselves are

intractable, failing to yield the gold that they, theoretically, con-

tain, so is the wisdom of the Canon and of the alchemical treatises.

The art of alchemy promises the Yeoman wisdom, revelation, and a mas-

tery over the external world that would allow him to define the world's

value in terms of personal gain. Yet alchemy has thwarted the Yeoman

and his bitterness and hostility exist in direct proportion to the
promised good.

It is no wonder, then, that the Yeoman speaks of learning and
wisdom only with contempt for its uselessness:

> Whan we been there as we shul exercise
> Oure elvysshe craft, we semen wonder wise;
> Oure termes been so clergial and so queynte.
> (VIII. G, 750-52)

The Yeoman concludes the "Prima Pars" of his tale with a more far-
reaching devaluation:

> And whan we been togidres everichoon,
> Every man semeth a Salomon.
> But al thyng which that shineth as the gold
> Nis nat gold, as that I have herd it told;
> Ne every appul that is fair at eye
> Ne is nat good, what so men clappe or crye.
> Right so, lo, fareth it amonges us:
> He that semeth the wiseste, by Jhesus!
> Is moost fool, whan it cometh to the preef;
> And he that semeth trewest is a theef.
> That shul ye knowe, er that I fro yow wende,
> By that I of my tale have maad an ende.
> (VIII. G, 960-71)

Because the learning that promised him material and intellectual wealth
has failed him, the Canon's Yeoman ends by devaluing it. On one
level, his words warn against the false gold produced by fraudulent alchemists; this gold is a base metal whose surface has been colored but
whose essence, whose intrinsic worth, has not been changed. This gold,
when "it cometh to the preef," will not prove its authenticity. Like
the wisdom of the Yeoman's master, it will not withstand the test.
Within the Yeoman's idiom, the wisdom intended to produce gold becomes
likened to the gold itself. The Canon and the Canon's learning, like
the Yeoman himself, have become elements in the alchemical process. If
the Yeoman has been turned into lead, his master, he implies, has

proven to be counterfeit gold.

The Yeoman, whose only possession is words that fail to transform his ambivalence, warns against a wisdom constituted, as he perceives it, only of language, of "termes . . . clergial and . . . queynte." These words should have signified a wisdom that could translate itself into mastery over the external world. Instead, for the Yeoman, they signify a wisdom that must necessarily be a valueless counterfeit if it fails to succeed. The Yeoman's concluding observations in the "Prima Pars" express an attitude toward language, similar to that explored in The Shipman's Tale, that questions language's referentiality, its ability to name value. Because the Canon's language and the wisdom signified by his words do not transform extralinguistic reality, the Yeoman concludes that the learning is a counterfeit equivalent to the second canon's confidence game. This confidence game is of course, only a veil of language hiding deception.

In the Canon's Yeoman's Tale, as in The Shipman's Tale, intention is a crucial determinant of language's creditability. Although Chaucer is aware of the deceptiveness of language, he is also aware that the intention of the speaker determines the faith that we can place in his language. The second canon means to deceive, yet the embittered Yeoman fails to see, or, more specifically, he does not want to see that a difference of intention distinguishes his master's language and learning from the second canon's. The Yeoman's bitterness, rather than his ignorance, has "blered" his vision. His attitude toward wisdom and language and people has undergone the same inversion of the alchemical transformation that he himself has experienced. The man who believed, seven years ago, that all base elements potentially signified value, potentially contained an intrinsic worth greater than their surfaces would indicate, now believes that no surface can contain value. For the Yeoman, if all lead is not gold, then all gold must be lead. Both attitudes toward the world and toward language are equally reductive.

But if Chaucer underlines the reductiveness of the Yeoman's devaluation of wisdom and language, he also underlines the way in which alchemy itself contributes to that reductiveness. Alchemy is the most ambitious of medieval sciences, but the nature of its goals determines the magnitude of its failure. Alchemy, the wisdom of its practitioners, and the language into which this wisdom is translated present, perhaps, the supreme example of the word failing to be cousin to the deed, because the deed itself may not exist; it may be an impossibility. Alchemy may represent the ultimate failure of referentiality, because, if it promises value, gold, it signifies, in reality, impossibility, futility, nothingness. Alchemy may, in the end, be a word with no referent.

But, through his presentation of alchemy, Chaucer also asks if the failure of the alchemical word to correlate with the deed necessarily means that the words and the wisdom which they signify are counterfeit. If all alchemical wisdom and its "queynte" terms are counterfeit, then, by extension, all human wisdom and its linguistic manifestations must be counterfeit, because they attempt to express that which man cannot know with certainty. As in The Shipman's Tale, Chaucer raises the issue of faith and its relationship to referentiality. For such faith--faith that there is a meaning to which our words refer; faith that intellectual or spiritual endeavor refers to a meaning or value, even if we cannot define it; faith that the configuration of the external world refers to a divine order unclear to us--is all that keeps us from seeing the world as counterfeit. Faith in referentiality would allow the Yeoman to see the value of his Canon's language and his wisdom.

If the Canon's Yeoman seeks to resolve his own ambivalence by denying referentiality, he also tries to resolve it by presenting himself to his audience as a victim of the external world. In order to explain the failure that he has experienced, the Yeoman blames the instruments, the procedures, the alchemical texts, and the Canon. He even blames the Philosopher's Stone itself:

> . . . the philosophres stoon,
> Elixer clept, we sechen faste echoon;
> For hadde we hym, thanne were we siker ynow.
> But unto God of hevene I make avow,
> For al oure craft, whan we han al ydo,
> And al oure sleighte, he wol nat come us to.
> He hath ymaad us spenden muchel good,
> For sorwe of which almoost we wexen wood,
> But that good hope crepeth in oure herte,
> Supposynge evere, thogh we sore smerte,
> To be releeved by hym afterward.
>   (VIII. G, 862-72)

In his description of the Philosopher's Stone, the Yeoman refers to the Stone as "he," rather than as "it." By attributing to the Stone an independent consciousness that deliberately seeks to thwart the alchemists,[54] the Yeoman can blame it, rather than them. The Canon's Yeoman's Tale presents numerous strategies that allow the Yeoman to

---

54. Gardner, 12; Bruce A. Rosenberg, "Swindling Alchemist, Antichrist," Centennial Review of Arts and Science, 6 (1962), 573.

deny his own culpability. He displaces his own covetousness onto the
"sely" priest. He attributes his failure to his "lewednesse" in the
context of an enterprise that even the most learned cannot learn. He
is unwilling to claim responsibility if, in fact, the fire caused the
eruption in the laboratory: "Thanne was I fered, for that was myn
office" (VIII. G, 924). Even his physical and spiritual blindness is
caused by external forces: by the alchemical fire and by the seduction
of alchemy itself. Through his strategies the Canon's Yeoman tries to
convince himself and his audience that he is, above all, a victim.

In his attribution of blame to the intractable external world,
the Yeoman fails to see that alchemy originates in the self. As Jung
argued, it is a projection of the self upon the chaos and undifferen-
tiated mass of the external world.[55] Alchemy promised the Yeoman a
means to make the world yield the value that he sought within it.[56]
Because the Yeoman perceived the world as an extension of himself and
of his imagination, the world, he believed, should have reference to
the meaning that he projects upon it. The Yeoman, in fact, does not
see what Chaucer, who has been studying the formulation of value
throughout The Canterbury Tales, knows all too well: that the individual defines meaning for himself, according to personal needs, and

---

55. Carl Jung's essay, "The Idea of Redemption in Alchemy" in
The Integration of the Personality, trans. Stanley Dell (London: Routledge and Kegan Paul, 1950), pp. 205-81, finds in the alchemical quest
the desire to explore the unknown within the self through an exploration of the unknown, that is, the matter of the external world, outside
the self. According to Jung, "The relation to the invisible powers of
the psyche constituted the actual secret of the magistery" (p. 221).

56. See Jung, pp. 219 and 222.

then seeks to find that meaning mirrored in the external world. Alchemy, like art or economics, is a construct created by man in order
to differentiate and thereby to give value to the potentially valueless chaos of the external world.

In The Shipman's Tale, the monk and the wife find no value in the
external world, except as they can appropriate phenomena of that world
to satisfy their own desires. The Wife of Bath, whose world is structured by a set of conventions and values that would deny her own value
as a woman, attempts to remake the world in her own image, in accordance with her own value and values. Yet the Wife of Bath's bout with
Jankyn, which shatters the narcissism of the antifeminist tradition
and of her own desire for maistrie, leads her to a system of valuation
equitable in its acknowledgment of otherness and of the need for reciprocity. The Yeoman's failure has shown him the autonomy as well as
the intractability of the external world. He, however, ends, not by
adjusting or criticizing his own expectations, but by condemning the
world whose surfaces are false because they do not reflect the value
that he seeks. Yet, at the same time that the Yeoman shirks blame, he
condemns himself to his ambivalence. Because alchemy is an imaginative
and intellectual response to the external world, the Yeoman cannot al-
leviate ambivalence by blaming alchemy. Nor can he leave alchemy by
presenting a verbal condemnation of it. What is more, as a manifestation of the self's quest for value and for the power to transform, alchemy must necessarily evoke ambivalence because both possibility and
limitation are intrinsic to the quest.

The "Secunda Pars" of The Canon's Yeoman's Tale presents a continuation of his efforts to resolve his ambivalence. The "Secunda
Pars" is a fabliau which, like The Miller's Tale, The Reeve's Tale, and
The Shipman's Tale, presents a confidence game designed to trick another in the name of personal gain. Not enough critical attention has
been paid to the genre of the "Secunda Pars" or to Chaucer's reasons
for selecting it. The Canon's Yeoman's story is Chaucer's adaptation
of the fabliau to suit the personality of his teller. Within this
fabliau, it is appropriate although not unusual that an intellectual,
scientific, and spiritual pursuit, like alchemy, is debased into a confidence game for the sake of personal profit. Courtly love and astrology, marriage and cosynage, suffer similar debasements in the tales
of the Miller and the Shipman. What is exceptional in The Canon's
Yeoman's Tale is the animosity of the narrator toward the trickster.
In Chaucer's other fabliaux, the narrator applauds the trickster's
wiliness, deceit, and success. He projects himself into the trickster's
personality and thus enjoys, in the world of his fiction, his trickster's mastery and self-determination. Regardless of the audience for
which it was intended, the fabliau is, essentially, a bourgeois genre.
The narrative patterns of the fabliau offer a wish-fulfillment of the
bourgeois desire for self-determination, of the desire to appropriate
the world, to buy it and master it through language.

In the "Secunda Pars" of The Canon's Yeoman's Tale, Chaucer has
transformed the fabliau's conventional representation of the relationship between narrator and narrative. The Canon's Yeoman's bitterness
and hostility extend to his fictional trickster. Because his own

alchemical quest has brought him neither mastery nor money, he damns
the second canon's successful deceit. The Yeoman envies the control
that his character wields through deception as much as he envies the
profit that accrues to him. Moreover, if the Yeoman damns the trickster, he sympathizes and identifies with the tricked.[57] It is clear
that he would rather attribute responsibility for the priest's loss to
the second canon's deceptiveness than to the priest's gullibility and
greed. To blame the priest would hit too close to home for the Yeoman,
who has an immediate stake in convincing his audience to sympathize
with the "sely innocent," and, by extension, with himself.[58] The Yeoman needs sympathy (and perhaps hard cash) to compensate for the losses
he has suffered.

The Yeoman's ambivalence and his need to reject responsibility
for his own loss explain the critical problem of a second canon in the
second part of the Tale.[59] When the Yeoman disclaims identification
between the second canon and his master, the information in the "Prima
Pars" of his Tale demands that we should believe him:

> This chanon was my lord, ye wolden weene?
> Sire hoost, in feith, and by the hevenes queene,
> It was another chanoun, and nat hee,
> That kan an hundred foold more subtiltee.
> He [second canon] hath bitrayed folkes many tyme . . .
>   (VIII. G, 1088-92)

---

57. See Gardner's discussion of this identification, 11-12.
Gardner also extends this identification to include the Yeoman's Canon.

58. Lumiansky also makes this observation about the Yeoman's
desire for sympathy, p. 228.

59. Ralph G. Baldwin, in "The Yeoman's Canon: A Conjecture" presents the difficulties raised by the presence of the two canons within
the Prologue and Tale, 233-34.

Of course, as critics have pointed out, there is no need for either
Chaucer or his Yeoman to have made the bogus alchemist a canon (thereby
adding confusion to an already confusing tale) unless the two canons
are identical.[60]   But if there is no logical or poetical need for this
confusion of canons, there is an emotional and intellectual need deriving from the Yeoman's ambivalence. The Yeoman is not unaware of
the discrepancy between the practices of his two canons. His recurrent
emphasis upon the falseness of the second canon and his ruse (an emphasis absent from the "Prima Pars") underlines not only the second
canon's treachery, but also a spuriousness that distinguishes him from
the Yeoman's Canon. Nevertheless, the tale in which the Yeoman has
projected his own sense of victimization onto the "sely" priest demands
that the victimizer be a canon. The Yeoman has proceeded over a hundred lines into his fiction before he becomes aware of what he is doing. His awareness and his ambivalence oblige him to dispel the confusion for his audience.

Once he has eliminated this confusion, however, the Yeoman cannot
resist taking a last shot at his master. The Yeoman derides his master's intelligence by attributing greater "subtilitee" to his fictional
alchemist. Within his fiction, the Yeoman can present a canon more
learned than his master, one whose alchemy always succeeds. But the
Yeoman, who has told us at the end of the "Prima Pars" that words are
empty, knows that linguistic revenge cannot assuage his own loss or
resolve his ambivalence. Three times he tells his audience that the
tale of the second canon's falseness dulls him (at lines 1093ff.;

---

60. See Baldwin, 233.

1172ff.; 1306ff.). His conflict with his own ambivalence and his futile attempts to exorcise it linguistically exhaust him. As the Yeoman proceeds further into his own psyche and into the fictionalization of his experience in his tale, he becomes more dulled by the conflict and by the absence of a resolution. Although, empirically, he knows that the Canon does not share the con-man's falseness, the conflict between experiential and psychological truth blurs the Yeoman's vision and the boundary between fiction and experience.[61]

The virulence of the Canon's Yeoman's condemnations in the "Secunda Pars" is necessary if he is to convince himself of alchemy's ultimate worthlessness. In order to resolve his own ambivalence, the Yeoman must perform, in his Tale, a transformation that follows the pattern of all the transformations within his experience. This transformation is, in essence, a devaluation similar to the devaluation of wisdom at the end of the "Prima Pars." In the "Secunda Pars," the Canon's laboratory becomes that of the second canon as experiment is transformed into deception. The failure in the first part becomes the success produced by bogus alchemy in the second. The Yeoman avenges himself on his master by granting the second canon success. But, in order to resolve his ambivalence, the Yeoman must not only transform the results in the laboratory; he must transform alchemy itself. Just as the Wife of Bath quites the antifeminist tradition for its devaluation of her, the Yeoman quites alchemy in kind. He devalues it, as it has devalued him, by transforming it from a potentially intellectual

_____

61. See Donald Howard's discussion of the "Secunda Pars" as an objectification of the Yeoman's experience, pp. 294-95.

and spiritual quest into a confidence game that reflects his own feel-
ings of deception and loss. In the process, he presents a prostituted
form of alchemy that cannot fail to be condemned by himself and by his
audience. This is not his Canon's alchemy, as the Yeoman rationally
knows, but the Yeoman wants the bogus alchemy to stand for the whole.
He wants the confidence game to represent all of alchemy so that he can
easily reject it. In the end, this effort at transmutation, like all
other efforts in the Yeoman's career, fails. It succeeds only in dull-
ing him, and in reminding him of his own devaluation.

Within this context, the Yeoman's recurrent warnings against alchemy are interesting. Ostensibly, his purpose in presenting his confession and his tale are didactic. He wishes to instruct his audience
by his example. After his final articulation of exhaustion at telling
his tale, he says:

> And nathelees yet wol I it expresse,
> To th'entente that men may be war therby,
> And for noon oother cause, trewely.
>   (VIII. G, 1305-07)

In her _Prologue_, the Wife of Bath also underlined the purpose of her
confession:

> "If that I speke after my fantasye,
> As taketh not agrief of that I seye;
> For myn entente is nat but for to pleye."
>   (III. D, 190-92)

The Wife of Bath's "pleye" consists, in fact, of an "ernest" presentation of the values that she has sought to formulate for herself. It
is doubtful that the Yeoman's assessment of his "entente" is any more
accurate than Alison's. Before he begins the allegorical conclusion to
his _Tale_, the Yeoman launches into an extended warning against alchemy:

O! fy, for shame! they that han been brent,
  Allas! kan they nat flee the fires heete?
  Ye that it use, I rede ye it leete,
  Lest ye lese al; for bet than nevere is late.
  Nevere to thryve were to long a date.
                        (VIII. G, 1407-12)

Indeed, as he has said at the beginning of the "Prima Pars," among

alchemists, misery loves company. If the Yeoman does not want to

seduce his audience into lending him money, he does want to seduce

them into lending him a sympathy that would resolve his indecision.

His warnings and the apostrophe to his audience that closes his Tale

are, in essence, both warnings to himself and signs of his own ambiv-

alence. For, in the end, his condemnation of alchemy in the "Secunda

Pars" has been as ineffective as all his previous attempts at trans-

formation.

The conclusion of The Canon's Yeoman's Tale presents his quota-

tions from alchemical authorities, from the "philosophres" who, he be-

lieves, conclusively define the impossibility of finding the Philos-

opher's Stone. The Canon's Yeoman's citation of the philosophers and

his purpose in quoting them has caused as many critical problems as

other aspects of his tale. Many critics find these citations too

learned to be assigned to the "lewed" Yeoman.[62] Others believe that,

at this point, the poet Chaucer interrupts his Yeoman's narrative in

order to offer his own assessment of alchemy.[63] But, as I have argued,

the Canon's Yeoman is not so "lewed" as he and his critics have billed

---

    62. On the inappropriateness of the Tale's conclusion to the
Yeoman, see Hartung, 126 and Herz, 236-37.

    63. Rosenberg, 580; Herz, 236-37.

him. Because he is sufficiently acquainted with alchemical lore to
list the allegorical names of the elements, it is not improbable for
him to cite alchemical authorities. (Few critics find the Wife of
Bath's quotation of texts improbable.) In addition, the texts from
which the Yeoman quotes represent the more widely read alchemical
treatises of his time.[64] Yet, if the Canon's Yeoman has the knowledge
to quote authorities, he, like the Wife of Bath, does so for his own
purposes. Because his diatribe against the false canon and his bogus
alchemy has not resolved the Yeoman's indecision, he turns to the alchemical authorities in order to convince himself of the impossibility
of success. In the process, he, like Alison, misreads texts as he im-
poses an interpretation on them that derives from his personal needs.

The context in which the Yeoman quotes alchemical texts transforms
their meaning at the same time that it reflects the Yeoman's own interests and needs. The Yeoman prefaces his final warnings against
alchemy and his citation of the philosophers with these words:

> Philosophres speken so mystily
> In this craft that men kan nat come therby,
> For any wit that men han now-a-dayes.
> They mowe wel chiteren as doon thise jayes,
> And in hir termes sette hir lust and peyne,
> But to hir purpos shul they nevere atteyne.
> (VIII. G, 1394-99)

The last three lines of this passage describe the Yeoman's purpose in

---

64. Thorndike cites Arnold of Villanova as one of the "revered
masters . . . of contemporary alchemists" (Vol. III, p. 47) and goes
on to say: "Whether Arnauld's Rosarius is the first considerable alchemical treatise to bear that title and passed it on to the other
Rosaries, is hard to say with certainty. If so, their adoption of that
name would be a sign of the diffusion and popularity of the original
treatise" (Vol. III, p. 57).

his tale at the same time that they present his recognition that his
language and his "termes" are as empty as he has found his master's to
be. The first three lines of this passage, however, read like a complaint against the philosophers who refuse to yield him the desired
knowledge. In this instance, the external source that thwarts the
Yeoman is alchemical authority itself.[65] Ironically, the Yeoman does
not see that the way in which he reads (or fails to read) the philosophers accounts for his failure as an alchemist. The Yeoman may not
be "lewed" in relation to alchemical technique, but he is "lewed" in
relation to the scope and to the spiritual dimension of the art to
which he has apprenticed himself. If the Yeoman's motives for pursuing
the alchemical quest are not as sordid as those of the characters in
his Tale, they remain focused on the empirical reality of the world
around him. The Yeoman looks for answers within the external world,
and, if it does not yield him the answers that he seeks, he concludes
that its surfaces are deceptive or that answers are permanently inaccessible to him.

The Yeoman's quotations from the philosophers demonstrate, once
again, his pride in his ability to regale his audience with erudition.
Interestingly enough, the character who complains about the philosophers' incomprehensibility is able to gloss the allegorical references
of "Arnold of the Newe Toun." He knows that the dragon is mercury and
that his brother is brimstone. Yet the Yeoman uses these quotations

---

65. Paul Taylor writes of the Yeoman: "His failure is, allegor-
ically, a failure to achieve his own grace. . . . His epilogue fits
neither his 'confession' nor his tale. It is, simply, sour grapes"
(387).

for a specific and limited purpose: to warn against wasting one's

"thrift" (VIII. G, 1425) in an impossible enterprise. Arnold of the

Newe Toun, the Yeoman implies, interprets alchemy in the same way that

he does:

> "Lat no man bisye hym this art for to seche,
> But if that he th'entencioun and speche
> Of philosophres understonde kan;
> And if he do, he is a lewed man.
> For this science and this konnyng," quod he [Arnold]
> "Is of the secree of secrees, pardee."
> (VIII. G, 1442-47)

The Yeoman is willing to admit that he is the "lewed" man who cannot

understand the "entencioun and speche" of the philosophers, for his

admission posits responsibility for his failure with their incomprehen-

sibility.

In his rationalization of the causes for his failure, the Yeoman

would even blame God, who is the final cause of the Philosopher's

Stone's inaccessibility. According to Plato, the Philosopher's Stone

is so dear to Christ

> "That he wol nat that it discovered bee,
> But where it liketh to his deitee
> Men for t'enspire, and eek for to deffende
> Whom that hym liketh . . ."
> (VIII. G, 1468-71)

And the Yeoman concludes:

> . . . sith that God of hevene
> Ne wil nat that the philosophres nevene
> How that a man shal come unto this stoon,
> I rede, as for the beste, lete it goon.
> (VIII. G, 1472-75)

The Yeoman's acknowledgment of the divine regulation of alchemy may

be, as some critics have suggested, his professional swan song; it may show his resignation to God's power.[66]   But his resignation is, at best, grudging and it does not resolve his ambivalence in relation to his craft.   The acknowledgment of God's power entails a recognition of one's own powerlessness and lack of self-determination, a recognition against which the Yeoman has struggled throughout his Tale.   Moreover, the acknowledgment of God's association with and protection of alchemical secrets counterbalances the infernal quality that the Yeoman has attributed to alchemy in his fabliau.   After his devaluation of alchemy in the "Secunda Pars," the Yeoman reinvests it with value by associating it with God.   The Yeoman's citation of the alchemical authorities underlines his awareness of the limitations and frustrations attendant upon intellectual endeavor.   But his citations also demonstrate that others have succeeded where he has failed.   The Yeoman cannot be unaware that he cites those sources that present alchemy as a potentially successful, divinely sanctioned art.   Yet he uses the alchemical sources for his own purposes, to convince himself and his audience of the impossibility of the quest.

Ironically, however, the philosophers' obscurity allows them to hide alchemical secrets from men such as the Yeoman.   The Yeoman, at one level, understands this.   Yet he does not explain why the Philosopher's Stone is precious to Christ nor why it is denied to the "lewed" men who cannot understand "th'entencioun and speche" of the philosophers.   The Yeoman suggests that the Stone is denied because of intellectual ignorance or because God reveals His secrets only to the chosen

---

66.   See Gardner's discussion of the Yeoman's error in the conclusion of his Tale, 13ff.

--that is, according to the Yeoman, the intelligent--few. He does not consider why God makes certain men "philosophres" nor why, aside from his own intellectual limitations and God's will, he himself has failed. The Yeoman does not see that the philosophers' obscurity is meant to illuminate the nature of the alchemical quest and to transform it from the materialistic construction that the Yeoman himself would place upon it. Because he reads the philosophers according to his characteristically limited vision, because he seeks within them the clue to material and intellectual gratification, his own quest is doomed to failure.

The alchemical treatises are written in allegorical language in order to preserve the secrets of alchemy from those who would reduce it to a materialistic science. According to the "philosophres," alchemy was a religious, often a mystical pursuit whose spiritual goals took precedence over the success of practical experimentation.[67] As Dorothée Metlitzki has shown, the religious and mystical goals of medieval European alchemy originated in the mysticism surrounding the science in Arabic alchemical treatises, the sources for alchemical learning in the West.[68] As alchemy became a part of occidental thought its religious overtones were, of course, modified according to the beliefs of a European Christian audience.[69]

---

67. For a summary of the spiritual aspect of alchemy and its relationship to experimentation, see Hutin, pp. 10-13.

68. Dorothée Metlitzki's article "The Code of Chaucer's 'Secree of Secrees'" presents a fully documented discussion of this transmission in relation to the material found in the conclusion of The Canon's Yeoman's Tale. See, especially, 261.

69. Ibid., 271.

The religious manifestation of alchemy corresponded to practical alchemy in its goals and purposes. E. J. Holmyard writes:

> . . . for many who practised it the transmutation of metals was symbolical of the transmutation of imperfect man into a state of perfection. Conversely, metallic transmutation could be brought about only by divine aid and by men of pure life. These two tenets reacted upon one another and were complexly interwoven in alchemical thought. The unity of the world and of all things in it was an unshakable belief; there was nothing illogical in the combination of mystical theology with practical chemistry . . . this combination . . . often makes it very difficult to decide whether a particular work of symbolism was intended to convey any real chemical information, or whether it was to be taken as speculative thought.[70]

The alchemists' theory of metallic conposition and their definition of the purpose of transmutation further clarifies the spiritual aspect of their goals. As Hopkins points out, according to the Aristotelian theory of matter adopted by the alchemists, "[t]he metals were striving to finish their peculiar cycle, tending toward perfection as fire seeks its source, toward the entelechy which is gold."[71] Serge Hutin summarizes the alchemists' theory of metallic composition:

> Gold is the perfection of the metallic realm, the constant objective of nature. But the attainment of this objective is delayed by numerous accidents and vicissitudes, which give rise to the imperfect metals. Gold, the living end of metallic perfection, is formed in the depths of the earth, from a primal matter ripened by the planets; but there are also "leprous," or base metals. Nevertheless, metals tend actively toward perfection . . . .[72]

For the alchemists, then, the natural world, like man himself, was fallen and was consequently striving toward perfection.[73] In their

---

70. Holmyard, p. 152.

71. Hopkins, p. 26.

72. Hutin, p. 84.

73. Ibid., p. 18.

efforts at transmutation, the alchemists assisted the metals in attaining their natural ends. According to Petrus Bonus, in the practice of alchemy, man, with the help of the divine will, only finished Nature's work.[74]

Of course, for the alchemical adepts, the acquisition of gold did not satisfy desire for material gain; it was sought only as proof that transmutation had been accomplished.[75] As Metlitzki writes, in the Islamic sources which influenced the formulation of European alchemy (and whose influence is present throughout the conclusion of The Canon's Yeoman's Tale), "[w]hat is important in the making of the elixir is not the process of transmutation to gold for the sake of its material value but the achievement of perfect religious knowledge, the penetration into the most sublime secret of mystical truth--the hidden Imam."[76] Repeatedly emphasized throughout alchemical literature (and in the Yeoman's closing lines) is the need for divine aid in order to accomplish transmutation. Given their own definition of purpose, the alchemists were involved, as Jung pointed out, in an act of redemption analogous to the act of transubstantiation which the priest accomplished in the Mass.[77] Jung wrote:

---

74. Holmyard presents this point in his discussion of Petrus Bonus, p. 140.

75. Jacques Sadoul writes: "L'or ou l'argent obtenus étaient pour l'alchimiste la preuve absolue qu'il avait bien réussi à fabriquer la Pierre philosophe, et désormais ces metaux précieux n'intéressent plus le véritable Adepte" (p. 55).

76. Metlitzki, p. 274.

77. Jung presents a detailed discussion of this analogy and its psychological ramifications in "The Idea of Redemption in Alchemy," pp. 237-39.

> . . . the Christian opus was an operari, to the honor of
> the redeeming God, on the part of the man who needs redemp-
> tion, while the alchemistic opus is the labor of man the
> redeemer in the cause of the divine world-soul that sleeps
> in matter and awaits redemption. The Christian earns for
> himself, ex opere operato, the fruits of grace. The alche-
> mist, on the other hand, achieves, ex opere operantis (in
> the literal sense), a "life remedy" . . . which seems to
> him either an ill-concealed substitute for the means of
> grace of the church, or a completion of, and a parallel to,
> the divine work of redemption that is active in man.[78]

If true alchemy was considered tantamount to the work of redemption

that the priest performed in the Mass, it is little wonder that the

alchemists deemed it necessary to keep this secret from the profane,

from the materialistic.

The "misty" terms against which the Canon's Yeoman complains are

a hallmark of alchemical writings. As Petrus Bonus points out, the

difficulty of alchemy is increased because, in the treatises, words

occur "not only in their ordinary sense but in allegorical, metaphori-

cal, enigmatical, equivocal, and even ironical ways."[79] As often as

the philosophers articulate the need for divine inspiration, they un-

derline the necessity of using allegorical language in order to pre-

serve their secrets. According to Roger Bacon, it is to everyone's

advantage that alchemical knowledge remain classified information:

"'By revealing the secret, one lessens its efficacy. The people can

understand nothing of it; they would make common use of it and take

away all its value. . . . the wicked, if they knew the secret, would

---

78. Ibid., p. 270.

79. Holmyard, p. 138. Thorndike (III, p. 155) also discusses
Petrus Bonus's observations about the allegorical language that was a
hallmark of alchemical treatises.

misuse it and overthrow the world.'"[80]

The allegorical language of the treatises is intended to preserve the sanctity, the secrecy, in short, the value of alchemy. Moreover, even the themes of allegories describing experimental procedures indicate the religious purposes toward which the philosophers directed their pursuit. A passage, from the Flower of Paradise, attributed in the Middle Ages to Arnold of Villanova, testifies to both the obscurity and the religiosity of alchemical allegories:

> . . . Father and Son and Holy Spirit are the same yet three.
> And so there are three of our stone. Moreover, the world
> was lost through a woman and hence should be recovered
> through a woman. Therefore take the pure mother and put her
> in bed with the son according to your intention and there
> let her do strictest penance until she is well cleansed of
> all sins. And then she will bear a son for certain who will
> preach to all saying, 'Signs have appeared in the sun and
> moon.' Therefore let him be taken and beaten well and
> scourged lest by reason of pride he perish. . . . while he
> is crucified, sun nor moon will be seen, and then the veil
> of the temple will be rent, and there will be a great earth-
> quake. So then the fire is to be increased, and thereupon
> he will give up the ghost.[81]

This densely allegorical passage justifies the Yeoman's confusion. But its theme, taken from Christ's nativity and passion, also demonstrates the conceptual framework within which the alchemists carried out their experiments. Of course, as Dorothée Metlitzki has pointed out, obscuring experimental procedures and swearing disciples to secrecy could have other than spiritual ends: "On the practical level, the injunc-

---

80. Roger Bacon, Opus Tertium. I quote this passage from Hutin, p. 25.

81. Thorndike quotes this passage in Vol. III, pp. 76-77. This passage is among many densely allegorical writings attributed to Arnold of Villanova and utilizing themes from the nativity, passion, and resurrection of Christ (Thorndike, Vol. III, pp. 75-77).

tion to secrecy in the transmission of alchemy may be regarded as the need to guard professional knowledge from outsiders."[82] The allegorical language of the alchemical texts has accomplished its purpose in relation to the Yeoman's quest for the Philosopher's Stone.

But the Canon's Yeoman's failure to understand the philosophers' allegorical language is not due entirely to his limited intellectual abilities. Rather, as his use of the philosophers indicates, the Yeoman's mind is not so limited as his spirit. His is a failure of interpretation that ultimately derives from his spiritual limitedness. Petrus Bonus wrote: "'The inconsistencies that critics found within the Stone cannot be explained on natural grounds but must be accepted by faith, which has no difficulty in accepting the Christian miracles. In alchemy work without faith is foredoomed to failure. . . .'"[83] I would suggest that the Yeoman's enterprise is such a work without faith. That he plans to leave alchemy because only God can give the answer implies his lack of faith that God will give the answer to him. In contrast, the Canon's perseverance, foolhardy as it seems to the Yeoman, is a sign of his master's faith. For the Yeoman, God does not represent the source of revelation if one possesses the spiritual fibre to be worthy of it. Rather, He is part of, as well as the reason for, the intractability of the material world. Once again, the Yeoman does not see that the cause of failure lies within himself, within his own definition of alchemy and of the value that it can afford him.

---

82. Metlitzki, 274.

83. This passage from Petrus Bonus is quoted from Holmyard, p. 140.

The Yeoman does not see that the authorities whom he cites point to the spiritual nature of the quest and to the redemption that, within a Christian cosmology, is the highest form of transformation available to man. The sources which could delineate a realm of spiritual possibility instead, he believes, warn him of materialistic impossibility. The sources which should direct him to his own transformation become instead an obfuscating force that brings him, he believes, his own devaluation. The philosophers should be a repository of hope and encouragement which would transmute the alchemical quest for the Yeoman. Instead, they spell failure to him because he reads them according to his own limited interpretation.

The Yeoman has been wasted by the alchemical quest because he does not see that success lies, not in the attainment of gold, but in the seeking and in the self-transformation that the quest entails. The Canon's Yeoman, as the concluding lines of his Tale indicate, is aware of alchemy's dependence upon the divine will. Yet he chooses to see this dependence as the final cause of his own failure and powerlessness, of his own victimization by the external world. And within this attitude lies the cause of the Canon's Yeoman's own devaluation, both as an alchemist and as a man. A passage from the Latin Geber summarizes the reasons for his failure:

> Our Art is reserved in the Divine Will of God, and is given to, or withheld from, whom he will; who is glorious, sublime, and full of all Justice and Goodness. And perhaps, for the punishment of your sophistical work [i.e., work directed solely toward material transformation], he denies you the Art, and lamentably thrusts you into the by-path of error, and from your error into perpetual infelicity and misery: because he is most miserable and unhappy, to whom (after the end of his work and labor) God denies the sight of the Truth. For such a man is constituted in perpetual

labor, beset with all misfortune and infelicity, loseth
the consolation, joy, and delight of his whole time, and
consumeth his life in grief without profit.[84]

All that the Canon's Yeoman has left is his empty wallet, his emptied spirit, and a sense of his own powerlessness. And, as his Prologue and Tale suggest, he has language with which he can express the
emptiness caused by alchemy. If, as some critics suggest, the Yeoman
is going straight, if he has seen his own limitations and the possibility of redemption amidst the pilgrims on the road to Canterbury, then
his language should express this transformation of attitude. But, as I
have argued, language is yet another instrument that fails the Yeoman.
The language of his Tale, which should effect or at least signify the
approach of his spiritual transformation, only ends by underlining his
ambivalence. Moreover, within his Tale, the Yeoman not only adopts
various strategies in order to resolve his ambivalence. He also adopts
and adapts various literary genres in his attempts to convince his audience and himself of his bitterness and of his rejection of alchemy's
deceptiveness. Just as he exhausted his material and intellectual resources in the alchemical quest, so too, in his Tale, he exhausts his
linguistic and artistic resources without reaching his "conclusioun."

Chaucer uses a change of genres to underline a transformation of
ethical values in the poetic unit formed by The Wife of Bath's Prologue
and Tale. The Wife of Bath's Prologue, although confessional in form
and delivered ostensibly, in response to the Pardoner's request, as a
sermon on love, reads like a fabliau in its attention to detail, to

---

84. This passage from the Latin Geber is quoted from Holmyard,
p. 154.

deception, to love and lust and rapid-fire movement. The fabliau of
her Prologue is a bourgeois woman's representation of her commercially
dominated world. But, as I discussed in Chapter II, Alison demonstrates her own capacity for change and moral growth in the romance
which she chooses as her tale. In addition, Alison's Tale underlines
Chaucer's transformation of genres to serve his own thematic and artistic purposes. Chaucer parodies the romance throughout The Canterbury
Tales, in The Miller's Tale, The Nun's Priest's Tale, and The Tale of
Sir Thopas, for example. These parodies (many of them found within
fabliaux) may be read as a bourgeois response to an aristocratic literature whose values are at variance with its own social and economic
concerns. Yet Chaucer's use of romance in relation to the bourgeois
Wife of Bath is not parodic; the poet and his character present the
conventional apparatus of romance uncritically: the testing, the
quest, and, at the conclusion of the quest, the attainment of greater
moral awareness.[85] Nonetheless, in her Tale, The Wife of Bath has re-
valued the conventional elements of romance, or, more specifically,
Chaucer has adapted them, to express the needs, values, and vision of
a bourgeois woman. Even if Alison retains the courtly setting for her
romance, her own bourgeois consciousness emerges from behind the tale's
setting and its characters to present the values of the woman whose
history we have just heard. Yet, in The Wife of Bath's Tale, Chaucer
has not only adopted and adapted the content of the conventional

----

    85. My discussion of the structure of romance relies on Northrop
Frye's "The Mythos of Summer: Romance," in Anatomy of Criticism: Four
Essays (Princeton: Princeton Univ. Press, 1973), pp. 186-206.

romance to suit his uncourtly character. He has presented a romance whose ethical themes--the importance of intrinsic worth and the value of reciprocity--transcend Alison's social class or commercial mentality.

The Canon's Yeoman also uses a change of genres to organize the content of his Tale, but the progression of these genres does not correspond to a transformation of values, to a movement toward the enlightenment evident in The Wife of Bath's Prologue and Tale. In The Canon's Yeoman's Tale, the generic movement is, in fact, a mirror image of that found in The Wife of Bath's Prologue and Tale. If she progresses from citations of authority through fabliau to romance, the Canon's Yeoman moves from romance to fabliau to citations of authority. By the end of his Tale, the Yeoman not only fails to affirm a more personally and spiritually satisfying system of values. The citations from the philosophers which should attest to his enlightenment end by emphasizing the absence of ethical transformation. For the Yeoman, the progression from romance to fabliau to allegory underlines a movement from a genre in which value is sought to one in which it is lost to one in which it is hidden and therefore inaccessible.

Throughout this chapter, I have referred to the alchemical enterprise as a "quest," a term which I have used to indicate the search attendant upon alchemy. I would like to define the alchemical "quest" more specifically, that is, in relation to romance and to the quests which structure medieval romance. Donald Howard and Winthrop Wetherbee have noted that, in The Canon's Yeoman's Tale, alchemy is a paradigm for the process of intellectual questing.[86] Other critics of the tale

have alluded to the structural similarities between the alchemical en-

terprise and the quest romance, specifically the Grail romance.[87] The

parallels between the esoteric alchemical quest and the Grail romances

can provide an illuminating context in which to place Chaucer's trans-

formations of the romance in the "Prima "Pars" of The Canon's Yeoman's

Tale.[88]

Within the tradition of the Grail romances as within the tradition

of esoteric alchemy, the questers after the Grail or the Philosopher's

Stone needed to possess certain virtues in order to succeed. Faith,

patience, perseverance, and a lack of attachment to worldly goods were

required of both alchemists and knights.[89] Those who sought the Grail

86. Donald Howard, p. 298. Winthrop Wetherbee, "Some Intellectual Themes in Chaucer's Poetry," Geoffrey Chaucer, ed. George D.
Economou (New York: McGraw-Hill Book Co., 1975), p. 90.

87. Although critics have mentioned the romance structure of the
alchemical quest, they have not presented a full discussion of its significance in relation to the Tale's themes or the characterization of
the Yeoman and his Canon. See Reidy, 34 and Rosenberg, 568. Judith
Herz discusses the stylistic elements of romance found in the Tale,
but compares alchemy not to a Grail quest but to a courtly love romance
in which alchemy becomes the elusive mistress (233-35).

88. Northrop Frye associates the quest with alchemy in his discussion of The Faerie Queene: "St. George's emblem is a red cross on
a white ground, which is the flag borne by Christ in traditional
iconography when he returns in triumph from the prostrate dragon in
hell. The red and white symbolize the two aspects of the risen body,
flesh and blood, bread and wine. . . . The link between the sacramental
and the sexual aspects of the red and white symbolism is indicated in
alchemy, with which Spenser was clearly acquainted, in which a crucial
phase of the production of the elixir of immortality is known as the
union of the red king and the white queen" (p. 195).

89. Roger Sherman Loomis discusses the virtues required of the
Grail knights in his interpretation of the Queste del Saint Graal in
The Grail From Celtic Myth to Christian Symbol (New York: Columbia

or the Stone must either be spiritual paragons or they must struggle
to attain the appropriate state of perfection in the course of their
quest. Moreover, as the alchemical treatises and the Grail romances
make clear, both the alchemists and the knights of Arthur's court
needed courage to confront the intractability and the obscurity of the
world around them. Both needed the wisdom and the faith to interpret
their experience and to ask the right questions of it.[90] In fact, in
some versions of the Grail quest, the failure to speak and to ask the
right questions blights the Fisher-King's lands. (The Canon's Yeoman's
failure to ask the right questions of the alchemical authorities produces the blight which besets his experience.) The man who succeeded
in either quest was able to transform value, to restore abundance, to
accomplish redemption. The Grail knight would restore to the Fisher-
King not only the fertility of his land; he would also restore the
Fisher-King's youth and vitality after the latter had received a cas-
trating wound.[91] The esoteric alchemist also performed an act of redemptive transformation. He released the perfection inherent in base
metals; he transformed the dross of the world around him into abundance, into value.[92] Moreover, both the Grail romances and the alchemical treatises described their redemptive processes in figures

---

Univ. Press, 1963), pp. 183-84.

90. Jessie L. Weston examines the importance of the hero's question and its relationship to the Grail quest in Chapter II, "The Task
of the Hero," From Ritual to Romance (Garden City, N.Y.: Doubleday and
Co., 1957), pp. 12-24.

91. Weston, pp. 12-24.

92. Hutin, p. 84.

associated with marriage, sexuality, and fertility.[93] If the Grail
knight restored fertility to the king and his kingdom, the alchemist,
as he himself described it, performed a marriage of the elements whose
fruitfulness gave yet another meaning to the term "multiplicacioun."[94]
Both the knight and the alchemist, then, were sources of creativity in
the worlds in which they accomplished their quests. Moreover, in the
process of restoring abundance to the world around them, both would
accomplish their own spiritual perfection and redemption.

The parallels between alchemy and the Grail romances extend to
the objects of their respective quests. Both the Philosopher's Stone
and the Grail possessed the capacity to effect a redemptive transformation. The Grail, whether it assumed the form of a plate or of a
chalice (reminiscent, of course, of the chalice of the Last Supper and
thought by some to be identical to it), was a source of nourishment as
it fed the company in the Fisher-King's hall or served as a receptacle
for the eucharist, the only food of the Fisher-King.[95] The Grail sig-

---

93. For these motifs in the Grail romances, see Weston, pp. 12-24
and Chapter IX, "The Fisher-King," pp. 113-36. Bruce Rosenberg gives
a brief description of these motifs in relation to alchemy: ". . .
what the experiment involved was a conjunction of opposites: male and
female, fire and water, sun and moon, spirit and body. This will produce the stone. Norton, Ripley, and Flamel stated that the stone was
the product of the union of masculine and feminine elements. Many of
the other alchemical workers speak of a brother-sister duality who must
unite sexually to produce the lapis. Arisleus tells the parable of an
old impotent king (the Fisher-King?) whose lands are sterile and who
cannot save himself or his country until his son and daughter cohabit"
(p. 568). For further discussion of the Arisleus parable, see Metlitzki, pp. 265-67.

94. Rosenberg, p. 568.

95. Loomis offers a summary of the various forms that the Grail
could assume in romance on p. 223 of The Grail from Celtic Myth to

nified abundance and sustenance for all of men's needs or desires.[96]

Interestingly, in Wolfram von Eschenbach's Parzival, the Grail is de-scribed, not as a chalice or a plate, but as a stone with the power to sustain and to restore life.[97] Of course, the Philosopher's Stone was no more a stone than was the Grail. It was a compound which, when manufactured after a long and arduous search for the correct procedures, could effect transmutation.[98] It, like the Grail, was a source of abundance capable of satisfying all of man's needs. In addition, it is important to note that the Philosopher's Stone, "elixer clept" (VIII. G, 810), was not only able to transmute base metals into gold. Known as the Fountain of Youth and the Elixir of Life, it was also con-sidered capable of prolonging life, restoring youth, and healing any disease despite its seriousness or duration.[99] I am not suggesting that the Philosopher's Stone was identical with the Holy Grail. I underline the similarities in their powers in order to emphasize the fundamentally romantic nature of the alchemical enterprise. By now it

---

Christian Symbol.

96. Ibid., pp. 183-84.

97. Ibid., p. 207.

98. Ideas about the components of the Philosopher's Stone changed throughout the Middle Ages. The earlier belief that it was formed by combining quicksilver and sulphur with silver or gold gave way to the idea that mercury alone, in conjunction with silver or gold, could pro-duce the elixir. Thorndike discusses this change in relation to John Dastin's writings, Vol. III, p. 86.

99. Thorndike, Vol. III, p. 87; Sadoul, pp. 57-58. Sadoul ar-gues that the major reason for the adepts' involvement with alchemy was their interest not in gold, but in the elixir as the Fountain of Youth.

is a commonplace in the study of romance to point to its archetypal
structure. Within this frame of reference, the goals of both the alchemical and the Grail quests would allow men to answer their deepest
fears and desires: the desire for unlimited abundance and immortality
and the desire to possess a transforming power over the external world.

The similarities between the Grail romance and the alchemical
quest provide a context within which to assess the Yeoman's rendering
of the alchemical romance in the "Prima Pars" of his Tale. As Judith
Herz has pointed out, conventional stylistic features of romance recur
throughout The Canon's Yeoman's Tale: in his descriptions of the Canon
as his "lord," in the long catalogues of elements and procedures, in the
comparisons which he chooses to describe the priest's happiness in the
"Secunda Pars."[100] But in the "Prima Pars" of the Yeoman's Tale,
Chaucer has once again transformed the content and the structure of
romance to fit a bourgeois character and his materialistic concerns.
As the romance of the "Prima Pars" progresses towards the climactic
confrontation in the laboratory, the Yeoman's bourgeois impatience
with the individual's powerlessness over the material world is antithetical to the perseverance of the true alchemist or of the Grail
knight. His engagement with the physicality of his craft, with practice rather than with theory, reflects the materialistic orientation
of his own values. Although the "Prima Pars" of The Canon's Yeoman's
Tale presents his own version of the alchemical romance, it does not
conclude with the attainment of value. Rather, it ends with the explo-

----

100. Herz, 233-35.

sion in the laboratory that replaces the desired transformation with yet another loss of material goods.

Absent from the Yeoman's bourgeois alchemical romance is an awareness of or appreciation for the spirituality that should accompany the pursuit of the Philosopher's Stone just as it accompanies the search for the Grail. This spirituality is necessary to accommodate the hardship endemic to both quests, a hardship that constitutes a testing and perfecting of the self. Absent, too, from the Yeoman's response to alchemy is his master's patience. The bourgeois romance of the "Prima Pars" fails to offer a movement toward ethical or spiritual value because the only augmentation of value that the Yeoman seeks is material. The Yeoman's definition of the alchemical quest is material and intellectual, rather than intellectual and spiritual; it is focused on the elements of and the values inherent within the circumambient world. The "Prima Pars" of his Tale not only undercuts the movement of romance toward value by emphasizing the Yeoman's lament over the material failure of the quest. I would suggest that the bourgeois romance of the "Prima Pars" is, in fact, an anti-romance, not so much because it presents a quest for material rather than spiritual value, for gold rather than God.[101] The Yeoman's romance is, essentially, an anti-romance because it ends by denying value: the value of the quest, of language, of wisdom, of intellectual endeavor.

Unlike the Wife of Bath's romance which affirms the presence of

---

101. Bruce L. Grenberg, in "The Canon's Yeoman's Tale: Boethian Wisdom and the Alchemists," 37-54, discusses the tension between worldly goods and spiritual Good in the Tale. See especially, 54.

value beneath the most unlikely surfaces and, by extension, the intrinsic worth of the things of this world, the closing lines of the "Prima
Pars" suggest valuelessness, that is, the absence of value beneath even
the most likely surfaces. Whereas the Wife of Bath's romance reinvests
the world of her Tale with value--with magic, love, reciprocity, and
beauty--the Canon's Yeoman's anti-romance empties the world of value
because alchemy has emptied his purse. The end of the alchemical
romance of the "Prima Pars" posits valuelessness because the world has
failed to yield the Yeoman an abundance of value and because it has
failed to accommodate itself to the demands of his imagination.

The Canon's Yeoman's portrayal of valuelessness and his impulse
to empty the world of value to avenge himself for his own impoverish-
ment continues in the "Secunda Pars" of his Tale. Although I have discussed Chaucer's selection of a fabliau for the Canon's Yeoman's story,
it is important to consider the fabliau in relation to the anti-romance
which has preceded it. The alchemical romance of the "Prima Pars"
should have ended by affirming value; instead, it becomes transformed
into a fabliau, into a genre whose purpose is to celebrate trickery,
deception, and wiliness. The fabliau of the "Secunda Pars" follows the
program of devaluation that the Yeoman established at the end of the
"Prima Pars." Within the story of the canon and the priest, the quest
for the Philosopher's Stone and the intellectual and spiritual commitment that should attend it are emptied of value as they are transformed
into cunning and avarice. In the fabliau, reward, defined solely in
materialistic terms, has ceased to encompass the gratification of an
intellectual and spiritual quest. Read as the conclusion of the alchem-

ical quest described in the "Prima Pars," the fabliau underlines valuelessness in its presentation of a counterfeit alchemy whose surface camouflages an absence of intrinsic worth. Ironically, the second canon does produce genuine silver; but he can produce value only because it was there in the first place. Intellectual questing, as the Yeoman implies, cannot discover value. It can, however, produce a trickery and deceit which perverts value. In addition, the "Secunda Pars" underlines the strength of human gullibility, in itself a perversion of the faith necessary to the alchemical quest. The Yeoman's fabliau, I would argue, is the only sequel available to him after the anti-romance of the "Prima Pars." Chaucer has performed his own transformation of genres to underline the consequences of his narrator's ambivalence.

Before he presents his quotations from the philosophers, the Canon's Yeoman offers his explanation for the current paucity of gold, attributing it, of course, to alchemy:

> Considereth, sires, how that, in ech estaat,
> Bitwixe men and gold ther is debaat
> So ferforth that unnethes is ther noon.
> This multiplying blent so many oon
> That in good feith I trowe that it bee
> The cause grettest of swich scarsetee.
> (VIII. G, 1388-93)[102]

The irony within these lines is, in part, intentional; the Yeoman is once again emphasizing the loss attendant upon "this multiplying." But there is another irony at work here which the Canon's Yeoman does not acknowledge: an economic irony that may explain, at least in part,

---

102. Hartung, 121.

the alchemists' desire to maintain the secrecy of their trade. In his quest for an unlimited supply of gold, the Canon's Yeoman does not see that, according to the materialistic terms in which he defines alchemy, the success of his enterprise would lessen the value of his goal. The growing scarcity of gold (which, he believes, is caused by his craft) increases the value of gold and therefore the energy and commitment with which he seeks it. According to the Yeoman's explanation of the gold shortage, alchemy would create rather than destroy value by creating a demand for the material that it consumes. As the Wife of Bath knows, supply and demand, inopia and copia, influence both the market price of goods and the customer's desire for them. Scarcity raises value; abundance diminishes it. If gold were as plentiful as lead, it might well have the value of lead. Whether or not the Canon's Yeoman finds the Philosopher's Stone, the quest for value, as he defines it, can only produce valuelessness, in both Christian ethical and in economic terms.

The development of genres within The Canon's Yeoman's Tale concludes, of course, with the Yeoman's citation of alchemical authorities and with his emphasis on the mystification caused by their allegorical language. I have discussed the ways in which the Yeoman's response to these authorities reveals his own interpretative limitations and his failure to transform alchemy into a spiritual quest. That Chaucer concludes the Tale with the Yeoman's citation of authorities is central to his characterization of the Yeoman. The Wife of Bath began her Prologue by quiting auctoritee and by revaluing it on the basis of her own experience. For her, authority exists to be interpreted. The

Canon's Yeoman's reading of authorities is diametrically opposed to
that of the Wife of Bath.[103] He accepts the limitations which authority would place upon him. The Canon's Yeoman's refusal to interpret
allegory constitutes a refusal to see beyond surfaces, a refusal to
look for meaning unless the surface readily yields meaning to him.
His interpretations are limited by his belief that surfaces are either
deceptive or illegible. For the Yeoman, the allegory of the philosophers represents neither our ability to interpret nor the necessity
of interpreting in order to discover meaning. Allegory, as the Yeoman
reads it, is a linguistic analogue to the intractability of his science
and of the material world. Like alchemy, allegory promises a meaning
that it ultimately denies the Yeoman.

Throughout his Tale, the Yeoman struggles to resolve ambivalence,
not by interpreting it, but by placing a reductive definition upon it.
By denying the value of alchemy, of wisdom, of language, the Canon's
Yeoman denies intellectually and psychologically what his experience
has shown him: that the world is multivalent, that answers do not come
easily, that we need to interpret in order to find meaning. Interestingly, the Canon's Yeoman resembles, in his mode of interpretation and
in his relationship to reality, a disenchanted counterpart of the pilgrim-Chaucer.[104] They are, as it were, obverse sides of the coin of

103. Lawler presents another interpretation of the Yeoman's acceptance of the limitations of authority, pp. 133-34.

104. My interpretation of the pilgrim-Chaucer's character is
based on E. Talbot Donaldson's discussion, "Chaucer the Pilgrim,"
Speaking of Chaucer (New York: W. W. Norton and Company, 1970), pp. 1-
12.

one interpretative personality. The Canon's Yeoman apologizes for
being unable to list his elements in order and he attributes this
failure to his "lewednesse":

> Ther is also ful many another thyng
> That is unto oure craft apertenyng.
> Thogh I by ordre hem nat reherce kan,
> By cause that I am a lewed man,
> Yet wol I telle hem as they come to mynde,
> Thogh I ne kan nat sette hem in hir kynde . . .
> (VIII. G, 784-89)

In the General Prologue to The Canterbury Tales, the pilgrim-narrator
offers a similar apology, and for a similar reason. The pilgrim-narrator fails to order the elements within his Prologue because of his
own "lewednesse":

> Also I prey yow to foryeve it me,
> Al have I nat set folk in hir degree
> Heere in this tale, as that they sholde stonde.
> My wit is short, ye may wel understonde.
> (I. A, 743-46)

The Canon's Yeoman's catalogues, as I have discussed, point to the vascillation within his own consciousness as he confronts the materiality
of alchemy that has both obsessed and thwarted him. Similarly, the
pilgrim-Chaucer's presentation of portraits within the General Prologue
reflects a consciousness fascinated with surfaces, with the materiality
of the world around him.

Both the Canon's Yeoman and the pilgrim-Chaucer admit to and display a professional incompetence rare among the Canterbury pilgrims.
Their inability to order the elements of the world around them reflects
their inability to interpret the meaning and value of these elements:
no minor deficiency in either an artist or an alchemist. In both cases,
incompetence derives from a reductive response to ambivalence, both

within the self and within the external world. The way in which the
pilgrim-Chaucer interprets ambivalence is apparent in his evaluations
of the pilgrims in the General Prologue. His response to the Prioress
is a classic example of his interpretative difficulties. Although the
Prioress's behavior and costume do not correspond to the piety incum-
bent upon her occupation, the pilgrim-Chaucer does not address this
incongruity. He is willing to judge a character's moral value on the
basis of external attractiveness. He is willing to believe that surfaces indicate value, just as he is willing to believe that the word
is cousin to the deed. The pilgrim-Chaucer's evaluations are accurate
only if, by chance, surface correlates with substance (which it seldom
does in the world of The Tales). In the end, the pilgrim-Chaucer responds to ambivalence by denying it, by finding intrinsic worth in
nearly all of his companions. His denial of ambivalence produces the
lack of discrimination apparent in his first contribution to the story-
telling competition. The pilgrim-Chaucer, who finds value in everything, cannot understand the Host's reaction to The Tale of Sir Thopas.

In his attempt to resolve his own ambivalence toward alchemy, the
Canon's Yeoman also denies it, but he does so by adopting the opposite
strategy from that of the pilgrim-Chaucer. The Yeoman denies value.
Through his presentation of the fraud of the "Secunda Pars," he attempts to impose a condemnation on alchemy and alchemists which would
eliminate the need to make discriminations of value. The intractability of the external world has thwarted the Yeoman. He, unlike the
pilgrim-Chaucer, has learned that surfaces do not always yield the
value that we would project upon them. Yet his experience has not

taught the Yeoman the necessity of interpreting rather than denying

ambivalence in order to discover meaning and value. Instead, his

frustration inverts the manner in which he reads surfaces without

bringing him closer to an ability to interpret them. The Yeoman's

dismissal of surfaces as deceptive or obfuscating is as reductive as

the pilgrim-Chaucer's belief that surface correlates with, that it

reveals substance, that all that glitters is gold.

The pilgrim-narrator is present throughout The Canon's Yeoman's

Prologue, providing information, responding and reacting to the ap-

pearance of the newcomers, attempting to interpret them. We are con-

scious of his presence for the first time since he embarassed himself

in the story-telling competition. The interruption of the newcomers

necessitates the re-emergence of the pilgrim-narrator as he tries to

incorporate them into the gallery of portraits which he offered in the

General Prologue. The pilgrim-narrator's response to the Canon and

his Yeoman shows that he has not been transformed on the way to Canter-

bury. He still believes that surfaces are trustworthy indices of

character. He is delighted with the sweat, the haste, and the ragged

clothing; he has trouble deciding what the Canon is. He tells us that

the Canon eavesdrops because he is guilty. The reappearance of the

pilgrim-narrator at this juncture of The Canterbury Tales underlines

his resemblance to the Canon's Yeoman, and that resemblance is signifi-

cant. The pilgrim-narrator, who "'semeth elvyssh by his contenaunce'"

(VII. 703) is the interpretative alter ego of the practitioner of "oure

elvysshe craft" (VIII. G, 751). Nowhere else in The Canterbury Tales

does Chaucer use the word "elvyssh," a word connoting mysteriousness and elusiveness. It is significant, I believe, that he underlines the connection between his poet-surrogate and the Yeoman, between poetry and alchemy, through the repetition of this word in The Canon's Yeoman's Tale. Alchemy, its concern with intrinsic worth and its unstable referentiality, resembles Chaucer's own poetry. Chaucer, of course, is more adept at interpretation and more conscious of the implications of trusting surfaces than either his Yeoman or his pilgrim-surrogate. But, as I will discuss in the Epilogue, The Canon's Yeoman's Tale underlines an ambivalence not only toward alchemy, but toward his own art that grows throughout the remaining Canterbury Tales until Chaucer attempts to resolve his ambivalence in his Retraction.

Epilogue

CHAUCER'S POETIC ALCHEMY AND THE TRANSFORMATION
OF THE CANTERBURY TALES

Alchemy, its goals, and its representation in The Canon's Yeoman's Prologue and Tale provide a means of understanding Chaucer's poetic interests as well as the transformation that The Canterbury Tales themselves undergo after the interruption of the pilgrimage by the Canon and his Yeoman. Within the Yeoman's Prologue and Tale, the preoccupation with testing and preef, whether of the first Canon's wisdom or of the second canon's gold, raises the question of authenticity in relation to intellectual endeavor. It is a question which, I would suggest, became increasingly important to Chaucer as he approached the end of his last poetic enterprise. The Retraction states explicitly what The Canon's Yeoman's Prologue and Tale imply: that, as he approached the end of The Canterbury Tales, Chaucer was not only ambivalent toward the efficacy of intellectual endeavor in general, but toward the subject and purpose of The Canterbury Tales in particular.[1] For the medieval poet, however, reservations about the authenticity and the intrinsic value of his own art did not indicate a crisis of poetic identity

---

1. Robert B. Burlin, Chaucerian Fiction (Princeton: Princeton Univ. Press, 1977), pp. 242-43, presents a discussion of Chaucer's ambivalence toward his own poetry at the end of The Canterbury Tales which resembles my own, but which does not place that ambivalence within the context of Chaucer's exploration of value throughout The Canterbury Tales.

that can be evaluated in solely personal terms. These reservations

and the ambivalence that they produced were inherent in medieval atti-

tudes toward art itself, toward a human endeavor that Jean de Meun

chose to describe in relation to coining, counterfeiting, and alchemy.

Art, like alchemy, evoked ambivalence throughout the Middle Ages be-

cause both sought, through the mediation of human intellectual and

creative effort, to reveal the intrinsic worth, the meaning that re-

sided within the phenomena of the sublunary world.[2]

Two medieval discussions of poetry, one from the thirteenth and

one from the fourteenth century, represent the conflicting perceptions

of poetry, its power, and its purposes during the late Middle Ages.

Moreover, these discussions, from Boccaccio's Defense of Poetry and

from Jean de Meun's continuation of the Roman de la Rose, approach

their topic in terms appropriate to Chaucer's thematic and artistic

concerns in The Canterbury Tales. The more affirmative of these dis-

cussions, the one, that is, more cognizant of the autonomy of artistic

creativity and of the integrity of art, appears in Boccaccio's Defense

of Poetry. Boccaccio writes:

> This poetry, which ignorant triflers cast aside, is a sort
> of fervid and exquisite invention, with fervid expression,
> in speech or writing, of that which the mind has invented.
> It proceeds from the bosom of God, and few, I find, are the
> souls in whom this gift is born . . . This fervor of poesy
> is sublime in its effect: it impels the soul to a longing
> for utterance; it brings forth strange and unheard-of

2. See Winthrop Wetherbee, Platonism and Poetry in the Twelfth Century: The Literary Influence of the School of Chartres (Princeton: Princeton Univ. Press, 1972), pp. 49ff., 152ff., 255ff. See also Wetherbee's article, "The Function of Poetry in the 'De Planctu Naturae' of Alain of Lille," Traditio, 25 (1969), 87-125 for a discussion of the background of late medieval attitudes toward poetry.

creations of the mind; it arranges these meditations in a
fixed order, adorns the whole composition with unusual
interweaving of words and thoughts; and thus it veils truth
in a fair and fitting garment of fiction. Further, if in
any case the invention so requires, it can arm kings, marshall them to war, launch whole fleets from their docks,
nay, counterfeit sky, land, sea, adorn young maidens with
flowery garlands, portray human character in its phases,
awake the idle, stimulate the dull, restrain the rash, subdue
the criminal, and distinguish excellent men with their proper
meed of praise . . .[3]

And Boccaccio concludes his exaltation of poetry with a quotation from

Cicero:

He says: "And yet we have it on the highest and most learned
authority, that while other arts are matters of science and
formula and technique, poetry depends solely upon an inborn
faculty, is evoked by a purely mental activity, and is in-
fused with a strange supernal inspiration."[4]

Not only does Boccaccio's description of poetry emphasize the power of

invention with which the poetic mind is endowed. His quotation from

Cicero describes the poet in terms appropriate to the esoteric alchem-

ist who devotes himself to an art surpassing all others because it is

sanctioned by divine inspiration. It is within the poet's power, Boc-

caccio believes, to create, or rather, to recreate the world by repre-

senting its diversity and multiplicity. Chaucer himself has, of course,

shown his awareness of this power as he exercises it throughout The

Canterbury Tales. Moreover, Boccaccio's poet has the ability to impose

an imaginative and artistic order upon his representations and, in his

---

3. The passage from Boccaccio's Defense of Poetry is quoted from
Robert P. Miller's edition, Chaucer: Sources and Backgrounds (New York:
Oxford Univ. Press, 1977), pp. 89-90. The passage, from The Defense
of Poetry, XIV, 7, is presented in Charles G. Osgood's translation.

4. Ibid., pp. 89-90.

systems of ordering, to transform the value of the world that he has
represented: "to awake the idle, stimulate the dull . . . and distinguish excellent men with their proper meed of praise. . . ." Moreover, the poet can communicate his ordering, his valuation of the
world, in a language which itself transforms by adorning: "Such then
is the power of fiction that it pleases the unlearned by its external
appearance, and exercises the minds of the learned with its hidden
truth. . . ."[5] In its purposes, the language of the poet is thus identical with the language of the alchemist, for both draw the learned to
a quest for the value hidden beneath surface forms. In its ability to
represent a world, poetry has, for Boccaccio, a power analogous to that
of the Philosopher's Stone, as Petrus Bonus describes it:

> Our Stone, from its all-comprehensive nature, may be compared
> to all things in the world. In its origin and sublimation,
> and in the conjunction of its elements, there are analogies
> to things heavenly, earthly, and infernal, to the corporeal
> and the incorporeal, to things corruptible and incorruptible,
> visible and invisible, to spirit, soul, and body, and their
> union and separation, to the creation of the world, its ele-
> ments and their qualities, to all animals and vegetables and
> minerals . . . to life and death, to virtues and vices, to
> unity and multitude, to actuality and potentiality, to con-
> ception and birth, to male and female, to boy and old man
> . . . to the beauty of Paradise, to the terrors of the infer-
> nal abyss.[6]

If the Philosopher's Stone can be compared to and can thus represent
all things in the universe, then poetry, for Boccaccio, has the same
powers of representation.

---

5. Ibid., Defense of Poetry (XIV, 9), p. 87.

6. This passage from Petrus Bonus is quoted from Joseph Grennen,
"The Canon's Yeoman and the Cosmic Furnace: Language and Meaning in the
'Canon's Yeoman's Tale,'" Criticism, 4 (1962), 233-34.

In the <u>Roman de la Rose</u>, Jean de Meun describes, in a catalogue
similar to that of Boccaccio in <u>The Defense of Poetry</u>, the multiplicity
and diversity that art can present and represent. Jean de Meun writes
that Art attempts

> de fere choses, quex qu'el saient,
> quelques figures qu'eles aient,
> paigne, taigne, forge ou antaille
> chevaliers armez en bataille
> seurs biaus destriers tretouz coverz
> d'armes indes, jaunes ou verz,
> ou d'autres couleurs piolez
> se plus pioler les volez,
> biaus oisillons en verz boissons,
> de toutes eves les poissons,
> tretoutes les bestes sauvages
> qui pasturent par leur boschages,
> toutes herbes, toutes floretes
> que valletons et puceletes
> vont an printans es gauz cueillir,
> que florir voient et fueillir,
> oiseaus privez, bestes domesches,
> baleries, dances et tresches
> de beles dames bien parees,
> bien portretes, bien figurees,
> soit en metaill, en fust, en cire,
> soit en quelconque autre matire,
> soit en tableaus, soit en paraiz,
> tenanz biaus bachelers a raiz,
> bien figurez et bien portrez . . . .

> (. . . with great study and effort, to make anything what-
> ever, no matter what shapes they have--whether she paints,
> dyes, forges, or shapes armed knights in battle, on handsome
> chargers all covered with arms, and worked in blue, yellow,
> or green or variegated with other colors if you want to mix
> them; or beautiful birds in green groves; or the fishes of
> all waters; all the wild beasts that feed in their woods;
> all plants, all the flowers that little boys and girls go to
> gather in the spring woods when they see them in bloom and
> leaf; tame birds and domestic animals; balls, dances, and
> farandoles with beautiful and elegantly dressed ladies, well
> portrayed and well represented, either in metal, wood, wax,
> or any other material, in pictures or on walls, with the
> ladies holding handsome bachelors, also well represented and
> portrayed, in their nets . . . .)[7]

---

7. Jean de Meun, <u>Le Roman de la Rose</u>, ed. Felix Lecoy, II (Paris:

But in the lines that precede this catalogue of Art's multifarious accomplishments, Jean de Meun significantly undermines the artist's creative achievement. His description of artistic endeavor begins by emphasizing its secondariness in relation to Nature's creativity. He writes of Nature:

> Quant autre conseill n'i peut metre,
> si taille anpraintes de tel letre
> qu'el leur doune fourmes veroies
> an quoinz de diverses monoies,
> don Art fesoit ses examplaires,
> qui ne fet pas fourmes si vaires;
> mes par mout antantive cure
> a genouz est devant Nature,
> si prie et requiert et demande,
> comme mandianz et truande,
> povre de sciance et de force,
> qui d'ansivre la mout s'efforce,
> que Nature li veille aprandre
> conment ele puisse conprandre
> par son angin an es figures
> proprement toutes creatures;
> si garde conment Nature euvre,
> car mout voudroit fere autele euvre,
> et la contrefet conme singes;
> mes tant est ses sens nus et linges
> qu'el ne peut fere choses vives,
> ja si ne sembleront naives.
>
> (15983-16004; emphasis mine)

(When she can bring no other counsel to her work, she cuts copies in such letters that she gives them true forms in coins of different monies. From these, Art makes her models, but she does not make her forms as true. However, with very attentive care, she kneels before Nature and like a truant beggar, poor in knowledge and force, she begs and requests and asks of her. She struggles to follow her so that Nature may wish to teach her how with her ability she may properly

---

Librairie Honoré Champion, 1965), 16007-31). The translation is taken from Charles Dahlberg's English language version, The Romance of the Rose (Princeton: Princeton Univ. Press, 1971), p. 272. Throughout this epilogue, I refer to the Lecoy edition and the Dahlberg translation. Quotations from the Roman will be cited within the body of the text by line number for the French and by page number for the translation.

subsume all creatures in her figures. She also watches how
Nature works, and she imitates her like a monkey. But her
sense is so bare and feeble that she cannot make living
things, no matter how newborn they seem.--pp. 271-72)

Art, then, in the Roman de la Rose, is not only a futile enterprise

that produces poor imitations. The economic tropes within this passage

underline the absence of value within artistic creations. If Nature is

a coiner of species within the sublunary world, then Art is a counter-

feiter who can produce only inauthentic works. Absent from Jean de

Meuns's passage is the idea, prominent in Boccaccio's Defense of

Poetry, that art is a divinely inspired invention of the human mind.

In the Roman de la Rose, Art is dependent, not upon God's influence or

desire to inspire Art's efforts, but upon Nature's tutelage, to which

she is an incompetent pupil.[8]

Chaucer was, of course, familiar with the Roman de la Rose. At

the beginning of his Physician's Tale, Nature presents a speech that

repeats the attitudes toward the relative worth of natural and human

creativity that Jean de Meun had presented:

"Lo! I, Nature,
Thus kan I forme and peynte a creature,
Whan that me list; who kan me countrefete?
. . . .
. . . for I dar wel seyn,
Apelles, Zanzis, sholde werche in veyn
Outher to grave, or peynte, or forge, or bete,
If they presumed me to countrefete.
For He that is the formere principal

---

8. The prototype for the presentation of Nature as coiner occurs
in its most influential form, of course, in Alan of Lille's De Planctu
Naturae. For a discussion of the development of the medieval concep-
tion of Nature, see George D. Economou, The Goddess Natura in Medieval
Literature (Cambridge: Harvard Univ. Press, 1972), especially pp. 58ff.
See also Wetherbee, Platonism and Poetry, pp. 188ff.

Hath maked me his vicaire general,
To forme and peynten erthely creaturis
Right as me list . . ."
                                    (VI. C, 11-21)[9]

Although traditional in its content, the speech of Chaucer's Nature is

interesting in its emphases. Because she addresses the audience di-

rectly, beginning her speech with an exclamation and challenging man

with the question "'who kan me countrefete?,'" Nature in The Physician's

Tale appears more powerful than she does in Chaucer's source. Although

she is God's "vicaire general" and He, "the formere principal," Nature

states twice that she works according to the dictates of her own will

("whan that me list"; "Right as me list"). The autonomy of her crea-

tive enterprise presents man as the only imitator within God's uni-

verse; only human art is secondary and inauthentic. Nature, as Chaucer

has presented her, defies imitation. For her, all human art is, of

necessity, futile and "countrefete" and therefore, presumptuous in its

very efforts to create.[10] There is no echo, in Nature's speech, of the

divine inspiration that Boccaccio had posited as the source of human

art.

     Nature's emphasis, in The Physician's Tale, upon the presumptuous-

---

     9. All quotations from The Canterbury Tales refer to the second
edition of F. N. Robinson's The Works of Geoffrey Chaucer (Boston:
Houghton Mifflin, 1957) and will be cited by fragment and line number
within the body of the text.

     10. Although "countrefete" can connote both "to imitate" and "to
counterfeit" (see A Chaucer Glossary, ed. Davis, Gray, Ingham, and
Wallace-Hadrill [Oxford:The Clarendon Press, 1979]), the economic
trope of Nature as coiner in Chaucer's source, Le Roman de la Rose,
suggest that we should keep both connotations in mind when reading
Chaucer's description of Nature.

ness of artistic endeavor and the counterfeits that it can produce makes it clear that, at the height of the Middle Ages, art, like economics, was a fundamentally ethical discipline.[11] If the merchant fell under the suspicion of immorality because he seduced or was seduced by man's natural inclination toward avarice, the artist was also subject to suspicion because he could tempt or be tempted by man's natural inclination toward pride. Art and commerce were thus susceptible to the two deadly sins that vied for pre-eminence in the fourteenth century.[12] The artist was subject to pride and presumption because, in his creations, he might attempt to rival or to usurp Nature's appointed position as vicar of God, as mediator between God and man. He might try to replace her order with his own. The artist would assume the role of Nature by stamping his own images upon the matter of the external world. According to Boccaccio, man's creativity and his prerogative to represent and to order the world through his art derives from God. But if, according to less laudatory appraisals of artistic endeavor, man was a counterfeiter, then he, unlike Nature did not coin divine ideas. Rather he minted the matter, the unrealities of his own imagination.

By applying the economic metaphors provided by the Roman de la Rose and The Physician's Tale to Chaucer's own art in The Canterbury

---

11. See the discussion of art as an ethical discipline in Judson B. Allen and Theresa Anne Moritz, A Distinction of Stories: The Medieval Unity of Chaucer's Fair Chain of Narratives for Canterbury (Columbus: Ohio State Univ. Press, 1981), pp. 65ff.

12. Morton W. Bloomfield, The Seven Deadly Sins: An Introduction to the History of a Religious Concept (Lansing: Michigan State Univ. Press, 1967), p. 95.

Tales, we not only gain an apprehension of Chaucer's poetic methods.

These metaphors also illuminate Chaucer's artistic interest in coining

and commerce and in the ethics of economic relationships throughout

The Canterbury Tales. Chaucer, as poet, would place the stamp of his

own imagination and of his interpretations upon the matter derived

from prior literary conventions. But, to continue the metaphor, Chau-

cer did not simply remint the old coins of prior traditions to provide

the currency of his own artistic economics, that is, the ycons of his

poetry. As I have discussed throughout the previous chapters, often,

when Chaucer adopts or adapts, he ends by making anew. He mints new

literary forms that represent the intrinsic worth of his own imagina-

tive vision. In the process, he creates new literary values. More-

over, The Canterbury Tales as a whole are not only an example of a new

literary form.[13] The subjects of many of his Tales also present new

substance. The Canterbury Tales reflect the social, ethical, and eco-

nomic transformations of Chaucer's late fourteenth-century world and,

in the process, they use the matter of that world as mintable species.

The poetry of The Canterbury Tales transforms Chaucer's world into art.

In the end, Chaucer is not simply the coiner/counterfeiter who risks

producing the poor imitations of reality that Nature derides. His own

artistic enterprise is more closely analogous to that of the alchemist

who, in many respects, bears the same relationship to the created world

as does the poet Chaucer. Interestingly, the role of Chaucer as al-

---

13. Robert Armstrong Pratt and Karl Young, "The Literary Framework of The Canterbury Tales," Sources and Analogues of Chaucer's Canterbury Tales, eds. W. F. Bryan and Germaine Dempster (New York:
Humanities Press, 1958), p. 33.

chemist is nowhere clearer than in the form and content of his tale on alchemy. Not only do The Canon's Yeoman's Prologue and Tale have no literary analogue. As E. Talbot Donaldson has noted, they transform, by their interruption of the pilgrimage, the form and value of Chaucer's own artistic project in The Canterbury Tales.[14]

The use of alchemy as an analogue to art has its place within the tradition of medieval attitudes toward art that I have outlined. Following the passage in the Roman de la Rose that figures Nature as coiner and Art as counterfeiter, Jean de Meun compares the respective powers of alchemy and art:

>   Ou d'alkemie tant apreigne
>   que touz metauz en couleur teigne,
>   qu'el se porroit ainceis tuer
>   que les especes transmuer,
>   se tant ne fet qu'el les ramaine
>   a leur matire prumeraine:
>   euvre tant conme ele vivra,
>   ja Nature n'aconsivra.
>   Et se tant se vouloit pener
>   qu'el les i seust ramener,
>   si li faudroit espoir sciance
>   de venir a cele atranpance,
>   quant el feroit son elixir,
>   don la fourme devroit issir
>   qui devise autr'eus leur sustances
>   par especiaus differances,
>   si conme il pert au defenir,
>   qui bien an set a chief venir.
>   Ne porquant, c'est chose notable,
>   alkimie est art veritable.
>   Qui sagement an ouverroit
>   granz merveilles i troverroit . . . .
>   (16035-56)

>   (She may learn so much about alchemy that she may dye all
>   the metals in color--for she could kill herself before she

---

14. E. Talbot Donaldson, Chaucer's Poetry: An Anthology for the Modern Reader (New York: The Ronald Press Company, 1958), p. 946.

could transmute the species, even if she didn't go to the
extent of taking them back to their prime matter--but she
may work as long as she lives and never catch up with Nature.
And if she did want to exert herself until she knew how to
take them back to it, she would still perhaps lack the knowledge of how, when she made her elixir, to arrive at that
suitable proportion of elements that should result in the
form, a proportion that distinguishes their substances among
themselves by their individual differences, just as, if one
knows how to arrive at a result, it appears in the definition.
   Nevertheless, it is a notable thing that alchemy is a true
art. Whoever worked wisely in it would find great miracles . . . .--p. 272)

In this passage, Jean de Meun's attitude toward alchemy and its effi-

cacy is unambivalent. Alchemy is an art that cannot only tinge and

color. It can actually accomplish the transmutation to which it lays

claim. It can change both intrinsic and extrinsic worth. Art, on the

other hand, is secondary not only to Nature, but also to alchemy. Al-

though, like alchemy, art can tinge and color surfaces, it cannot ac-

complish transformations. Art fails, specifically, because it does not

comprehend and therefore define "especiaus differances." The implica-

tion of the passage is, of course, that Art can only manipulate sur-

faces. Art does not understand or address the question of substance,

and more specifically, of the "especiaus differances" between substances

that define their intrinsic value. Consequently, art is incapable of

accomplishing alchemy's transformation of value. Jean de Meun's deni-

gration of the powers and efficacy of art precedes his statement that

no artist, except God, could represent Nature's loveliness, "si tres

grant biauté portrere" (16179). He himself refuses to attempt such an

undertaking. He expresses his artistic failure in the face of Nature's

splendor in terms that echo the Canon's Yeoman's articulation of his

own failure:

Et por ce que, si je poisse,
volantiers au mains l'antandisse,
voire escrite la vos eusse
se je poisse et je seusse,
je meismes i ai muse
tant que tout mon sens i use
conme fos et outrecuidiez;
.c. tanz plus que vos ne cuidiez;
car trop fis grant presumpcion
quant onques mis m'antancion
a si tres haute heuvre achever . . . .
                    (16181-91)

(Therefore I would willingly at least have tried if I had
been able; indeed I would have described her to you if I
could have and had known how; I have even wasted my time
over it until, like a presumptuous fool, I have used up all
of my sense, a hundred times more than you suspect. I made
too great a presumption when I ever set my intent on achieving so very high a task.--p. 274)

Chaucer, unlike Jean de Meun, presents an ambivalence toward alchemy, or rather, toward the manifestations of alchemy that are analogous to aspects of his own artistic enterprise in The Canterbury Tales.
Chaucer's Yeoman acknowledges legitimate forms of alchemy, especially
as it is practiced by the adepts and the philosophers whom he cites in
the closing lines of his Tale. Nonetheless, the Yeoman needs to condemn alchemy as it has manifested itself in his experience. Similarly,
in his Retraction, Chaucer acknowledges legitimate forms of artistic
endeavor, such as his translation of the De Consolatione Philosophiae
and his other conventionally moral works. Interestingly, he claims as
legitimate forms of artistic endeavor those works which involved least
creativity and least imaginative invention, in which artistic transformation was limited to translation, to imprinting genuine gold with a
new configuration of language that did not obscure its meaning. But
Chaucer has not only written morally didactic works and translations
nor is the only kind of alchemy practiced in the fourteenth century

that which takes the matter of this world as a pretext for divine in-
vestigation.   There are many kinds of art and many kinds of alchemy.
If Chaucer had not been ambivalent toward his art when he wrote The
Canon's Yeoman's Prologue and Tale, he would not, I believe, have included a spectrum of alchemical practices in his Tale.   In The Canon's
Yeoman's Tale, Chaucer, I believe, explores a variety of alchemical
practices and purposes as he tries to come to terms with art as he has
practiced it in The Canterbury Tales.   Chaucer's ambivalence, like his
Yeoman's, derives not only from the kind of enterprise with which he
has been involved, but from the purposes that motivate his involvement.

The art which Chaucer has produced in The Canterbury Tales resembles alchemy in its purposes and goals.   As I have discussed in Chapter
IV, alchemy would, according to the adepts, release the value inherent
within the elements of the external world.   Alchemy would redeem the
base elements composing the external world by transmuting them into
gold.   Moreover, alchemy underlines the theme of transformation and
conversion which, as Lawler has noted, is central to the pilgrimage
and particularly appropriate to its end.[15]   The poem which Chaucer devotes to pilgrimage as both subject and theme should have underlined
the transformation, the movement toward spiritual perfection that is
the purpose of the pilgrimage as well as the purpose of the alchemical
quest.   But a question arises concerning the nature of the transformation of value which Chaucer has shown in The Canterbury Tales.   Have
the pilgrims, as Chaucer depicts them, experienced a spiritual trans-

---

15.   Traugott Lawler, The One and the Many in The Canterbury
Tales (Hamden: Archon Books, 1980), p. 145.

formation? Have poetry and poetic language had the power to convert, to change, to transform?

In the General Prologue to The Tales, Chaucer has, as it were, usurped the role of Nature. He has assumed Nature's function as coiner as he creates a social microcosm and imprints its members with the stamps of their personalities. Of course, his poet-surrogate, a puffer as a poet just as the Yeoman is a puffer as an alchemist, would find gold in all of the pilgrims. He does not see that some of these characters may be counterfeits, or, at least, genuine scoundrels. Chaucer's irony in the General Prologue underlines the lesson that the Canon's Yeoman has learned after seven years of loss: that all that glitters is not gold. But despite Chaucer's orthodox Christian admonition that the surfaces of this world are deceptive, his art has addressed these surfaces throughout many of The Canterbury Tales. Chaucer's art, in many of his pilgrims' stories, is as rooted in the materiality of this world and in the question of its value as the Canon's Yeoman's enterprise has been. Chaucer, like the Yeoman, has tried to find value behind the chaos and the multiplicity, behind the baseness of the elements constituting the social and economic milieu around him, and he has tried to order those elements according to his own quest for value. Chaucer's quest has been defined by his effort to make the often base mettle of his characters yield the value of sentence.

By studying, in The Canterbury Tales, a multiplicity of pilgrims, professions, and of emotional and spiritual dilemmas, Chaucer has explored the ways in which value is formulated in response to interpreta-

tion of experience. Moreover, the relationship between teller and tale
allows Chaucer to explore the etiology of values, the ways in which
ethical values arise in response to experience and to personal and
psychological need in the same way that commercial values depend upon
and arise from market conditions. He has shown value beneath surfaces
which would seem to hide it, as in the case of the Wife of Bath and of
the Canon. He has shown instances in which no value exists behind surfaces, in which there is a moral bankruptcy as disturbing as that evi-
denced by the Shipman. And he has shown us everything in between.
Most often, Chaucer has shown that meaning and value are difficult to
find or are not what we would expect because surface does not correlate
with substance. Meaning in this world can be found only after a process of interpretation that has penetrated beneath surfaces.

When the Yeoman tells the pilgrims that his master could pave the
road to Canterbury "'al of silver and of gold,'" many critics have
pointed to the discrepancy between the literal gold and silver to which
the Yeoman refers and the spiritual gold and silver paving the way to
the New Jerusalem.[16] But Chaucer, too, is trying to pave the way to
Canterbury with the silver and gold of his art, with the value of the
meaning which inheres within his characters and within his artistic
production. But as the Retraction shows and The Canon's Yeoman's Tale
implies, Chaucer, as he nears the end of the Canterbury pilgrimage, is
ambivalent about his art, about his ability to reveal meaning, and
about the nature of the meaning which he has revealed throughout The

---

16. Paul B. Taylor, "The Canon's Yeoman's Breath: Emanations of
a Metaphor," ES, 60 (1979), 384.

Canterbury Tales. Chaucer asks himself whether he, as poet, is the true alchemist who releases the gold, the redeemability within the material world and who, in the process, achieves his own spiritual perfection as he approaches an understanding of the order of God's creation; or whether he is an alchemist like the Canon's Yeoman who expects the world to conform to the desires of his imagination and to yield the meaning that he would seek within it; or whether he is the confidence man of the "Secunda Pars," who has mastered a technique, but who can produce the silver of sentence only when it is already in his crucible. Chaucer wonders if his art reveals a meaning inherent within the material world or whether that meaning is the invention of his own imagination, a counterfeit mirroring his own image back to himself rather than the reflection of a divine meaning and order which he has failed to understand and to communicate.

The question arises, then, concerning Chaucer's estimation of the value and values which he has represented throughout The Canterbury Tales. For much of Chaucer's art has focused on ambivalence, or, more specifically, on multivalence and the interpretative problems posed by a multivalent world. Ambivalence makes alchemy and Chaucer's art in The Canterbury Tales possible. Both enterprises direct their attention to the coexistence of different, often conflicting values within one phenomenon, within one sign. Chaucer has deliberately created ambivalence in his General Prologue portraits. He has underscored ambivalence in his complex psychological portraits like those of the Wife of Bath, the Pardoner, and the Canon's Yeoman. We can condemn many of Chaucer's characters according to an orthodox Christian definition of morality. But, by revealing the psychological and social reasons for their behavior, Chaucer makes a prima facie condemnation of these pilgrims an inadequate response to their complexity. The Pardoner may never be redeemed, but the fact that he can offer us sentence raises the question of whether the most damned of the Canterbury pilgrims has value. If, through interpretation, we can find sentence in the tale of a reprobate character, does this tale have value? Is it "writen for oure doctrine" (X. I, 1083)? Chaucer, with his irony, his punning, and his sophisticated apprehension of behavior and of the motives behind behavior, is, in the end, a poet of ambivalence.

But, as I have argued, ambivalence can lead to a distorted perception of value. It can produce a lack of discrimination that spells the end of our ability to evaluate and to order. In his struggle to resolve his own ambivalence, the Canon's Yeoman has ended by denying value. Chaucer fears that, in his treatment of ambivalence, of the changing nature of value, and of the deceptiveness of the signs by which we read value, he, like the Yeoman, may have ended by finding no enduring value at all.[17] Through his language and his art, Chaucer, like the Canon's Yeoman, has sought to transform the value of the world around him. But Chaucer is afraid that he, too, ends with the loss of value that the Canon's Yeoman experiences after his long quest. The Canterbury pilgrimage may be nothing more than a bourgeois romance like the "Prima Pars" of The Canon's Yeoman's Tale, a poem too preoccupied with the materiality of the external world, and with his own

---

17. David Aers, Chaucer, Langland, and The Creative Imagination (London: Routledge and Kegan Paul, 1980), p. 102.

efforts at poetic self-determination. Or, Chaucer fears, The Canterbury Tales may turn the pilgrimage into an anti-romance that ends by
positing the deceptiveness of surfaces and the lack of inherent value.

The Canon's Yeoman calls alchemy a "slidynge science," one which
promises to yield value if one has wisdom, but which constantly eludes
its practitioners. It is a phrase which, I believe, Chaucer would also
apply to his art.[18] His poetry is "slidynge" because, if it promises
the artist the power to create worlds that Boccaccio described, it can
only produce counterfeits, imitations of translations of a divine
ideal. As The Shipman's Tale makes clear, Chaucer was aware of the
"slidynge" quality of language, of the material of his art. And he
was aware that words can fail to reveal meaning. His art, like the
Canon's Yeoman's, is disillusioning because it is founded upon the
illusion that the artist can create a world ordered by his imagination
and reflecting the meaning that he finds within the world outside himself. But the meaning that the medieval artist finds within the external world and that he attempts to represent through the evasive
medium of his art may itself be counterfeit, for it may not accurately
represent the world's intrinsic value. Chaucer has, throughout The
Canterbury Tales, presented the tales of pilgrims who assign value
according to their own needs, desires, and imaginations, and who therefore make the world in their own images. Chaucer, as a medieval man,
could not have escaped the fear that he had done the same thing. It
is, on the one hand, difficult for the artist to reveal the meaning

---

18. Lawler, p. 137 and Burlin, p. 242.

inherent within the created universe and assigned by a prior and
supreme artificer when his language betrays him just as the elements
in the Canon's laboratory erupt in his face. Moreover, the difficulty
of revealing authentic value is compounded by the fact the artist is
a mortal man whose vision is de facto "blered" by his mortality.
Knowledge of the truth, as the Yeoman has implied, is inaccessible to
all but the adepts. Consequently, the attempt to discover and to represent the meaning beneath the shifting and deceptive surfaces of the
external world may yield only dross or a counterfeit of value stamped
with the imprint of the artist's own imagination. The romance of the
Canon's Yeoman's career degenerates into fabliau. So too, Chaucer's
confidence in the power of poetry to translate meaning into art has
been burned away, I would suggest, by his quest along the road to
Canterbury.

According to Jean de Meun, although art can never accomplish alchemical transmutations, it can learn from alchemy a skill in tinting
and in coloring. Yet it was specifically this ability that aroused
suspicion among the critics who would accuse all alchemists of counterfeiting.[19] The changing of colors, the ornamentation of surfaces,
cannot produce a change in essence. It cannot convert; it can only
conceal. Poetry is an art concerned with ornamentation, with transforming surfaces. The term used to designate rhetorical ornamentation
is "colours," as the Franklin notes in the Prologue to a tale concerned
with the deceptiveness of surfaces and the ultimate inability of lan-

_____

19. John Webster Spargo, "The Canon's Yeoman's Prologue and Tale,"
in Sources and Analogues to Chaucer's Canterbury Tales, p. 687.

guage to transform. The concern with testing and authenticity in The Canon's Yeoman's Prologue and Tale reflects Chaucer's fear that the art which he had used to show the deceptiveness of surfaces may, in itself, be only a deceptive surface created by language. His poetry may be only a rhetorical show, that hides dross beneath a gilding of language, that creates a counterfeit promising more value than it can deliver. He may fear that, like the second canon, he too may only traffic in a linguistic sleight-of-hand.

Chaucer's reservations about language become increasingly apparent in The Manciple's Tale, which presents the most cynical attitude toward language and poetry of any of The Canterbury Tales.[20] The Manciple also expresses his belief that the word must be cousin to the deed (IX. H, 207-10), but he does not find this correlation operative in experience. According to the Manciple, only the name distinguishes the adulterous lady from the whore, the name and the social class. Words, for the Manciple, obscure essential difference or lack thereof and they thus thwart our attempts to evaluate. In The Manciple's Tale, moreover, Apollo turns his dulcet-toned white bird into a black, cawing crow for telling the truth. The moral of The Manciple's Tale effectively puts an end to Chaucer's art before the final movement of The Canterbury Tales into The Parson's Tale and the Retraction: "My sone, be war, and be noon auctour newe/ Of tidynges, wheither they been false or trewe" (IX. H, 359-60). Significantly, the prologue to The Parson's Tale rejects poetry as the Parson says: "'I kan nat geste rum, ram,

---

20. For a similar discussion of The Manciple's Tale, see Burlin, pp. 243-44.

ruf, by lettre;/ Ne, God woot, rym holde I but litel bettre'" (X. I,
43-44). The Parson's comment not only mocks the alliterative tradition. It reduces poetry to sound, to a surface with no meaning beneath
its configuration of sounds.

The Canon's Yeoman's Tale ends with the Yeoman's presentation of
the allegory which, he believes, hides meaning unless that meaning is
revealed by divine inspiration. But it is here, within the allegory
that represents the final obstacle to the Yeoman's success, that Chaucer finds a justification of the art and of the intellectual quest
that art can entail. This justification of the quest would for Chaucer,
as for the Yeoman, deepen the ambivalence toward art and its poten-
tialities. This ambivalence would make Chaucer concur with the Yeoman
about their respective enterprises: "'I koude nevere leve it in no
wise.'" Chaucer cannot leave his art until he has pursued his own intellectual and spiritual, if not poetic, quest until the end of the
pilgrimage. For Chaucer, unlike the Yeoman, can transform his own
quest from an artistic into a spiritual one. It is within the allegory
and within the true alchemy presented by this allegory that Chaucer
finds the energy and the direction to complete the romance of his pilgrimage.

The allegory at the end of The Canon's Yeoman's Tale legitimizes
poetry and poetic language for the last time in The Canterbury Tales.
Allegory is, of course, a transformation of surface, a rhetorical embellishment; but, at the same time that it demands interpretation, it
delivers the gold of meaning that its ornamented surface promises.
Allegory tells us that meaning is hidden, that there is meaning beneath

the surface of language. Moreover, although allegory demonstrates the multivalency of language, its surfaces do not deceive. In the case of the true alchemists, as in the case of all moral writers throughout the Middle Ages, allegory hid a meaning which pointed toward God, toward redemption, toward the ineffable whose presence is masked by language just as it is masked by its translation into the imperfect forms of this world. Allegory also points to the need for interpretation if the mind is to understand and to perfect itself; it points, in fact, to the need for interpretation that Chaucer has underlined throughout The Canterbury Tales. Only through a quest for meaning accompanied by the faith that meaning exists can we reach the self-transformation which is the purpose of the pilgrimage toward Canterbury. Chaucer may not have presented this transformation of value in a work that treats the ambivalence of the material world. But that does not mean, as Chaucer knew, that perfection and self-transformation are unattainable or that some works of art might not aid in that attainment.

In order to rescue The Canterbury Tales from its own resemblance to a bourgeois romance, Chaucer must illuminate the way to this final transformation. Through the content of The Parson's Tale and of the Retraction, he annuls the commercial contract that was the original reason for the story-telling competition and that would have returned the pilgrimage to the Tabard Inn. Had Chaucer ended The Canterbury Tales as they began, as his own program in the General Prologue suggests, the reintegration into society that traditionally climaxes the romance would have returned his pilgrims to a commercial world in which value is as narrowly and as materially defined as it is by the Canon's Yeoman. Through the Parson's prose treatise, the most obviously moral and didactic piece in the Canterbury collection, Chaucer presents a tale that does not hide the gold of doctrine behind rhetorical gilding because its purpose is to transform by revelation.

As Chaucer moves away from the poetry of The Canterbury Tales into the prose of The Parson's Tale, he leaves his attempts to explore the multivalency of human life and to transform this multivalency into art. He moves into a tale that is unambivalent and that reaffirms a stable system of Christian values for right conduct in this world. Yet, as he moves away from the alchemy of his own poetry, Chaucer, like the Canon's Yeoman, must have felt a sense of loss, a sense that all one has left at the end of the effort is a torrent of language. This language, in a fallen world that constantly experiences "defaute" in human endeavor, cannot have the power to transform. All he has left is his language and his ambivalence. For Chaucer, however, there remains a consolation which the Yeoman does not have, a consolation that would maintain his ambivalence toward the value of his endeavor. That consolation lies in the awareness that the value of the enterprise is measured not by the transformations it accomplishes, but by the spirit of the quest that comprises the final test of authenticity.

BIBLIOGRAPHY

Abraham, David H. "Cosyn and Cosynage: Pun and Structures in the Shipman's Tale." ChauR, 11 (1977), 319-27.

Abram, A. "Women Traders in Medieval London." Economic Journal, 26 (1916), 276-285.

Aers, David. Chaucer, Langland, and the Creative Imagination. London: Routledge and Kegan Paul, 1980.

_____. "Criseyde: Woman in Medieval Society." ChauR, 13 (1979), 177-200.

Aiken, Pauline. "Vincent of Beauvais and Chaucer's Knowledge of Alchemy." SP, 41 (1944), 371-389.

Alan of Lille. Anticlaudianus or the Good and Perfect Man, trans. James J. Sheridan. Toronto: Pontifical Institute of Mediaeval Studies, 1973.

_____. The Complaint of Nature, trans. Douglas M. Moffat. Yale Studies in English. XXXVI. New York: Henry Holt and Company, 1908.

Alford, John A. "Literature and Law in Medieval England." PMLA, 92 (1977), 941-951.

Allen, Judson Boyce, and Theresa Anne Moritz. A Distinction of Stories: The Medieval Unity of Chaucer's Fair Chain of Narratives for Canterbury. Columbus: Ohio State University Press, 1981.

Thomas Aquinas. Summa Theologiae. Prepared by the Blackfriars. New York: McGraw Hill Book Company; London: Eyre and Spottiswoode.

_____. Summa Theologica. Trans. Fathers of the English Dominican Province. New York: Benziger Brothers, Inc., 1947.

Aristotle. The Art of Rhetoric, trans. J. H. Freese. Loeb Library. Cambridge: Harvard University Press, 1959.

_____. The Nicomachean Ethics, trans. Martin Ostwald. New York: The Bobbs-Merrill Company, Inc., 1962.

_____. The Nichomachean Ethics, ed. and trans. H. Rackham. Loeb
    Library. Cambridge: Harvard University Press, 1939.

_____. Politics, ed. and trans. H. Rackham. Loeb Library,
    Cambridge: Harvard University Press, 1959.

_____. The Politics, trans. T. A. Sinclair. New York: Penguin
    Books, 1979.

Augustine. De Doctrina Christiana, ed. Joseph Martin. Corpus
    Christianorum Series Latina, 32:1-167.

_____. On Christian Doctrine, trans. D. W. Robertson, Jr. New
    York: Bobbs-Merril Company, Inc., 1958.

Baldwin, Ralph G. "The Yeoman's Canons: A Conjecture." JEGP, 61
    (1962), 232-243.

_____. "The Unity of the Canterbury Tales." Chaucer Criticism
    Vol. I: The Canterbury Tales, ed. Richard J. Schoeck and Jerome
    Taylor. Notre Dame: University of Notre Dame Press, 1971, pp.
    14-51.

Barthes, Roland. Elements of Semiology, trans. Annette Lavers and
    Colin Smith. New York: Hill and Wang, 1979.

Baum, Paull F. Chaucer: A Critical Appreciation. Durham: Duke
    University Press, 1958.

_____. "Chaucer's Puns." PMLA, 71 (1956), 225-246.

Bender, D. R. "A Refinement of the Concept of Household." American
    Anthropologist, 69 (1967), 493-504.

Benveniste, Emile. "Gift and Exchange in the Indo-European
    Vocabulary." Problems in General Linguistics, trans. Mary
    Elizabeth Meeks. Coral Gables: University of Miami Press, 1971,
    pp. 271-280.

Bloch, Marc. Esquisse d'une historie monetaire de l'Europe. Paris:
    Armand Colin, 1954.

_____. Land and Work in Mediaeval Europe: Selected Papers, trans.
    J. E. Anderson. Berkeley: University of California Press, 1967.

Bloomfield, Morton W. The Seven Deadly Sins: An Introduction to the
    History of a Religious Concept, with Special Reference to
    Medieval English Literature. 1952; rpt. Michigan: Michigan
    State University Press, 1967.

Boethius. The Consolation of Philosophy, trans. V. E. Watts.
    Baltimore: Penguin Books, 1976.

Bowden, Muriel. A Commentary on the General Prologue to the Canterbury Tales. New York: The Macmillan Company, 1954.

Brewer, D. S. Chaucer, third edition. London: Longman, 1973.

_____. "Class Distinctions in Chaucer." Spec, 43 (1968), 290-305.

Bridbury, A. R. Economic Growth: England in the Late Middle Ages. London: George Allen and Unwin, Ltd., 1962.

Bridrey, Émile. Nicole Oresme: Étude d'Histoire des Doctrines et des Faits Économiques. Paris: V. Giard et E. Brière, 1906.

Brown, Arthur C. L. The Origin of the Grail Legend. Cambridge: Harvard University Press, 1943.

Bryan, W. F., and Germaine Dempster, eds. Sources and Analogues of Chaucer's Canterbury Tales. New York: Humanities Press, 1958.

Burke, Kenneth. A Rhetoric of Motives. Berkeley: University of California Press, 1969.

Burlin, Robert B. Chaucerian Fiction. Princeton: Princeton University Press, 1977.

Cahn, Kenneth S. "Chaucer's Merchants and the Foreign Exchange: An Introduction to Medieval Finance." SAC, 2 (1980), 81-119.

Caldwell, Robert A. "Chaucer's Taillynge Ynough, CTs, B^{2}1624." MLN, 55 (1940), 262-265.

Carruthers, Mary. "The Wife of Bath and the Painting of Lions." PMLA, 94 (1979), 209-222.

Carus-Wilson, E. M., ed. Essays in Economic History: Reprints Edited for the Economic History Society. London: Edward Arnold (Publishers), Ltd., 1954.

_____. Medieval Merchant Venturers, second ed. London: Methuen, 1967.

Chaucer, Geoffrey. The Works of Geoffrey Chaucer, ed. F. N. Robinson. Second Edition. Boston: Houghton Mifflin, 1957.

_____. The General Prologue to the Canterbury Tales and the Canon's Yeoman's Prologue and Tale, ed. A. V. C. Schmidt. London: University of London Press, 1974.

Clark, Susan L., and Julian N. Wasserman. The Poetics of Conversion: Number Symbolism and Alchemy in Gottfried's "Tristan." Bern: Peter Lang, 1977. Utah Studies in Literature and Linguistics, Vol. 7.

Colmer, Dorothy. "Character and Class in the Wife of Bath's Tale."
    JEGP, 72 (1973), 329-339.

Courtenay, W. J. "The King and the Leaden Coin: The Economic Background
    of 'sine qua non' Causality." Traditio, 28 (1972), 185-209.

Curry, Walter Clyde. Chaucer and the Mediaeval Sciences. New York:
    Barnes and Noble, Inc., 1960.

Curtius, Ernst Robert. European Literature and the Latin Middle Ages,
    trans. Willard R. Trask. New York: Harper and Row, Publishers,
    1963.

David, Alfred. The Strumpet Muse. Bloomington: Indiana University
    Press, 1976.

Davis, Norman, Douglas Gray, Patricia Ingham, Anne Wallace-Hadrill,
    eds. A Chaucer Glossary. Oxford: The Clarendon Press, 1979.

Donaldson, E. Talbot. "Chaucer the Pilgrim," Speaking of Chaucer.
    New York: W. W. Norton and Co., Inc., 1972, pp. 1-12.

_____, ed. Chaucer's Poetry: An Anthology for the Modern Reader.
    New York: The Ronald Press Co., 1958.

DuBoulay, F. R. H. The Age of Ambition: English Society in the Late
    Middle Ages. London: Nelson, 1970.

Duby, Georges. Rural Economy and Country Life in the Medieval West,
    trans. Cynthia Postan. Columbia: University of South Carolina
    Press, 1968.

Duncan, Edgar Hill. "Chaucer and 'Arnold of the Newe Toun.'" MLN,
    57 (1942), 31-33.

_____. "The Literature of Alchemy and Chaucer's 'Canon's Yeoman's
    Tale': Framework, Theme, and Characters." Spec, 43 (1968),
    633-656.

Economou, George D., ed. Geoffrey Chaucer: A Collection of Original
    Articles. New York: McGraw-Hill Book Co., 1975.

_____. The Goddess Natura in Medieval Literature. Cambridge:
    Harvard University Press, 1972.

Elliott, Ralph W. V. "'Faire Subtile Wordes': An Approach to Chaucer's
    Verbal Art." Parergon, 13 (1975), 3-20.

Ferrante, Joan. Woman as Image in Medieval Literature. New York:
    Columbia University Press, 1975.

Finkelstein, Dorothée. "The Code of Chaucer's 'Secree of Secrees':
    Arabic Alchemical Terminology in The Canon's Yeoman's Tale."
    Archiv Für Das Studium Der Neueren Sprachen und Literaturen,
    207 (1970), 260-276.

Fisher, Ruth M. "'Cosyn' and 'Cosynage': Complicated Punning in
    Chaucer's 'Shipman's Tale.'" N&Q, CCX (1965), 168-170.

Freud, Sigmund. Wit and Its Relation to the Unconscious, in The Basic
    Writings of Sigmund Freud, trans. and ed. A. A. Brill. New
    York: The Modern Library, 1938, pp. 633-803.

Frye, Northrop. Anatomy of Criticism: Four Essays. Princeton:
    Princeton University Press, 1973.

Gardner, John. "The Canon's Yeoman's Prologue and Tale: An
    Interpretation." PQ, 46 (1967), 1-17.

Geoffrey of Vinsauf. Poetria Nova, trans. Margaret F. Nims. Toronto:
    Pontifical Institute of Mediaeval Studies, 1967.

Grenberg, Bruce L. "The Canon's Yeoman's Tale: Boethian Wisdom and
    The Alchemists." ChauR, 1 (1966), 37-54.

Grennen, Joseph E. "The Canon's Yeoman's Alchemical 'Mass.'" SP, 62
    (1965), 546-560.

_____. "The Canon's Yeoman and the Cosmic Furnace: Language and
    Meaning in the 'Canon's Yeoman's Tale.'" Criticism, 4 (1962),
    225-240.

_____. "Chaucer's Characterization of the Canon and His Yeoman."
    JHI, 25 (1964), 279-284.

Hamilton, Marie P. "The Clerical Status of Chaucer's Alchemist."
    Spec, 16 (1941), 103-108.

Hanning, Robert W. "The Theme of Art and Life in Chaucer's Poetry."
    Geoffrey Chaucer, ed. George D. Economou. New York: McGraw-
    Hill Book Co., 1975, pp. 15-36.

Hartung, Albert E. "'Pars Secunda' and the Development of the Canon's
    Yeoman's Tale." ChauR, 12 (1977), 111-128.

Heinzelman, Kurt. The Economics of the Imagination. Amherst:
    University of Massachusetts Press, 1980.

Herlihy, D. "Three Patterns of Social Mobility in Medieval History."
    Journal of Interdisciplinary History, 3 (1973), 623-647.

Herz, Judith Scherer. "The Canon's Yeoman's Prologue and Tale." MP,
    58 (1961), 231-237.

Hilton, Rodney. Bond Men Made Free. London: Temple Smith, 1973.

Hoffman, Arthur W. "Chaucer's Prologue to Pilgrimage: The Two Voices."
    Chaucer: Modern Essays in Criticism, ed. Edward Wagenknecht.
    London: Oxford University Press, 1970, pp. 30-45.

Holmyard, Eric J. Alchemy. Baltimore: Penguin Books, 1957.

Hopkins, Arthur John. Alchemy: Child of Greek Philosophy. New York:
    Columbia University Press, 1934.

Howard, Donald. The Idea of the Canterbury Tales. Berkeley:
    University of California Press, 1976.

Huizinga, Johan. The Waning of the Middle Ages. Garden City:
    Doubleday and Co., Inc., 1954.

Huppé, B. F. A Reading of the Canterbury Tales. Albany: State
    University of New York, 1964.

Hutin, Serge. A History of Alchemy, trans. Tamara Alferoff. New
    York: Walker and Co., 1962.

Jones, Claude. "Chaucer's Taillynge Ynough." MLN, 52 (1937), 570.

Jordan, R. M. Chaucer and the Shape of Creation. Cambridge: Harvard
    University Press, 1967.

Josipovici, Gabriel. The World and the Book: A Study of Modern Fiction.
    Stanford: Stanford University Press, 1971.

Jung, Carl G. "The Idea of Redemption in Alchemy." The Integration
    of the Personality, trans. Stanley Dell. London: Routledge and
    Kegan Paul, Ltd., 1950, pp. 205-281.

Justman, Stewart. "Literal and Symbolic in the Canterbury Tales."
    ChauR, 14 (1980), 199-214.

Kaske, R. E. "Chaucer's Marriage Group," ed. Jerome Mitchell and
    William Provost. Chaucer: The Love Poet. Athens: University
    of Georgia Press, 1973.

Kean, P. M. Chaucer and the Making of English Poetry. London:
    Routledge, 1972.

Keiser, George R. "Language and Meaning in Chaucer's Shipman's Tale."
    ChauR, 12 (1977), 147-161.

Kernan, Anne. "The Archwife and the Eunuch." ELH, 41 (1974), 1-25.

Kirk, R. E. G., ed. Life Records of Chaucer, IV, Chaucer Society.
    London: Kegan Paul, Trench, Trübner and Co., 1900.

Knight, Stephen. "Chaucer and the Sociology of Literature." SAC, 2 (1980), 15-52.

Langholm, Odd. Price and Value in the Aristotelian Tradition: A Study in Scholastic Economic Sources. Bergen: Universitets forlaget, 1979.

Lawler, Traugott. The One and the Many in The Canterbury Tales. Hamden: Archon Books, 1980.

Leff, Gordon. The Dissolution of the Medieval Outlook: An Essay on Intellectual and Spiritual Change in the Fourteenth Century. New York: New York Press, 1976.

Leicester, H. Marshall, Jr. "The Art of Impersonation: A General Prologue to the Canterbury Tales." PMLA, 95 (1980), 213-224.

Levy, Bernard S. "The Quaint World of The Shipman's Tale." Studies in Short Fiction, 4 (1966-1967), 112-118.

Little, Lester K. Religious Poverty and the Profit Economy in Medieval Europe. Ithaca: Cornell University Press, 1978.

Loomis, Roger Sherman. The Grail from Celtic Myth to Christian Symbol. New York: Columbia University Press, 1963.

Lopez, Robert S. The Commercial Revolution of the Middle Ages, 950-1350. Englewood Cliffs: Prentice-Hall, Inc., 1976.

deLorris, Guillaume, et Jean de Meun. Le Roman de la Rose, 3 vols., ed. Félix Lecoy. Paris: Librairie Honoré Champion, 1965.

_____. The Romance of the Rose, trans. Charles Dahlberg. Princeton: Princeton University Press, 1971.

Lumiansky, R. M. Of Sondry Folk. Austin: University of Texas Press, 1955.

Macfarlane, A. The Origins of English Individualism: The Family, Property and Social Transition. Oxford: Blackwell, 1978.

Malone, Kemp. Chapters on Chaucer. Baltimore: The Johns Hopkins University Press, 1951.

Mann, Jill. Chaucer and Medieval Estates Satire: The Literature of Social Classes and the General Prologue to The Canterbury Tales. Cambridge: Cambridge University Press, 1973.

Margulies, Cecile S. "The Marriages and the Wealth of the Wife of Bath." Medieval Studies, 24 (1962), 210-216.

Mathew, Gervase. The Court of Richard II. New York: W. W. Norton
     and Co., Inc., 1968.

McCracken, Samuel. "Confessional Prologue and the Topography of the
     Canon's Yeoman's Tale." MP, 68 (1970-71), 289-291.

McGalliard, John C. "Characterization in Chaucer's Shipman's Tale."
     PQ, 54 (1975), 1-18.

McKisack, May. England in the Fourteenth Century 1307-1399. London:
     Oxford University Press, 1959.

Menut, Albert D., ed. and trans. Maistre Nicole Oresme: Le Livre de
     Yconomique d'Aristote. Transactions of the American
     Philosophical Society., New Series, Vol. 47, part 5 (1957).

Metlitzki, Dorothée. The Matter of Araby in Medieval England. New
     Haven: Yale University Press, 1977.

Miller, Robert P., ed. Chaucer: Sources and Backgrounds. New York:
     Oxford University Press, 1977.

Miskimin, Harry S. The Economy of Early Renaissance Europe, 1300-1460.
     New York: Cambridge University Press, 1975.

Mumford, Lewis. The City in History: Its Origins, Its Transformations,
     and Its Prospects. New York: Harcourt Brace Jovanovich, 1961.

Murray, Alexander. Reason and Society in the Middle Ages. Oxford:
     The Clarendon Press, 1978.

Muscatine, Charles. Chaucer and the French Tradition: A Study in
     Style and Meaning. Berkeley: University of California Press,
     1973.

_____. Poetry and Crisis in the Age of Chaucer. Notre Dame:
     University of Notre Dame Press, 1972.

Myers, A. R. England in the Late Middle Ages. Eighth edition.
     Baltimore: Penguin Books, 1971.

Noonan, John T. The Scholastic Analysis of Usury. Cambridge: Harvard
     University Press, 1957.

O'Brien, George. An Essay on Medieval Economic Teaching. London:
     Longmans, Green, and Co., 1920.

Olmert, K. Michael. "The Canon's Yeoman's Tale: An Interpretation."
     AnM, 8 (1967), 70-94.

Oresme, Nicholas. De Moneta, trans. Charles Johnson. London: Thomas
     Nelson and Sons, Ltd., 1956.

Owen, Charles A., Jr. Pilgrimage and Storytelling in The Canterbury Tales: The Dialectic of "Ernest" and "Game." Norman: University of Oklahoma Press, 1977.

Ozment, Steven. The Age of Reform 1250-1550: An Intellectual and Religious History of Late Medieval and Reformation Europe. New Haven: Yale University Press, 1980.

Parker, David. "Can We Trust the Wife of Bath?" ChauR, 4 (1970), 90-98.

Palmer, Philip Mason, and Robert Pattison More. The Sources of the Faust Tradition: From Sinon Magus to Lessing. New York: Oxford University Press, 1936.

Patch, Howard R. The Goddess Fortune in Mediaeval Literature. Cambridge: Harvard University Press, 1927.

Payne, R. O. The Key of Remembrance: A Study of Chaucer's Poetics. New Haven: Yale University Press, 1963.

Peck, Russell A. "Chaucer and the Nominalist Questions." Spec, 53 (1978), 745-760.

_____. Kingship and Common Profit in Gower's Confessio Amantis. Carbondale: Southern Illinois University Press, 1978.

Pirenne, Henri. Medieval Cities: Their Origins and the Revival of Trade, trans. Frank D. Halsey. Princeton: Princeton University Press, 1974.

_____. Economic and Social History of Medieval Europe. New York: Harcourt, Brace and World, Inc., 1937.

Postan, M. M. Essays on Medieval Agriculture and General Problems of the Medieval Economy. Cambridge: Cambridge University Press, 1973.

_____. Medieval Trade and Finance. Cambridge: Cambridge University Press, 1973.

_____. The Medieval Economy and Society: An Economic History of Britain in the Middle Ages. London: Weidenfeld and Nicolson, 1972.

_____, E. E. Rich and Edward Miller, eds. Economic Organization and Policies in the Middle Ages. Cambridge Economic History of Europe, Vol. III. Cambridge: Cambridge University Press, 1963.

_____, and E. E. Rich, eds. Trade and Industry in the Middle Ages. Cambridge Economic History of Europe, Vol. II. Cambridge: Cambridge University Press, 1952.

Power, Eileen. Medieval Women, ed. M. M. Postan. Cambridge: Cambridge University Press, 1975.

Quintillian. Institutio Oratoria, trans. H. E. Butler. Loeb Classics Library. New York: G. P. Putnam's Sons., 1921.

Read, John. The Alchemist in Life, Literature, and Art. London: Thomas Nelson and Sons, Ltd., 1947.

Reidy, John. "Chaucer's Canon and the Unity of the Canon's Yeoman's Tale." PMLA, 80 (1965), 31-37.

Reisner, Thomas A. "The Wife of Bath's Dower: A Legal Interpretation." MP, 71 (1973-74), 301-302.

Reiss, Edmund. "Chaucer and Medieval Irony." SAC, 1:67-82.

Richardson, Janette. "The Facade of Bawdry: Image Patterns in Chaucer's Shipman's Tale." ELH, 32 (1965), 303-313.

Robertson, D. W. A Preface to Chaucer: Studies in Medieval Perspectives. Princeton: Princeton University Press, 1962.

DeRoover, Raymond. La pensée economique des scholastiques, doctrines et méthodes. Montréal: Institut d'Études Médiévales, 1971.

_____. San Bernardino of Siena and Sant'Antonino of Florence: The Two Great Economic Thinkers of the Middle Ages. Boston: The Kress Library of Business and Economics, 1967.

_____. "The Scholastics, Usury, and Foreign Exchange." Business History Review, 41 (1967), 257-271.

_____. "The Concept of the Just Price: Theory and Economic Policy." Journal of Economic History, XVIII (1958), 418-434.

_____. L'Évolution de la Lettre de Change XIVe-XVIIIe siècles. Paris: Librairie Armand Colin, 1953.

_____. "What is Dry Exchange? A Contribution to the Study of English Mercantilism." Journal of Political Economy, 52 (1944), pp. 250-266.

Rosenberg, Bruce A. "Swindling Alchemist, Antichrist." Centennial Review of Arts and Sciences, 6 (1962), 566-580.

Ruggiers, Paul G. The Art of the Canterbury Tales. Madison: University of Wisconsin Press, 1967.

Ryan, Lawrence V. "The Canon's Yeoman's Desperate Confession." ChauR, 8 (1974), 297-310.

Sadoul, Jacques. Le grand art de l'alchimie. Paris: Éditions Albin Michel, 1973.

Saussure, Ferdinand de. Course in General Linguistics, trans. Wade Baskin; eds. Charles Bally, Albert Sechehaye in collaboration with Albert Rudlinger. New York: McGraw-Hill Book Co., 1966.

Scattergood, V. J. "The Originality of the Shipman's Tale." ChauR, 11 (1977), 210-31.

Schneider, Paul S. "'Taillynge Ynough': The Function of Money in The Shipman's Tale." ChauR, 11 (1977), 201-209.

Shoaf, R. A. Dante, Chaucer, and the Currency of the Word: Money, Images, and Reference in Late Medieval Poetry. Forthcoming from Pilgrim Books, 1983.

_____. "Notes Towards Chaucer's Poetics of Translation." SAC, 1 (1979), 55-66.

Shell, Marc. The Economy of Literature. Baltimore: Johns Hopkins University Press, 1978.

Shumaker, Wayne. "Alisoun in Wander-land: A Study in Chaucer's Mind and Literary Method," in Discussions of the Canterbury Tales, ed. Charles A. Owen, Jr. Westport: Greenwood Press, 1961.

Silverman, A. H. "Sex and Money in Chaucer's Shipman's Tale," PQ, 32 (1953), 329-336.

Silverstein, Theodore. "The Wife of Bath and the Rhetoric of Enchantment; Or, How to Make a Hero See in the Dark." MP, 58 (1961), 153-173.

Simmel, Georg. On Individuality and Social Forms, ed. Donald N. Levine. Chicago: University of Chicago Press, 1971.

Singer, Kurt. "Oikonomia: An Inquiry into Beginnings of Economic Thought and Language." Kylos, 11 (1958), 29-54.

Slaughter, E. E. Virtue According to Love--In Chaucer. New York: Bookman Associates, 1957.

Southern, R. W. The Making of the Middle Ages. New Haven: Yale University Press, 1978.

Speirs, John. Chaucer the Maker. London: Faber and Faber, 1972.

Stephenson, Carl. Mediaeval Institutions: Selected Essays. Ithaca: Cornell University Press, 1967.

Taylor, Paul B. "The Canon's Yeoman's Breath: Emanations of a
     Metaphor." ES, 60 (1979), 380-388.

Thorndike, Lynn. A History of Magic and Experimental Science. Vol.
     II, New York: The Macmillan Co., 1929. Vol. III, IV, New York:
     Columbia University Press, 1934.

Thrupp, Sylvia. The Merchant Class of Medieval London. Chicago:
     University of Chicago Press, 1948.

Vance, Eugene. "Love's Concordance: The Poetics of Desire and the Joy
     of the Text." Diacritics, 5, 1 (Spring, 1975), 40-52.

Waite, Arthur Edward. The Secret Tradition in Alchemy: Its Development
     and Records. New York: Alfred A. Knopf, 1926.

Weissman, Hope P. "Why Chaucer's Wife is from Bath." ChauR; 15
     (1980), 11-36.

_____. "Antifeminism and Chaucer's Characterizations of Women."
     Geoffrey Chaucer, ed. George D. Economou. New York: McGraw-Hill
     Book Co., 1975, pp. 93-110.

Weston, Jessie L. From Ritual to Romance. Garden City, New York:
     Doubleday and Co., Inc., 1957.

Wetherbee, Winthrop. "Some Intellectual Themes in Chaucer's Poetry."
     Geoffrey Chaucer, ed. George D. Economou. New York: McGraw-Hill
     Book Co., 1975, pp. 75-91.

_____. Platonism and Poetry in the Twelfth Century: The Literary
     Influence of the School of Chartres. Princeton: Princeton
     University Press, 1972.

_____. "The Function of Poetry in the 'De Planctu Naturae' of
     Alain of Lille." Traditio, 25 (1969), 87-125.

Young, Karl. "The 'Secree of Secrees' of Chaucer's Canon's Yeoman."
     MLN, 58 (1943), 98-105.

For Product Safety Concerns and Information please contact our EU
representative GPSR@taylorandfrancis.com
Taylor & Francis Verlag GmbH, Kaufingerstraße 24, 80331 München, Germany